"...This morning we sighted a bo. Deep in wolf territory. Beware not only of the boar, but of our enemy. If they catch a gryfon on the ground, they will not be merciful. I know this..."*

~ ~ ~

"ONLY A FOOL WOULD STAND ground alone against old Lapu," a female voice said.

Shard whirled, hissing, and saw no one.

"I'm glad to see you aren't a fool, Rashard son-of-the-Nightwing."

"Show yourself!" He turned in a circle, wings half open, though he didn't dare try to fly in the woods again. All the other gryfons pursued the boar to the meadow. He was alone. A scent washed him, musky, woodsy.

Wolf...

~ ~ ~

WHAT PEOPLE ARE SAYING:

"...Very talented author, both creative and relatable. Stunning craft..."

"...The world that Jess E. Owen creates is at least as fascinating as the story, if not more so... The time I spent in this world was awesome and I loved every minute of it. It was fantastic to fly with the Gryfons and run with the wolves...I could feel the wind, hear the wolves howl and a Gryfon roar.... It was totally and utterly perfect!"

SONG OF THE SUMMER KING

JESS E. OWEN

five elements press

Five Elements Press
Suite 305
500 Depot Street
Whitefish, MT 59937
www.fiveelementspress.com

five elements press

PUBLISHER'S NOTE

This is a work of fiction. Any references to historical events, real people, or real locales are used fictitiously. Other names, characters, places, or incidents are the product of the author's imagination, and any resemblance to actual events, locales, or persons, living or dead, are purely coincidental.

Cover art by Featherdust Studios.
Cover typography and interior formatting by Terry Roy.
Edited by Joshue Essoe
Final copy edit by AnthroAquatic LiteraryEditing

ISBN-13: 978-0-9967676-6-8
ISBN 10: 0-9967676-6-5

SECOND PAPERBACK EDITION

This book is dedicated to my sister,
who will always read first.
To my husband, who is my wingbrother.
And to Mom and Dad
who knew it was never just a hobby.
You are the wind under me.
Thank you.

Contents

CONTENTS, continued

PREFACE

W ELCOME TO BOTH NEW MEMBERS of the gryfon pride, and old. As we grow, so do our stories and ideas. I first published *Song of the Summer King* in 2012, launching with a wonderful team, a successful Kickstarter campaign to fund a hardback edition, and beautiful cover art that I adored. I still adore it! And I'm leaving it available in print as an option for readers. It's rich and beautiful, and illustrates every emotion I felt for the story at the time.

However, as I have grown in my publishing savvy and Jennifer Miller has continued to astonish and amaze with her beautiful artwork, I found myself wanting to explore options for a new cover. Studying other covers in my genre led me to ponder brighter colors to catch the eye, a different, exciting pose for Shard, and a background that depicted a little more of the Silver Isles as an introduction to the landscape. We have both grown since 2012, and this new cover, on the six year anniversary of the original publication, is a product of that growth.

Jennifer agreed to create the new cover for a second edition paperback and ebook edition, so along with that, I have gone through and fixed some of the beloved old typos and mistakes that still appear in the hardback and the first edition for a new, improved, shinier book.

The decision to publish my own work and hire my own team means the freedom to make changes that I hope will improve the life of the story and draw in new readers as the years pass.

To all those who supported the Kickstarter for this new cover art, thank you, and welcome back home.

To new readers discovering the Silver Isles for the first time, thank you! Welcome to the Gryfon Pride.

~Jess

THE SONG OF THE SUMMER KING

BY

Jess E. Owen

A gryfon's view of

The Silver Isles

Starward

Nightward

Dawnward

Windward

Pebble's
Throw

Talon's
Reach

Star Isle

Crow
Wing

The gryfon colony of
Windwater

Sun Isle

The White Mountains

Black Rock

The Nightrun River

The Nesting Cliffs

The Windward Sea

1

THE RED KING

FRESH MORNING AIR LIFTED CLOUDS and gulls above the glimmering sea, and drew one young gryfon early from his den. Too early, just before sunrise when forbidden darkness still blanketed the islands.

The sun rose unhurriedly from the sea, and Shard strained against the steep sky, breathing deep, challenging himself to the highest possible dive. The sea spun below him. His mind flickered lightly in the thin air and he shoved down panic. Some would call it too high.

His wings drew in and flapped out sluggishly, feeling separate from his body. He had to bank, to get lower, breathe the deeper air.

Night sparked at the edge of his mind. His dreams flocked up from the night before. Nightmares of the impending initiation hunt.

The hunt! What's the sunmark?

Dreams scattered like crows from Shard's mind. He gave up on grace and tucked his wings to dive. His thoughts collapsed for three breaths as he plummeted on faith toward the sea, blind and gasping. Plenty of sky stretched below him. Plenty of room to fall, to breathe, to regain safe air.

Terrifying chills laced his muscles. The hunt, the hunt haunted him. In his dream he'd been late, missed it completely and faced banishment from the pride. But as Shard fell lower, he realized that the sun still hovered, dipped in the sea, that the dawn rippled softly across the water. Not as much time had passed as he'd thought.

The ocean swelled toward him and Shard shrieked into the morning to warn gulls from his path. He shoved his wings and feathered tail to flare, the hard stop shocking his muscles.

It was never the dive that was dangerous, his nest-father had taught. It was the landing. Shard laughed, raw and breathless, and turned to regain some sky. He angled his tail to help him turn. His tail swept long like a mountain cat's for balance, but feathers lay over the length, and could fan wide at the end to help with flying.

Shard floated higher on gentler, warmer air, still far above land.

Small, bright breezes pushed under his wings and buffeted the soft feathers of his face, bringing him scents from all the islands. He reveled in the damp spring air, still edged with winter in its coldest gusts, and wheeled through the tattered clouds that had left rain the night before. He flew high enough to see the whole cluster of the Silver Isles, bunched like the stamp of a gryfon's hind paw. They stood alone in the cold starland sea.

An eagle scream pierced his thoughts and in the high, thinner air above, it sounded like his name.

Shard!

Ocean rolled under him. He shouldn't have flown out so far or so high, but Shard only felt truly free up in the wind, and he had to practice high flying to keep up with his larger peers. He peered down at the islands. Today, a hunt on one of those isles would determine his future.

"Shard!"

It was his name. And whoever called it sounded worried.

Shard's ears twitched as he tucked his long wings and dove for the nesting cliffs on the dawnward side of the massive Sun Isle. Not the fast, plummeting dive he had planned, to clear his head, but straight and steady.

Shame at his cowardice wriggled. *Next time.*

"Shard!"

This time he knew the voice, and keened a response. A mote of gold circled below him, what looked like a huge fishing eagle. It wasn't.

The broad, bronze-black faces of the nesting cliffs glittered in the low morning light. Shard stretched his talons forward, laughing into the wind that beat back his long, feathered ears and rippled the last of the winter coat on his flanks and hind legs. He aimed for the gold gryfon below him, who was shouting.

"You're late!"

"Not yet, Kjorn!" Shard laughed at his gold friend, and before Kjorn realized Shard wasn't slowing, Shard slammed into him from above and sent them both sprawling lock-claw toward the sea.

"Get off!" Head tossing, tail lashing, Kjorn shrieked and tried to pry free.

"Did you see how high I flew?"

"You're a mudding genius. Shard, *listen!*"

They fell, a tangle of gray and golden feathers, wings flashing and snapping. Salt waves leaped and crashed toward them. Kjorn wrenched free and wheeled away. Shard corrected and glided up beside him.

"Did you forget the sunmark?" Kjorn was a third again Shard's size, gold as the morning and with eyes a rare summer blue.

"No," Shard murmured, gulping a breath. "I had to clear my head."

"That shouldn't have taken long."

Shard laughed and banked to catch Kjorn's wing, but Kjorn shoved higher, avoiding another spar. "The others have gathered already."

"But we weren't going to present until the sun reached middlemark!"

Kjorn stretched his talons. "It was changed. Didn't you hear?"

"No. Is your father there yet?"

"My father the *king*."

"Your father the king," Shard corrected, perking his ears toward the nesting cliffs as he and Kjorn glided in. Gryfons moved about on different levels of the cliffs, little bits of color waking, stretching deeply, bowing to the morning sun. Shard and Kjorn floated on the buoyant air over the rocks to the highest cliff overlooking the dawn-ward quarter of the sea.

"No," Kjorn said. "He hasn't come back yet. He flew along the coast at sunrise, to ask Tyr's blessing for the hunt."

"Then I'm not late." Irritation sizzled under his feathers, and worry. *Why wouldn't I have heard of the time change? Did someone say something, Mother or Thyra, and I forgot it?*

He shook off worry as they glided in.

Copper Cliff shone like its namesake in the dawn. A flat, grassy round formed the top of a cliff that dropped sharply into the sea, and a tumble of stones from the First Age sat in rough display near the edge. A perfect place for the king of the pride to stand and speak.

Or judge.

Shard and Kjorn angled toward the broad sloping meadow that stretched deeper inland from the cliff, and landed together. Kjorn thumped hard on the rocky peat, Shard a falcon's touch beside him.

Kjorn eyed his landing and ruffled. "Are you prepared? I thought we were going to spar this morning."

Shard folded his wings and dipped his head. "I had to fly," he murmured. The rush of flight seeped out of him and anxiousness slithered back in its place. Exile didn't hover over Kjorn's head if he did poorly on the initiation hunt, only embarrassment. Shard could lose everything. "I'm prepared." *I hope.*

He remained one of the few males in the pride not friend or kin to Sverin, the king. Since he had come of age, he could only stay if he proved himself useful and loyal. "But I'm worried," he said, softly so only Kjorn and the wind would hear.

"I'm with you, brother," Kjorn stared him in the eye, "whatever happens. I told my father I wouldn't hunt without you."

Shard perked his ears, and stretched out a gray wing. Kjorn fluffed happily and extended his own golden wing to eclipse it. "Wind under me when the air is still."

Shard took up the wingbrother pledge. "Wind over me when I fly too high."

"Brother by choice."

"Brother by vow."

"By my wings," they said together, "you will never fly alone."

"Kjorn—"

"After the hunt," Kjorn said, folding his wing, "you'll show me how you flew so high, and that fast dive—"

"If I'm still here," Shard tried to joke.

Kjorn bumped at Shard's ear with his beak. "Go."

Shard bounded up the slope toward the king's rocks. He didn't see the king yet, but three other young males waited in a line below them. A coppery male several years Shard's junior, almost too young to hunt, looked relieved to see him trot up. He and Shard exchanged a nervous look, but before Shard remembered his name, the young gryfon looked away and whispered to the gryfon ahead of him, also copper-brown.

"Is it true that the king killed three wolves on his initiation hunt?"

"No," drawled an answer before the older copper could speak. All three looked to the green gryfon who stood first in line. A year Shard's junior, bright emerald, his name was Halvden. A son of the Conquering. Shard flattened his ears. All three gryfons ahead of him were bigger, even the youngest, for half their breeding was of Sverin the king's pride, called the Aesir, from across the Windland Sea. Of all the young gryfons in the pride, only Shard's blood was fully of the Silver Isles, of the smaller, conquered pride, called the Vanir.

Halvden continued, carelessly using the king's full name. "Sverin's initiation came when he and his father conquered the Silver Isles. We might take a great beast," he said with a knowing glint, "but the king took a kingdom. Hello, Shard."

Shard tensed his wings. Everyone knew Halvden was a braggart; it was why Shard avoided him most of the time. But there was no avoiding this. "Fair winds, Halvden."

Halvden turned fully, as if he couldn't care less when the king arrived, to face Shard and the other two gryfons. "Fair winds, son-of-Sigrun." The word cut. His mother's name. No one knew his father's. "I saw you flying. Were you hoping Sverin would be so impressed that he would allow you to skip the hunt? Or that your nest-father would excuse you on account of your disadvantage?"

Heat burned under Shard's feathers. "I hunt as well as you."

"Yes, the field mice of Sun Isle live in terror of you." Halvden flicked his tail, idly fanning the feathers at the end to show off the colors. He even had a handsome tail, Shard thought in dismay.

A breeze picked up between them. The cool weedy scent of the Nightrun river drifted to them and Shard tried to let it calm him.

"Quail and mice," Halvden continued when Shard didn't rise to his first insult. "I heard that old Caj and your nest-sister spotted a boar on Star Island. That beast would strip your feathers to line its den before you could take to the sky."

"I wouldn't fly." Shard bristled, raising the longer hackle feathers behind his ears and down his neck.

"Have you ever seen such a beast?"

"Have you?"

Halvden flared his wings, advancing a step. The younger gryfon in front of Shard crouched back and spread his wings a little in deference, stepping out from between them. The older copper gryfon didn't move to interfere, and Haldven raised his head higher than Shard's. "The only reason you're here is because the prince begged–"

"Prove that!" Shard crouched, ready to leap and fight. Against Halvden, he knew he would probably lose.

"Enough," rumbled the older copper gryfon, stepping forward so his shadow fell over Shard. He stood as tall as Halvden, though he looked older. "Prove yourself on the hunt, Halvden. Not here."

Halvden paused, sizing up the older gryfon. He seemed familiar to Shard, though he couldn't place why.

Halvden perked his ears in mock attentiveness. "I don't think I should follow the advice of *your* family—"

"The king comes," said the older gryfon. Halvden blinked and spun as they all perked ears toward the king's rocks. The king glided in from his morning flight, massive wings flaring, stirring the grass as he landed on the top of his rocks.

The largest of the pride, Sverin son-of-Per looked every bit a king. He wore gold, crusted with emerald and sparkling catseye, around his neck, and golden bands clamped to his forelegs just above the spread of black talons. Tokens from Sverin's grandfather's war with dragons in the farthest arctic lands across the sea. The dawn outlined his copper flanks, throwing sheen across the scarlet feathers of his shoulders and the deep crimson of his face.

Shard and the others bowed. Other gryfons in the distance paused their morning business to watch the judgments.

"Halvden, son-of-Hallr," rumbled Sverin, wasting no niceties. Halvden stepped forward and mantled, letting his green wings droop from his shoulders and spreading his long flight feathers in a handsome display of respect.

Shard tightened his own plain, gray wings to his sides.

Dull as a sparrow and about as useful. Halvden was right. What have I ever hunted but quail and mice?

Sverin regarded Halvden fondly. "Your father is a great warrior, and a friend. Your mother was wise to choose him. If you prove yourself half the gryfon he is today, I shall be proud to have you in my ranks."

Halvden fluffed and then let his feathers smooth to sleekness with more dignity, dipping his head. "Let's hope I can prove myself by more than half, my Lord." He mantled again and strutted off when the king flicked a wingtip in amused acceptance.

Shard perked his ears again, hopeful and attentive. Halvden had barely needed to say anything. *Maybe it won't be so hard.* Then the older copper in front of Shard stepped up and mantled.

Sverin's golden eyes cooled.

"Son-of-Vidar," he rumbled.

That was a Silver Isles name. A conquered name. Shard fought the urge to cower and pretended he was made of stone.

"Your father was of the Vanir of the Silver Isles. You've waited long enough to seek this honor."

"I thought it best," said the copper quietly. "To let things calm down."

"I remember your father."

"I don't, my Lord." The copper gryfon's voice remained blank. "My mother is a huntress of your clan. Your father's cousin."

And Shard remembered. Four winters ago, Sverin had banished a gryfon for flying at night, which was forbidden by their bright god, Tyr. Exile at any time meant questionable survival. Exile in winter meant death. The exiled gryfon had been this gryfon's father.

"Why didn't you seek to reconcile with me sooner?" The king's tail lashed. The large copper gryfon lifted his head, ears flattening.

"I wasn't flying at night, my king."

"You're of his blood. You should have sought honor. Apology. Redemption." The king raised his voice; it cracked and rolled down the slope. "Or were you afraid?"

"No!" snapped the copper, wings lifting in agitation. Shard forced his own feathers to stay smooth, calm, but saw the younger gryfon ahead of him step back, half-cowering.

The king lowered his head, eyes blazing gold. "You are a coward, the son of an oath-breaker, who now seeks to strut up to me and expect a place in this pride. I need strength in my pride. Courage. Loyalty."

"I am loyal!" But he flared his wings and crouched, his voice rising in threat.

"You will not hunt and fly in my ranks, son-of-Vidar. Your blood is poisoned by your father's betrayal and disregard for my law."

Silence.

Trying to take a breath against his tight throat, Shard then had to stifle a gasp. *Refused, before getting a chance to hunt?*

The larger copper gryfon stared at the king, eyes wide, the black centers pinpointed in the panic of a witless eagle. "What are you saying, my Lord?"

"Leave this pride. I will not have you."

"My mother, and brother—"

"Are better off without you."

Silence stretched taut across the slope and the rocks and for a moment Shard thought the copper gryfon would spring and challenge the king himself. His copper wings twitched. Then his gaze twitched to the younger gryfon behind him. He faced the king, and bowed. Shock rippled up Shard's skin.

"As—as you wish, my Lord. I am not worthy of the pride."

But Severin no longer heard his words. He had turned his head, looking away toward the sky as if the copper gryfon no longer existed. Shard blinked and looked away too. He heard the younger gryfon ahead of him whisper a name. *They must be brothers.*

"Fair winds," whispered the older, then shoved off from the ground, wings beating hard to gain sky. Shard ground his beak, not looking. His heart shoved ice through his body and heat roiled in his belly. He wondered, if that was the reception of one half-blood with a dishonored father, what would his be?

Gulls cried above. Shard thought one of them sounded in pain, then realized it was a female gryfon, a gryfess keening sorrow into the morning. Severin snapped his gaze around and all fell silent again. The younger copper in front of Shard cowered back. Then, for some reason, he glanced to Shard. Shard drew a breath and forced himself to nod encouragingly. He had never seen Sverin banish someone before even giving them a chance to hunt.

"*Second* son-of-Vidar," the king rumbled.

"My...my name is Einarr, my king." The young gryfon's voice trembled. Shard released a breath, willing him to be strong.

"You're young to be seeking glory."

"I seek honor, after..." Einarr trailed off. What was there left to say? His father exiled, his brother exiled right before his eyes. Shard stepped forward as if he could give Einarr strength.

"Yes," Sverin murmured. "I imagine you would." He stared down the young gryfon with cool golden eyes. "Your brother could have learned from your brave example." His tail twitched. His gaze didn't waver. The sound of waves breaking against the rocks shoved into the space of silence. "You may hunt. Let us hope you have more of your mother's blood than your father's."

"Thank you, my Lord," breathed Einarr. "My king." He scraped a low bow and turned, sprinting from the king's sight. Shard stared after him. One gryfon banished. Two kept. Why had he thought this would be easy? Flying with Kjorn had made him too confident. The king possessed more ferocity in a single tail feather than Shard had ever felt in his entire body.

Drawing breath, he gathered himself and looked up.

Sverin was staring at him.

Waiting.

2

A RAVEN SPEAKS

SHARD CHECKED HIS TERROR AND bowed low, wings splayed. His mother's honor, his place in the pride, and his life all depended on his resolve now.

"My Lord." *Your fear is only a wind,* his mother once said. *It may shape your flight, but not you.* "You know me—"

"Son-of-Sigrun."

Shard couldn't read the emotion in Sverin's low voice, but he made a point of using his mother's name. No one ever uttered his father's, if they knew it.

"As wingbrother to my son, I expected you first in line."

I would have been! If I'd known about the time change. But everyone else had known. Excuses were useless. Shard straightened, grinding his beak. The Red King looked huge in the dawn, heavy with gold and the edge of threat that gleamed whenever he looked at Shard. The gentle, chilly breeze stirred against him, and he found his voice.

"I hope to keep surprising you today, my Lord," he managed, then clamped his beak. The king flattened one ear, then chuckled with understanding, ears perking.

"You're a loyal friend to my son. His wingbrother. Not chosen lightly. You, I'm afraid, have more to prove than any other. Your father resisted mine. Your mother was blatant in her disregard for the ways of conquering—"

"Only by asking that I be permitted to live," Shard broke in, and his heart nearly stopped. He had interrupted the king.

Sverin's eyes narrowed and the next words tumbled out of Shard. "But she took a new mate, of the Aesir. Your own wingbrother. She serves you as healer. My father fought you, but that made him a warrior. There is courage in my line, my Lord. And loyalty. I don't know my father's name and I don't wish to. Let me prove myself to you. For Kjorn, my wingbrother."

He said the word again, just to remind the king. Breathless as if he'd flown six leagues, Shard thought it was best to stop there, and bowed so low his beak touched the ground.

The king spoke quietly. "Well said."

Shard didn't dare lift his gaze.

"My son loves you well. For my son's sake, you may hunt. For your sake and your mother's, prove your words true."

Dismissed, Shard dipped his head once and trotted away, every muscle screaming to scurry away just as Einarr had done. Relief slipped over him like cool water after flight. He didn't look at the king again, but felt the gold eyes burning him until he was out of sight.

When he looked up again he saw Kjorn, gold as the sun on the slope. Shard broke into an undignified sprint, shedding terror in the running.

"He said *yes*," he gasped, bowling into Kjorn.

"Of course he did!" The prince laughed, shoving Shard off with a thrust of his wing. "Now hurry. Caj and the others are meeting at the Star Cliff."

"Caj will wait on *you*." Shard laughed as they shoved into the sky.

The Day Star, easily seen in the brightest part of the day by a sharp gryfon eye, glimmered in the late dawn, guiding their flight. Just as the rising sun marked the dawnward quarter of the sky, and the setting sun marked nightward, the starward direction was so named because the star in that part of the sky always shone first in the evening and died the last at dawn. *If a gryfon flies far enough starward,* his mother once told him, *he will reach the freezing cold top of the world.* Shard's happy thoughts marveled as they flew starward.

The hunt! The thought rolled happily over his mind and Shard soared through the air, the terror of seeing another gryfon banished before him washed away in relief and hope. He laughed and chased Kjorn lower until they saw the group of hunters milling on Star Cliff. Shard counted only seven. Einarr and Halvden, four experienced gryfess hunters and of course, Caj.

"If his highness is quite ready now," Caj rumbled as Shard and Kjorn landed hard and loped over the stunted grass.

"We are," Kjorn said, including Shard. All but Caj mantled low as the prince approached. Instead, Caj loosed a short, disapproving huff.

Caj stood taller than most, his flanks scarred from countless battles with gryfons and other beasts, his broad wings bright as a cobalt sea under the sun, his lion haunches rich gold. The king's honored wingbrother flaunted no metal or gems. He probably saw Kjorn as nothing more than another bumbling young male adding weight to the hunt.

And Shard, he barely saw at all.

"Nest-father," Shard murmured, inclining his head. Caj lashed his tail in answer and he paced to higher ground. Not his true father, but his mother's mate.

Surely he doesn't begrudge my coming? More honor for our family, his nest?

"Shard!" One of the gryfess hunters bounded forward with a happy cry. Shard's nest-sister. Of course she would be hunting with them. She would probably help Caj to lead.

"Thyra!"

The daughter of Caj glimmered pearly lavender in the morning, and before Shard could offer more greeting, she slammed into him and they both rolled across the grass, laughing and kicking like kits. The other gryfons, irritated, cleared from their rollicking path, until Caj's short, deep-chested growl halted them.

"Save your energy. *Daughter.*"

At Caj's voice, Thyra raised her head, at once a huntress, sleek and proud. Caj snapped his beak and lifted his wings for attention.

"The boar will not be so playful." All the gryfons turned fierce eyes to Caj, watching him pace the edge of the cliff. Mostly he addressed the new males, his golden eyes only rarely checking the trio of younger females, and never Thyra. They all knew what to expect. Shard fluffed. His nest-sister was one of the finest hunters of the Sun Isle.

"This morning we sighted a boar on the nightward side of Star Island. Deep in wolf territory. Beware not only of the boar, but of our enemy. If they catch a gryfon on the ground, they will not be merciful." He cast sharp looks at the young males. "I know this."

Fights were inevitable on contested hunting grounds. Shard's gaze strayed to the scars on Caj's flank as the old warrior delivered a strategy for flushing the boar out of the tangled underbrush, thick rowan and pine. Dangerous ground for gryfons, perfect for wolves and boar.

Shard listened, determined to be a part of the victory, though the kill would go to Kjorn.

Caj paused, raking them with his gaze. Feathered ears snapped forward, heeding. Caj was more dangerous than any wolf.

"A boar is deadly, even to the strongest gryfon. You haven't hunted, any of you, until you've hunted boar. They have weapons to rival ours. Hooves sharp as ice. Tusks as strong and sharp as a gryfon claw and three times as long." He addressed that to Halvden, who stopped preening and blinked to attention. Caj went on. "Because of their thick skin, you cannot kill from above, like a deer. You must get underneath." Caj flexed his black talons against the peat, squeezing out rainwater as if he held the boar's throat before them. "You must fight on the ground. Boars are fast. They're also stupid, which makes them fearless. If we can't get the beast off its feet, we can't kill it." His gaze stopped on Kjorn. "We can only bring down our prey together."

He held Kjorn's gaze until the gold prince dipped his head. "If you survive," Caj rumbled coolly to all, "you will have proven yourselves worthy of the king's pride and he may choose to let you remain. Hunt well." Shard shifted his feet, anxious to move. Caj's next words blazed sunlight through his blood. "In the light of sun, with the grace of great Tyr, for the glory of the king, we hunt, we fly!"

Caj flared his bright wings and lifted from the ground with a ringing cry. The four females rose behind him. Kjorn and Shard leaped into the sky with the other young males, and all followed Caj's flight starward.

They ranged into the wind with Caj at point and Thyra far on the left flank. The six islands shone under them in the dawn, and Shard focused starward. With the others ranged out he flew nearly alone in the sky, and took the moment to gather himself. All he needed to do was stay at Kjorn's side. To go at all was an honor. If he helped to bring down the boar and managed not to die in the process, why…he tried not to think so far ahead.

The paw-print stamp of the islands floated under them. The great Sun Isle formed its heel, with the five toes of Star Isle, a crescent mass called Talon's Reach, then mountainous Pebble's Throw, Crow Wing, and Black Rock.

Aside from the Sun Isle where Sverin ruled, and the Star Isle, overrun with wolves, there was no good place for a gryfon to live. The other islands lay mostly barren, with sparse game and little shelter.

With the clouds still drifting clear of the sky over the islands, Shard could see nearly all of the Sun Isle, their home island and the largest. Most of it rolled in a grassy, rock-strewn plain of peat and rough earth, scattered with hills that led into a thrust of barren mountains. The Nightrun River split the land, rolling down from the White Mountains to plunge over a cliff into the sea. Birch and juniper forest rose up around it and little streams tendriled off into the rest of the isle.

Shard had spent most of his kithood in that wood, catching bugs and then hare and birds with Kjorn and Thyra. Only small game lived on Sun Isle but for the reindeer in the snowy, more dangerous mountains. The White Mountains in the far starward edge of the island lent cold rainy winters to Sverin's pride on the windland coast, and bitter cold and snow to the other side of them.

If exiled, Shard would have nowhere to live on Sun Isle. If he even stayed in the Silver Isles. Most exiles had fled. No one really knew if they even survived the flight oversea to somewhere beyond. Shard thought of the copper gryfon, exiled that very morning.

Where will Einarr's brother go?

A harsh cackle nearly sent Shard out of his feathers and he veered. A raven. A raven had called at him through the high air. *Why would a raven fly so high?*

"I'm not hunting," Shard growled. "I have no scraps for you, pest!"

"But you are hunting," the raven taunted. "Aren't you?" Shard glanced around to make sure no others saw him speaking to the bird. Kjorn would have laughed himself out of the air. Unlike lesser birds, ravens had learned the gryfon's tongue in the First Age. Shard knew they had only done it to be bothersome.

"No. Do you see anything up here to hunt? Leave me in peace."

"If you were in peace, I would leave you, son-of-Sigrun." The bird snickered, clicking its beak in good imitation of a chiding gryfon mother. Heat flushed under Shard's feathers.

"How do you know me?"

The raven studied him with one black eye. "You are Rashard, son-of-the-Nightwing, the last born Vanir of the Silver Isles?"

Shard ground his beak, gaze flicking about. If anyone saw him talking to a raven–but his curiosity bubbled. He had never heard of the Nightwing. Or anything else about his father. "I am Rashard. Speak plainly."

The bird snickered and dove back toward the islands. For a heart-beat Shard considered catching him, and his wingtips twitched. Only the thought of what Caj would say of him falling out of ranks to chase a mudding carrion-eater stopped him. He stared until the speck of raven disappeared into the bleak green of Star Island.

There were too many reputations to guard. His own, Kjorn's, his mother's. Even Caj. Shard knew nothing of his father, or this Nightwing, and he knew that was of his mother's design. *And didn't I just tell the king I didn't care?*

Caj gave the call to descend toward the forest. The call for the hunt to begin.

Shard narrowed his eyes, tucked his wings, and dove.

3
UNDER THE ROWAN TREES

S HARD'S WINGS CRAMPED IN THE chilly, damp woods. If he tried to
open them he would strike a tree on either side and tangle in the
wild, wiry underbrush. All stood bare yet from winter except for the
long pines and twisting, ancient red juniper that grew evergreen. Only
strange shapes of sunlight reached the ground, mottles of bright and
twists of shadow that could have been animals, or just breezes. Shard
was grateful to see that Kjorn was just as twitchy.

Star Island was larger than it appeared from above. The dark roll
of pine, birch and brush, and the river that snaked through them,
broken by short rocky cliffs and falls, were beautiful from above. They
became nothing but trouble for a gryfon on foot.

Shard remained at Kjorn's side as they ranged. No gryfon was
to hunt alone. Ahead of them, Thyra tracked. Shard slunk through
the trees, edgy in the cool shadows. He didn't care for this kind of
darkened stalking.

The witless birds were silent, watching them, and other lesser
creatures had fled. Shard peered around for ravens but saw none. At
his side, Kjorn shone like one of his father's golden bands every time

they walked through the dapples of sun. Shard's darker feathers and duller flanks seemed better suited to forest hunting.

But we aren't meant to hunt on the ground at all. Shard thought of a gryfess, plunging down on a deer from above. Hunting through the forest was a warrior's challenge. A gryfon, the king insisted, should be able to hunt on any ground he chose.

Ahead, Thyra paused. Shard nudged Kjorn, who'd kept walking. The prince hesitated, lowered his head and peered around, taking slow sniffs.

Shard smelled it too, a musky wash of scent.

"Wolves," whispered Kjorn.

Shard made note of the place. A round of pale, black-pocked birch and the trickle of water nearby. "We are in their territory," Shard said.

The prince swiveled a fierce blue gaze on him. "We're in *our* territory. The Silver Isles belong to my father and his pride. You can hunt wherever you like, Shard."

"I just meant—"

Thyra snapped her beak, cocking her head back at them. They fell silent, and all three crept forward again. If they sighted or scented the boar, they would raise a call, and all the hunters would drive it out of the trees. Until then it must be silent hunting.

Damp, spongy earth quieted their footfalls, though Shard kept seeing motion in the shadows at the corners of his vision. Every time he turned to look, all was still. Birch trees gave way to a ring of skeletal rowan, gnarled and dark. In autumn, their berries blazed like forest fires all over the islands, but now they only added to Shard's tension, for they offered shelter to enemies.

"I think we're being watched."

"Wolves," Kjorn said again, this time with disdain. "Too cowardly to try and fight us off. Maybe they hope to feed off our kill. I'd see them try!"

"You sound like you want to meet wolves here," Shard muttered. Kjorn cocked his head, eyes bright. Shard scrounged for even a speck of his friend's courage.

"And why not? Think if we took a wolf pelt to my father along with the boar's meat, think of the honors we—"

"Silence, idiots," Thyra hissed. Something moved two leaps ahead. They froze and crouched. Thyra perked her long feathered ears, tail-tip twitching, and lifted her beak to sniff.

Kjorn's tension felt like a ball of skyfire, ready to burst and light up the woods. His tail twitched, talons clutching the carpet of pine needles. Shard watched his prince warily, hoping he kept to Caj's instructions.

Thyra's tail flicked up to signal, feathers fanning open at the end for a half breath before she lowered it again. She had spotted the boar. Kjorn and Shard exchanged a look and parted from each other to circle around the sides. In a triangle, they could drive it out of the woods.

Shard's heart beat so thunderously through his ears he was surprised it didn't frighten the boar in the wrong direction. Shadows moved in the corner of his eye. He stopped, looked, and clamped his will against a warning snarl.

"*Now!*" Thyra's shriek dragged him back to the hunt.

Shard hadn't even seen the boar, and the wind was wrong for him to smell it, but he trusted her. He ramped up to stand on his hind legs and flared his wings, only to knock them against two trees. He stamped his feet to earth and bellowed, a young lion's roar deep in his chest. Kjorn's fierce cry answered his across the woods. The brush rustled between them and Shard leaped forward.

He saw a flash of hard gray hide, snarled and snapped his beak in threat. The boar wheeled to charge Kjorn. Shard leaped after it, and Thyra shouted.

"Stay! It's only threatening. We'll drive it out of the trees over there!"

Shard looked. Ahead, the trees broke to a rockier, grassy expanse of meadow. He heard Kjorn's shriek and forced himself not to run to help. He kept to the plan and waited, crouching, ready to harry the boar if it came back his way. The bright shine of gold ahead was Kjorn, and Shard watched over the underbrush. He heard Thyra fighting through underbrush and trees to get closer, trying to distract the boar away in the right direction.

Shard trotted forward. The woods remained still and silent. He lifted his ears and scented. The wind shifted, and the boar's scent struck like a wing blow. Shard froze.

Brush rustled and he saw the hump of the creature's back. He braced and roared a challenge.

The boar broke from the heavier brush straight to the trees where Shard crouched. His throat clamped against another roar. The boar's cloven hooves tore the earth. He stood as tall at the shoulder as Shard and glared with tiny, wet, red eyes. Skin as thick and hard as rock sheathed the muscled body, all as Caj said. Unable to roar, Shard ducked his head and opened his beak in a long hiss, clawing the damp earth.

The boar squealed. Shard knew Thyra and Kjorn had to hold their own ground. It was up to him to drive the beast back. In all the tales ever told of hunts, courage and glory, no one had ever warned of the tight, cold feeling Shard felt in his belly.

He forced a step forward, then another, raising his wings to make himself look bigger, stronger, and fearless, though terror arced through him.

The boar shook its ugly head and squealed, a split, three note, horrible sound. A horrible sound that, to Shard's awe, dissolved itself into words.

"*I will not die for your glory, thief.*"

Stupid, boars are supposed to be witless! Shard had no chance to balance his shock. The boar stamped the ground and charged, thundering forward through the brush. He drove through tangle and thorn, tusks tearing, hard shoulders snapping twigs.

Panic and confusion burst inside Shard, and he flared his wings without thinking, shoving up from the ground. The bare, wiry birch caught his wings, tangled his feathers. Rowan limbs bent and snapped. He could not beat the air to gain height. He clawed at the trunks and branches around him like a panicked kit, like a lesser wildcat, a squirrel. A coward. More branches snapped under his wings. The boar rammed its shoulder against the birch. Shard clung and tried mustering a roar. Nothing came.

The boar struck again. Bark and birch twig fluttered to the ground. Shard shoved his hind legs against the birch trunk, leaped and caught purchase on a thick, twisted juniper. Only one leap off the ground, but the boar couldn't reach him. It rampaged past with an evil, laughing squeal.

The colors of other gryfons flashed in the meadow beyond the trees. Braver gryfons. Einarr and Halvden were already proving themselves warriors.

Roars and shrieks met Shard's ears. Relief tingled in him, then shame. Cautiously he slid down from the tree, leaving long talon scars in the red trunk. He flexed his wings and found them undamaged, if a little bruised, and he felt calmer knowing he could fly. A broken paw mended easily. A broken wing mended with the help of a gryfon healer, or not at all, and being stranded flightless on Star Isle could mean death.

Shard turned toward the meadow, ready to make up for his cowardice.

"Only a fool would stand ground alone against old Lapu," a female voice said. Shard whirled, hissing, and saw no one. "I'm glad to see you aren't a fool, Rashard son-of-the-Nightwing."

"Show yourself!" He turned in a circle, wings half open, though he didn't dare try to fly in the woods again. All the other gryfons pursued the boar to the meadow. He was alone. A scent washed him, musky, woodsy.

Wolf.

When he stood still at last and moved only his ears he heard her, and turned.

In the woods she blended as well as a shaft of sunlight, or a shadow, or a leaf. The wolves of the Star Isle grew nearly as large as gryfons. Unlike the lesser beasts that ranged the little forests of the lesser islands, they also boasted bold coloring, had names, and spoke. What he could see of her coat was like the red heather of summer, but those spots in the sunlight shifted color like gryfon feathers, iridescent gray and gold. She stood under the tallest of the rowan trees.

"Who are you? Speak!"

She stepped forward, ears up, alert but not threatening, amber eyes bright. Her hackles remained smooth, her stance passive.

"I am Catori. Why do you hunt the great boar?"

"For meat," he lied, then, thinking of Kjorn, angled his head proudly. "For the great kill, to prove our worth. For the glory of the king." Even as he spoke he wondered why he was explaining himself to her instead of attacking, or leaving to join his fellows.

"Which king?" She stood rooted as a pine tree, inscrutable as the whispering birch. Shard hesitated. The wind shifted through the naked branches and pine boughs and seemed to echo her in tiny voices: *Which king? Which king?*

Snapping his gaze up, he saw only branches rustling in the whispering breeze, and birds. He looked back to the she-wolf, narrowing his eyes.

"The only king. Sverin son-of-Per, king of the Silver Isles."

Her nose wrinkled, showing the sharp points of her teeth. "King of the Sun Isle, you mean. King of thieves. There is already a king on the Star Isle. Gryfons don't belong here."

"We belong wherever we wish. Wherever we fly. Fight me if you don't think so."

Movement caught his eye and he looked up. A raven sat in the branches above, bobbling back and forth and chuckling. Shard wondered if it the same as earlier that morning. *Did it track me, tell the wolves, cause this trouble?*

"I have no wish to fight you." The wolf drew Shard's attention back down. "Though you trespass here, and your king has hunted my family."

"Trespass?" Shard forced a bold laugh, thinking of Kjorn. *These islands belong to us.* "As for the king, Sverin hunts wolves because you harry our hunts on Star Isle. It's your own fault."

"A vicious circle." She tilted her head. "But which came first, Rashard, the mountain, or the sea?" Above, the raven guffawed and sidled on his branch, echoing her.

Shard hesitated and fluffed. Her answer made no sense, and yet with the words came a memory, the low and thrumming voice of a male gryfon. *My father's voice?*

Which sprang first, Rashard, the mountain or the sea? Not even the eldest could tell, whether first came wave or tree.

"Which came first?" The raven winged to another branch.

Words Shard didn't remember learning clawed his mind and he whispered, "The silence, or the song…"

"Not even the rowan could say," murmured Catori, "had it a voice, and lived so long."

Shard backed down two steps, wanting to flare, to fly, staring at the wolf before him. This was madness, all of it. He needed to return to Kjorn's side.

Then an idea struck like skyfire. He could take a wolf as his prize today. Kjorn had said it himself. *What honors might Sverin give me, then?* He stamped a taloned foot.

"Enough of this wolf witchery. Drive me off if you don't like me here. Fight me. I challenge you!"

He snarled, flattened his ears and opened his wings. The wolf didn't move. Then he saw why. More movement. More shadows. The scent clouded him and warbled growls and mutters mocked him from the trees.

Wolves surrounded him. He just hadn't seen them.

"Now answer me truly, Rashard." Her eyes glowed in the slant of sun. "Why do *you* hunt the great boar?"

Aching to fly, to escape, or to leap and fight, Shard shifted, unable to stand still. *Why did I think I could hunt and fight alone?*

His breath short, he answered the truth in anger. "To prove my worth as a warrior. To earn a place in the pride, so I won't be exiled."

"Exile," murmured the she-wolf. He wondered if she would be so brave if she didn't have the support of the wolves in the trees. He doubted it. He noticed, after seeing the raven, that Catori wore two long, dark feathers twisted neatly into the heavy fur of her neck. Only bird talons could have done that work. She was in league with ravens.

"Exile might not be so bad, Rashard."

"Stop saying my name," he snarled. "How do you know me?"

She turned one ear to the raven, who cackled and babbled his name over and over. "For your honesty, and for your family, I will tell you how to kill the boar." Her amber eyes seemed mischievous, then fierce and sad. Shard grew alert in spite of himself. "He has had a life so long that he has outlived any kind of joy. Even we would be glad not to lose more cubs to his hooves."

Shard lifted his wings. "We know how to kill the boar."

She tilted her head. "Do you?"

He hesitated. It had to be some kind of wolf trick, to keep him away from the hunt, to keep him from helping Kjorn. *But then, wouldn't they have attacked by now?* The vicious wolves Caj described did not seem to be the same kind of wolf that stood before him now, speaking with quiet reason. He also hadn't expected the boar itself to speak. Shard feared more surprises. *Do we truly know how to kill the boar?*

The thought of attacking this wolf who knew his name, who had spoken as reasonably as any gryfon, didn't feel right.

Today was about the boar, about Kjorn, about supporting Kjorn. If this wolf knew how to kill the boar, then Shard had to learn.

"Tell me what you have to say." He lifted his head. A breeze sifted through the woods, ruffling his feathers. "Then leave me."

She yipped a laugh, then, to his surprise, stretched down and lowered her head in a mocking bow. "Why yes, great gryfon. Yes, of course, we will leave you to your most important business."

More yips rose, then full howls of laughter. Their ghostly voices sent shudders through his chest and the skin under his feathers flushed. Then the red she-wolf stepped forward from under the rowan tree, her soft fur making her silent in the underbrush, until she stood so close he could have stretched a talon to her throat.

She wasn't afraid of him, Shard realized. He knew then that she wouldn't be even if she faced him alone.

That near, her amber eyes glowing in the sun, she told him what he must do to kill the boar.

4
LAPU'S LAST WORDS

THE SMALL MEADOW ROILED WITH gryfon colors. Old Caj and Kjorn burned bright, blue and gold like the sky, Halvden green as the grass, Einarr as copper as stone. The females stood at four points on the edge of the meadow to guard against the wolves they'd heard and to keep the boar from escaping.

Lapu, the she-wolf had called him. She told Shard to remember his name, that he would answer to it.

Shard loped into the clearing with a shrieking snarl and heard Kjorn answer in relief. The boar stood in a ring of the males, his hide barely scored from their claws. The gryfons panted strategy to each other over his head. They didn't know what Shard knew. They didn't know Lapu understood their words.

There were three things he must do.

You must not speak what you don't want him to hear, the she-wolf had said. *Or he will know your plans. Lapu is proud, the wiliest creature on all the Star Isle, and he does not know fear.*

Shard shoved himself into the air, relieved that the meadow was wide enough. He keened a signal to Kjorn, whose head snapped up

27

in surprise. Caj barked at him to come down—hadn't he said they couldn't hope to kill from above? But Kjorn listened. He leaped from the ground and Shard saw in dismay that his shoulder seeped blood under the bright feathers.

You must make him charge, the she-wolf said. *In a rage, he is half blind.*

"Listen, Kjorn, my prince," Shard spoke over the wind, high where Lapu couldn't hear.

"Where were you? We heard wolves!"

"I'm fine. Fly higher with me. We're going to kill this monster."

Kjorn peered at him, then huffed and followed him up. Shard told him what he knew, Kjorn listened with surprise, and they made their plan.

Shard dove down and landed on the far side of the meadow near Thyra.

"Nest-sister! Do you think the boar is too stupid to run toward the trees, or just blind?" He forced a laugh, speaking too loudly. Thyra swiveled her head to stare at him. Then she also saw Lapu the boar whirl, thrusting tusks at old Caj, who was nearest. The blue warrior leaped aside, hissing.

"What are you doing?" Thyra flapped her wings once, and Shard saw in her face she knew that Lapu understood them. "If he charges, we'll lose him in the trees again."

Shard flattened his ears. "Trust me!" He crouched. *Lapu is proud.* "Einarr!" The younger gryfon's ears snapped up, heeding Shard even as Caj shouted at them. *I must make him charge. I must make him charge.* "Why do you think the other creatures of Star Island avoid this old beast?"

Einarr's eyes widened and he looked from Thyra to Caj and then ramped up to his hind legs, flashing his wingtips wide. He locked eyes with Shard, doubtful, but in a ringing voice snapped, "It must be the smell!"

Shard laughed, breathless. Lapu shrieked and whirled, swinging his tusks. The gryfons took up the insults. Shard dared him, called him a coward. *Lapu is proud. You must make him charge.*

His heart beat the words. *Why am I trusting the word of a wolf? She's probably trying to get me killed.* But if that were true, they would have simply killed him in the trees when they had him outnumbered. They were using the gryfons to kill the boar. They wanted to be rid of him. Shard didn't care, as long as it worked.

"I wonder why there are no young boars around?" He shouted toward the field, and paced four steps before crouching. "Maybe the old beast is too ugly. Or too stupid to find a mate. Or too blind."

"His brain is made of stone like his hide," one of the females called, and laughed. She squawked and darted aside as Lapu stamped and feinted an attack. Thyra shrieked in alarm as the boar broke through the male gryfons in the middle of the field.

"Shard!"

"Or not strong enough to get piglets on a sow?" Blood pumping wild, Shard flung his wings open, taunting, trying to draw Lapu's gaze. The other males harried the old boar at his sides, but he spun and slashed with his tusks until they fell back.

Before Shard could think of another insult, Lapu lowered his head, bellowed a squealing challenge that rocked the air, and charged.

Shard's breath left him. He crouched, digging his talons into the earth. *I will not fly. Not this time. I will not—I will not.* Gold flashed above him. He held his ground, flared his wings, lowered his head and hissed. To his own surprise, it deepened to a roiling, deep roar from his belly and then his chest, a sound like thunder over the sea.

Lapu's red eyes flickered at the sound. His step caught.

I must make him charge.

"Second thoughts, coward?" The air shifted and rustled above Shard.

"Never!" Hooves gouged the earth. The boar pounded down the last length of empty grass between them.

The scent washed him. The sight of blood on those long tusks.

The gleam in tiny, wet red eyes.

I will not fly!

A ball of sunlit fire and feathers slammed into the boar from the side, sending him rolling across the dirt. The crash of their impact sent flocks of birds from the trees, crying alarm.

Thyra leaped past Shard. "Kjorn!" The others ran forward now that the boar was off its feet.

Shard stood there, shuddering, then blinked and surged forward, leaping into the fray. *There are three things you must do,* Catori had said.

Three things.

You must not speak what you don't want him to hear.

Shard knocked Thyra aside. She fell back, surprised, but bowed her head to let him pass.

You must make him charge.

Caj stood in his path. "Move!" Shard bellowed, and strained his wings open to shove the blue warrior out of his way. He fell aside out of shock, then laid back his ears and shouted warning. But Shard was not clawing for glory. He saw only his friend, his prince, gold Kjorn rolling across the earth with an ancient, battle-scarred boar now mad for a kill. *You must not speak. You must make him charge. Three things.*

You must say these words.

Then the she-wolf had murmured gibberish into his ear. It was the language of wolves, boar, deer, and other mudding creatures bound to the dirt. He didn't understand it. She'd made him repeat the murmuring, throaty words three times to her even though he didn't understand.

You aren't listening, she had said. It was wolf language. It was earth language, mud language, not spoken by gryfons, not spoken by voices of the sky. Of course he wasn't listening. But he learned the words to say them.

Madness. I shouldn't have trusted her. But the boar was down, and Kjorn was in danger. There was no other choice. He couldn't take two steps down her path and then turn. It had to be done.

Kjorn shrieked in pain and Shard leaped over Halvden's head, landing nearly on top of the gray and gold tangle that was Kjorn and the boar.

"*Lapu!*" Shard slapped talons against the stone hide. Lapu shrieked and bellowed. "Hear me!"

Kjorn flicked a narrow look to him, panting, half mad with hunt-anger and fear, his ear torn from a slash that could have taken his eye. Lapu gurgled, struggling to rise to his hooves. Shard skidded around to his head.

"Kjorn, hold him!" Both gryfons dug talons into the boar's shoulder and neck. "Lapu," Shard muttered while the great boar squirmed, kicking sharp hooves and straining to toss his head and tear with his tusks.

Shard ground the hastily practiced, foreign words out of his beak. They whispered back into Shard's mind like tumbling rock and the whisper of paws in the grass, but he couldn't define their meaning.

Lapu blinked his tiny, hooded red eyes, shuddered, and seemed to collapse inside. Shard perked his ears and spoke the words again. Lapu tossed his head, but less in threat. Shockingly, he met Shard's eyes, and in the glazed red depths Shard saw centuries of a long and proud life as one of the mighty princes of Star Island, saw that Lapu remembered his name, that he knew wisdom. And, as Kjorn's talons clenched his throat, fear. Slow, hollow breaths lifted his ribs, each weaker than the last.

He grumbled something and foam dripped from his snout. Shard lifted his ears. Unlike Catori's words that he hadn't wanted badly enough to understand, he listened closely to Lapu's last words, and Lapu made himself understood.

"Nightwing," he rasped in disbelief, still clenching to life.

Shard's beak clicked twice before he could speak. *Are you Rashard, son-of-the-Nightwing?* The raven had asked. He wasn't sure if Lapu would understand in turn.

"No. His…his son."

"Then I am at peace." Lapu's red eyes, ancient, baleful, and clever, held Shard's gaze. "Thank you for a good death, brother."

Kjorn caught his breath at last and nudged Shard aside. The last words of Lapu of the Star Isle sent Shard reeling more than the push.

"For the king," Kjorn snarled before he swept in for the kill. Shard backed away, letting the others see the prince take the kill. Glancing around, he knew that he was the only one in the meadow who had understood Lapu's words. As when Catori had spoken he had only heard uttered growls, so, he knew, Kjorn hadn't understood him speaking to Lapu.

Their cry rose up, lion roars and eagle calls, echoing through the woods and rocks and streams to the sea. Shard gathered himself, lifted his voice with theirs, and flared his wings.

Kjorn stepped back after wiping his beak on the grass. Ragged and bleeding, he looked as savagely majestic as a legend from the pride's oldest songs.

Thank you for a good death, Lapu had said. *Brother.* Shard folded his wings and ducked his head when the prince looked his way.

"Shard," he whispered, blue eyes half wild from the hunt. "He just…died. He was gone before I bit. I know he was. He just laid down his head. What did you do?"

Shard perked his ears toward the carcass that had been Lapu. *Brother.*

"Nothing." He looked away from his prince into the dark, silent woods as the birds settled back into the trees. "I didn't do anything."

He thought he saw amber eyes glowing back at him from the woods, but it might have been sunlight on rowan buds, or shadows, or nothing at all.

5
THE WIDOW QUEEN

"A BOAR INDEED. SHARD, BLACK MOSS, please."

Shard sat on his haunches at the back of his mother's den, picking through her stores of astringents and moss compresses nudged into the layered rock wall. The den was larger than most, for she stored herbs in its bowled crevasses, splints of wood along jutting rock shelves, and batches of clay in scooped depressions. It was a healer's cave, delved deeper into the rock that held it with each new generation.

Sigrun shooed a fledgling apprentice out of the way and extended her talons to take the moss from Shard with a quick murmur of thanks. She didn't have to check if it was the right one. She had raised him to know them all. Shard had grown up to the sharp scent of herbs, sticky clay, and the blood of injuries. All of it whorled into his mother's scent and in that place, nothing seemed as strange or worrisome as it had before.

Einarr and Halvden had come and gone with bruises and strains, and now Kjorn stood near the entrance. The den lay on the edge of the cliff facing the dawnward sea, so was one of the first to grow gloomy and cool in the late afternoon. Sigrun's two apprentices, fledging females of questionable attention span, busied themselves cleaning up fallen feathers and the spill of bark and seeds. Shard puttered slowly, more or less helping but mostly in the way, as he thought back on the hunt.

Thank you for my good death, brother.

He didn't know what it meant. He had understood the boar's final words, but not what he himself had said. *What did he mean, brother?* There was no one he could ask. No one except the she-wolf, Catori. Or maybe one of the other old Vanir. Shard glanced furtively at his mother.

"I suppose," Sigrun went on as she gently lifted the prince's gold feathers to apply the thirsty moss to his wound, "next initiation it will be a flight to the White Mountains for the snow cats. Or caribou. So you may fight snow and height as well as deadly prey. Won't that be merry? Or wolves, I suppose."

"I hope," Kjorn growled, then winced when Sigrun prodded his left wing. "Did Shard tell you how they ambushed him?"

One ear slanted Shard's way, but she didn't answer as Kjorn went on, sounding more and more like his father. They bickered politely, Sigrun longing for the less deadly initiations of yesteryear, Kjorn arguing for challenge. Shard helped the apprentices to clean, and even managed not to snort when he saw the oldest tuck a fallen green feather, Halvden's, under her wing for keeping.

"Shard," said the younger. "Play riddles with us?"

Shard had enough riddles for the day. But her brown eyes pleaded, reminding him of Thyra at a younger age, and he relented. He had a new riddle they wouldn't have heard before.

"Which came first," he murmured, "the mountain or the sea? Not even the eldest could tell, whether first came wave or—"

"*Shard.*"

He and the fledges blinked at Sigrun. Her wings had tensed, her feathered tail quivered. She looked surprised at herself, then her feathers slowly rose to fluff. "Here, now. I need your help." She turned to Kjorn. "Your Highness, the wing is out of joint."

"I know," Kjorn said. "I felt it flying home. It'll sort on its own."

"It won't."

Kjorn shuddered a sigh. Shard trotted to them and he braced Kjorn's wing carefully, readying to tug while Sigrun gripped the prince's shoulder. "All right. On three now." She caught Shard's gaze and he dipped his head. "One…"

They wrenched together and Kjorn's sharp cry cracked through the cave. "*Windblown, mudding—*"

"Language, my prince." Sigrun eyed her ogling apprentices. Shard chuckled and butted Kjorn's shoulder.

Wings rustled, the shadow of an approaching gryfon darkened the cave, and at once, Kjorn rose to full height. He sleeked his feathers down, compact against his body so that he looked smooth and proud. He didn't even favor the wing.

"All part of it, of course. Little injuries like that." He stretched his wings to demonstrate his health, masking a wince. "A minor thing."

Shard ruffled and glanced to the mouth of the cave. Thyra stooped and landed. An amused sound rose in Shard's throat and he stifled it.

"Your Highness." Thyra lowered her head, and Shard saw that Kjorn was, in a rare moment, without words. He simply lifted his wings in acknowledgement, and winced at the motion while she stepped inside. "Mother. Is everyone sorted?"

"Well as can be," Sigrun said, turning to finish the last of the cleaning. She gave Shard a quick, sharp glance, and he looked to Thyra to avoid eye contact. Thyra appraised Shard, then addressed all of them.

"Then the king has asked everyone to gather on Copper Cliff before sunset for the tale."

"Shortly," said Sigrun, who hated rushing.

Shard noticed her look between Thyra and Kjorn, and the way they didn't quite meet each other's eyes. He couldn't tell if Sigrun was pleased over the prince's interest Thyra. Not by the expression on her face, anyway. Much of Sigrun's work depended on hiding a truth of how grim an injury might be, for the peace of mind of her charges, and so her expression was often impassive. Shard could read her wings, though, which laid relaxed along her back, short feathers fluffed, the long flight feathers brushing the floor.

She's pleased.

"You led us well today," Kjorn said to Thyra, when he found his voice at last.

Shard busied himself with his mother, and cuffed the staring apprentices into work. Thyra's eyes glimmered in the last light reaching the cave.

"Well. Thank you, my Lord. But then what hope would a lot of bumbling males have without the help of my sisters and I?"

"None at all. But you did see, of course, when I knocked the monster off its feet."

"Everyone saw, my Lord." But her gaze almost imperceptibly switched to Shard, who watched them sidelong, before the feathers of her face fluffed in amusement. She inclined her head. "A mighty victory."

Kjorn drew a breath. "You'll join us on the high rocks for the feast, of course? As one of the honored hunters."

Thyra mantled. "If my prince wishes."

Kjorn ruffled and Shard clinched his beak against laughter. His sister was bold. How many of the young females would simply roll at the prince's feet? *Not Thyra, daughter-of-Caj.*

"I do," Kjorn said. "That is, only if you–"

"Well then," chirped Sigrun, turning to behold her tidy, crowded den. "Shall we be off?"

"Please," said Thyra, then turned and dove from the cave before any of the others could speak.

Shard erupted into laughter. "You're smooth as swan down, wingbrother." Kjorn feinted an attack, loosing a mock snarl. Shard crouched, ready to spring away. "Will you give me tips for my own lady friends?"

Kjorn barked laughter and lunged. Shard dodged toward the back of the den, the two fledges scattered with delighted shrieks, and Sigrun threatened violence if they wrecked her cave. Kjorn herded Shard from the cave, and chased him all the way to the king's rocks.

SIGRUN WATCHED THEM GO before helping her flightless apprentices along crags to the top of the cliff. *Is this how it is to be, then?* She asked the pale sky. Kjorn was courting her daughter, and she didn't know what had come over Shard.

Which came first, the mountains or the sea?

Where had he heard that song?

Wolves ambushed him, indeed. Sigrun was convinced there was more to it than that. But Shard had never lied before. *But then, he hasn't lied yet.* She realized he truly hadn't yet said anything at all. Everyone else had spoken of what happened, and Shard neither confirmed nor denied.

"Hurry now," she whispered to her fledges as unease curled under her wings. "The king's patience is not to be tested."

SHARD AND THYRA PICKED their way through other gryfons settling into the grass below the rocks. Late afternoon light warmed against a cold starward wind, and rosy gray touched the sky. Kjorn had flown to the rocks to sit beside his father, who lounged on the lowest slab to be nearer to the pride and the storytellers. He looked informal, no gold and gems, ears laid back lazily as he waited for the last arrivals to settle.

"You should sit closer," Thyra murmured as Shard claimed a bare spot, kicking away a few pebbles. "You'll have a ways to walk when it's your turn."

"What will I say?" Shard muttered, shifting. His wings tensed at the thought. He looked nightward to the sun, then dawnward where the moon already hung at second mark. "I've never spoken to so many before."

Thyra flickered her ears, then dipped her head down to preen at his shoulder. She was going to outgrow him, he realized, like all the other Aesir females. "Then don't speak to so many. Just look to me when you tell your tale."

Shard laid one ear back in uncertainty, but before he could respond, the king spoke and his low voice carried long over the grass.

"Welcome, my family." He didn't stand. Shard perked his ears, curious at the informality. Everyone fell silent. The king seemed pleased. "Before this day, our thoughts of the hunt were only hopes. We only imagined what our young warriors could do." The king lifted his scarlet wings as if to enfold them all. "Now it is proven!"

Shard wondered at the king's manner, so relaxed and, for he couldn't think of a better expression, happy. Everyone had done well on the hunt, but now came the judgement, which was usually more somber. Sverin's fierce red face grew still. His golden eyes seemed to light on every alert face in the pride. "I know that many of you of the old pride still question the way of my forefathers. That you still wish to hunt from the sea."

The sudden, sharper tension among the gryfons at the words felt just as strong to Shard as he'd felt during the hunt. Many eyes averted, wings rustled, and some shifted nervously, as if they felt trapped.

But the king didn't seem angry. "To hunt on land, to know the fierce struggle of battle, is one of Tyr's great gifts to us. The sea," he paused, ears flickering back in the rarest moment of hesitation, "brings only chill and death."

A murmur chirruped and muttered through all. "He speaks of his mate," Thyra whispered, and perked her ears toward the king.

Shard did the same. Sverin never spoke so openly, so calmly, as if all who lay on the grass that evening were his wingbrothers and sisters.

"But now!" Sverin stretched his wings. "Let each come forward and tell his part in the hunt."

A nervous rustle rippled through the assembled gryfons. The king chuckled at the hesitation. Gryfons exchanged glances. They had never seen the king so cheerful after a great hunt. These tales and his judgment determined whether they remained with the pride or went into exile.

"After facing a boar, an old, wily, stone-strong boar, I've heard, no one will be the first to stand?"

"I will!" Halvden leaped to his feet, green feathers bright.

Gryfons churred and called encouragement as he padded up to the rocks, pausing to mantle and bow to the king before he turned to face the pride. The late light blazed on his wings and he looked the part of a fully-grown warrior. Shard curled his claws against the grass and checked a sigh.

"I sighted the boar first from the air as we scouted…"

When the pride encouraged him he grew bolder, both in his storytelling and, it seemed, on the hunt itself. Shard thought he took too long telling his part, and he drifted. *I should think what I will say.* He couldn't speak of the wolves. Or the words Catori the she-wolf had told him to say. He shouldn't have spoken strange words whose meaning he didn't know. Shard tried to think what part he could tell to make himself sound worthy.

I will have to lie.

He looked about as Halvden droned on, scarcely noticing when the next young male climbed onto the rock. His ear twitched to hear a more confident voice: Einarr. He would probably be a good singer. Everyone looked so happy. He saw siblings lounged together like himself and Thyra, he saw mated pairs, clumps of fledges just old enough to range from the nest and climb but not strong enough to fly, all with ears perked and beaks parted in awe at the tales.

How will they feel when Sverin announces who can stay, and who can't?

"Why are you so twitchy?" Thyra purred softly. Shard felt her contentment against his side. "Your tale will be the best." He blinked, swiveling his face back toward the rocks.

There was a moment of silence as copper Einarr hopped down from the rocks and took his place again in the listeners. Shard tilted his head and Thyra nipped his shoulder.

"Go!"

He blinked and clawed to his feet, stepping forward, around other gryfons who dozed, or listened raptly. He nearly tripped over an old female, who hissed grumpily, then looked curiously to the rocks. Shard followed her gaze.

A gryfon had already climbed onto the rocks. Kjorn. Shard froze. By rights, the prince should speak last. *Does he mean to skip me?* Shard stood there, stupid, then sank to his haunches as the prince spoke.

"We had a great hunt, with so many skilled warriors and the experienced gryfess hunters to guide us." He dipped his head and Shard looked about to see that the prince looked directly at Thyra. Thyra ruffled and looked away in modesty, while Shard felt his own feathers sleeking down, readying for a fight.

He acknowledged Thyra, but not me? Kjorn had never slighted him before. How could he now, when it was so important? Agitation crept up Shard's muscles and he strained to keep his wings closed as Kjorn continued.

"Some others, including my honored father who was not there, will tell you that my part in the hunt was the most dangerous, bold, and of course, I was given the killing stroke. But I know and am proud to say I couldn't have done any of it without the others. I couldn't have tracked and cornered the old beast."

His summer-blue gaze lit on many faces and he stood proud, tail low and confident. "I could not have driven it into the meadow, or gotten it off its feet. Truly, I couldn't have delivered the killing bite without the help at my side. Without all the hunters and, at the end, without my wingbrother. Tell us what befell you, Rashard, son-of-Sigrun."

Kjorn left that astonishing statement hovering in the air as he climbed back onto his higher rock and lay down, giving Shard the last part of the tale.

He did it for me. He knew I needed an extraordinary chance to prove myself to his father, and he did this for me.

Shard sat in the middle of the grass with his beak open and ears flat, uncertain. Gryfons peered around until it seemed every face was on him. The king's rocks felt leagues away. It would have taken forever to walk that distance. Instead, he rose to his feet where he was, swallowed whatever creature seemed to grasp his throat from the inside, and spoke from the middle of the pride.

"Ah, I helped Thyra and Kjorn to drive the boar into the meadow." That was hardly true. His voice sounded weak and far away. "Or—or at least, I got out of his way." Someone chuckled. A grizzled female near him shifted, bright eyes kind, others settled, more ears lifted to attend him closely.

But making them laugh wouldn't win him a place in the pride. Fear eddied around his words. He didn't feel like the same gryfon who had faced down a charging boar. *Lapu laid down his head for me.*

He tried to straighten up, opened his wings to catch some of the sunlight. "The boar charged me." He took a slow breath. Every face was on him. Those who had dozed were awake. Even the fledges watched him with wide, bright eyes. "I'm…ashamed to say that I tried to fly, that first time. You don't know fear," Shard said quietly to the nearest, wide-eyed kit, "until it's screaming toward you on sharp hooves." The kit burrowed into its mother's talons and Shard looked up again. "The boar escaped me, but others drove him to the meadow."

His heart thundered. His skin burned so hot under his feathers he thought he might burst into fire. Desperate, he glanced around until he caught Thyra's eye. *Just tell me your tale.* Her ears perked, rapt as the others, her wings lifted a little in encouragement.

"A pack…a number of wolves surrounded me. I got free of them and found the others in the meadow."

The words rolled out of him as if from somewhere else. Murmurs wove through the pride. After the bluff of the wolves, the rest came easily. He made the boar charge. He stood his ground. He and Kjorn got the beast off its feet. He didn't mention the foreign words, and finally, finally, the kill.

A buzzing sound made him flatten his ears. Not buzzing. Rustling. Churring. Sounds of respectful approval from his pride.

They don't know. They don't know that I treated with wolves, that I spoke earth words, that the boar we killed had a name.

He sank down to his belly in the grass, grateful it was done. If the king felt anything about Kjorn giving up his rights as the last speaker, it didn't show. He didn't rise from his comfortable position.

"Truly great tales, and a great hunt from all." Sverin swiveled to eye Kjorn. "And I'm glad to know my son understands that it is the pride that makes its king." At last he stood, pushing to all fours. "Take your leisure now. Feast. Enjoy this victory. I have many things to think over. We will gather again soon, to announce who has earned his place to remain on Sun Isle."

Shard's belly locked and the whole pride took a breath. The king had never delayed before. Never made them wait.

Talk erupted as gryfons rose, stretched, and padded to the meat gathered earlier—deer, rabbit, half a flock of geese. The boar was reserved for those on the king's rocks.

Sverin's judgement waited.

He could speak all he liked about glory and family, but Shard wasn't distracted. The hunt was about the judgement, about earning a place in the pride. Not just honor. Not just meat. He lay there on his belly on the cool grass, talons dug hard into the peat. They were fighting to earn their very life with their family. And he had *lied* about his part in the victory.

But it was still a victory. If he learned what bewitching words he'd said, Shard wondered if he could them again, if he might, in fact, have a great gift to offer the pride. Maybe there was some strength in his blood he hadn't known about.

Thyra bumped his shoulder with a purr as she trotted past to join Kjorn, the king, Caj and Sigrun in a place of honor on the rocks. In the corner of his eye Shard saw Halvden and his father and mother also climb to high spots, greeting and talking casually with the king. Kjorn sought Shard's eye contact over the field and tilted his head in invitation. Shard supposed he could've sat beside Kjorn, in a place of honor. But the way Kjorn stood to greet Thyra told Shard he didn't particularly want more company. Shard was happy to give them time.

And he wasn't hungry anyway.

A shadow fell over him and he looked up, then scrambled to his feet in surprise.

A gryfess stood there like a ghost in the late light. Her pale feathers weren't the startling white of an Aesir female but soft, like the foam that edged every wave in winter. She was a Vanir, a smaller gryfess of the original Silver Isles pride like Shard's mother. She was silent. She was Ragna, whom everyone called the Widow Queen.

Shard couldn't help but dip his head and mantle, at least halfway, to show his respect. She hadn't taken a new mate when Per the Red conquered. She'd refused. Her mate, the old king, was killed, but Per couldn't have killed or exiled her, for fear of the anger of the rest of the Silver Isles pride. He and his son could never truly have their loyalty if he'd killed their king *and* beloved queen.

Everyone knew the story, though Shard couldn't recall who had first told it to him. Sverin forbade speaking openly of the Conquering and what passed before it. The past was past, and such history endangered the unity of the pride.

"You hunted well." Her voice was measured and soft. Shard had never heard her speak before. Certainly not to him. Her eyes were the pale, pale green of autumn moss.

Shard searched for his voice. "I...thank you."

"Your storytelling could use some improvement." She cocked her head and Shard blinked. *Was that a joke?* Shard tried to figure out if she was teasing him. It hardly seemed dignified.

"Thank you. I mean—yes. I know." They stared at each other, and he resisted saying many things. All around them, gryfons chattered, laughing, some worried, some already sparring in the grass and planning for tomorrow.

Shard felt compelled to tell her the truth and he didn't know why. *Why her, when she's never spoken to me before?* The cold breeze shifted and he caught her scent, the warm fluff of feather and over it, wild sage.

The memory slapped his mind of Sigrun, standing over him, begging Per the Red to spare his life. As a kit he hadn't understood but he remembered her desperate tone. There had been another scent there too. Warmth and sage. A far away memory, he a half-blind kit, Sigrun begging. Standing beside her, Shard's senses told him, had been the white, Widow Queen. He wondered if they had been friends. *Wingsisters even? Why hasn't she spoken to me before?*

He realized his beak had fallen open in a nervous pant. He'd never remembered that before. But scents didn't lie.

"I'm proud of you, Rashard." Her pale eyes seemed far away, sadder, or younger, looking at a different point in time. "Whatever happens after this, know that, if it means anything to you."

Rather than pride, shame coiled in him again. Half of his victory was a lie. "Thank you," he whispered.

"Know also..." She hesitated and he lifted his head, ears perked, for some reason hungry for her words. She seemed to draw herself together from many places, and the light in her eyes softened. "Sigrun cannot speak of this, I know. But you should know how very much you resemble your father."

With that, she dipped her head and walked away, leaving Shard standing as blank and witless as a gull.

The sun seemed to slip lower too fast, and the starward wind brought cold.

The feast wore on toward evening as all seemed to forget the occasion. Shard forced down three gulps of rabbit meat and wrestled with the fledges, avoiding Kjorn the best he could for fear the prince would ask questions he couldn't answer.

As the sun touched the nightward horizon, parents herded kits and fledges away and the pride sought their dens. When Shard glided low to wing toward Sigrun's cave, he found Caj lounging fully in the way. Shard flapped once, wheeled and tightened to land, clinging to the rock face just outside the den.

"Nest-father," he said, one ear laying back in uncertainty. "May I—"

"As a grown warrior," Caj murmured, blue tail coiling and flicking out, "I expect you're old enough to find a new den."

Shard blinked, wings tense against his back. *Is he telling me I'm accepted into the pride?* Cautious joy wove up, but coupled with confusion. He hadn't expected to be kicked from the den.

Caj's tone and eyes were not cruel, but he didn't move. Beyond, Shard could see Thyra and Sigrun huddled and laughing over stories from the feast. Thyra scented him and glanced over with pity before looking away. A cold rock formed in Shard's belly.

"Shard," old Caj said, quieter, but hard as the rock on which he stretched, "It just won't do. On with you."

Hesitating, but not wanting to make a scene or seem like a yowling kit, Shard inclined his head and shoved from the rock face, freefalling toward the jagged rocks one hundred leaps below, until he felt a sliver of wind. Flaring, he caught it and rode along the face of the nesting cliffs until he came fully around to the starward side, where a few dens still lay empty.

Letting his wings choose, he flapped thrice and plunged into the first den he found with a large enough entrance. Old rodent bones and gull leavings scattered the floor. Shard didn't care. He picked through the gloom until he found the rotted remains of a nest, flopped down, and shut his eyes.

With no other gryfons near, the lack of Thyra's warm breathing at his side, his mother's twitching, even Caj's great, terrifying, comforting bulk, Shard felt less like an initiated warrior and more like a fallen fledge.

But at least he knew they were near. At least all of the pride was near. This was only a new den. Not exile. Shard stared hard through the darkening cave toward the opening of stars and sea. This den had a good view of the Star Isle, a dark lump against the night sky.

I can't be exiled.

He had to learn what power had made Lapu lay down his head. He had to learn if it was a trick he could use again, and why it seemed every beast but him knew his father's name, and if he possessed any of whatever power his father had. *You should know how much you resemble your father,* the Widow Queen had said. He'd told Sverin he didn't care about his father, but he had to know his own strengths.

The solemn, haunted howling of wolves rolled into his new den from across the league of sea between the islands. His ears perked. In the silence, he took its meaning. As Lapu's squeals had turned to words, he felt in his bones that this wolfsong was not for hunting.

Shard stared, sleepless through the dark, as understanding came. It was mourning.

On the eve of Lapu's death, the wolves who had *wanted* his death now sung mourning for him, honored him as a warrior. It made no sense. Shard had to go back.

6
AHOTE AND AHANU

S HARD FLEW UNTIL HE SAW the meadow where they fought Lapu. It was madness. The wolves would probably attack him. Shard wasn't sure he could even find them. It had been days since the hunt, nearly a fortnight before he could get away to fly on his own.

The king had yet to speak his judgment and the whole pride felt like a cramped winged muscle, tense and knotted from cold.

That morning Shard had left Sun Isle at first light, before Thyra or Kjorn could find him, ask questions, or follow. Kjorn had business that could keep him occupied, and Thyra and the other gryfesses would be hunting, far away near the coast of the island.

Winds tossed his flight as he peered down for any kind of movement below. The Star Island seemed bigger to him now, full of mystery and possibly magic. Shard was sure that's what the words had been, some kind of wolf magic.

Content that there were no wolves in the clearing, Shard drifted lower. Deer grazed in the woods. His belly snarled. He doubted he could take a deer on his own yet, and didn't like the idea of making a fool of himself by trying.

What will happen if I'm banished from the pride? He lighted, hind-paws finding earth first, flicking his wings once to soften the impact, and sunk his talons into the dirt and grass.

Birds flew, calling alarm through the trees as he landed. The deer sprang away. Shard perked his ears, every muscle taut. Wind rustled through the long yellow grass, bringing the scent of dirt, then pine and rain. It would come late in the night, he decided, or blow right by on the strong wind.

Spring leaped through the islands now in pale green buds and the floating feathers of molting gryfons. Shard sat down to scratch vigorously behind his right ear and watched some of his own pale down float away. Then he waited, still and silent. He didn't know the best way to find a wolf. He had no plan. They had just come to him before. Jays and sparrows swooped down to pluck his shed feathers for their nests.

"This is stupid," he muttered, flexing his talons. If wolves came this time, they would surely attack him. *If they come now, they'll surely attack. They don't need me to kill Lapu now.* Now he was a lone gryfon, trespassing in wolf hunting territory.

Our territory, Kjorn had growled. Lapu had called him a thief and Shard didn't understand what he meant. Shard lifted his head, opened his wings and spoke, trying to sound confident, as if he belonged there. He could see, then fly, from any wolf before they got close. *Yes, fly like a coward.*

"Catori!" He finally called the she-wolf's name toward the trees, then turned about, and called again. "Catori, of…of the Star Island wolves!" Grass rustled, wind sang through the trees and shadows shifted. "I am Rashard, come back to speak with you!"

Maybe he being was foolish. No, it he was certainly being foolish. What if they were on the other side of the island? Or down by the sea? They would never hear him, leagues away. But, feeling stubborn, Shard sat in the grass and waited.

As he sat and listened to the wind he felt slightly less foolish. He saw birds settle again in the trees. The witless things probably thought that since he had been still so long that he was a stone, or an odd feathered tree. Shard listened to their songs. A shadow in the woods moved and he focused on it, ears tuned. A doe. Even the deer had returned, for the wind was wrong to take them his scent.

Part of him enjoyed this silence, knowing no one would come along and heckle him as Halvden did, knowing he didn't have to speak to anyone. He was free to fly and range over the island or the sea. *Exile,* he remembered the red she-wolf saying. *It might not be so bad.*

The other part of him warned of hungry nights, dangerous nights without the other eyes and ears of his pride. He thought of how he woke with starts every night in his empty den, certain he'd heard voices that turned out to be dreams.

No, exile was not for him.

"*Catori!*" Finally impatient, he stood again, tail lashing. The birds yattered their alarm but didn't fly. The deer leaped away again. Shard sighed, and lifted his wings to fly. Then he saw a shadow in the trees.

"You!"

The raven peered at him, still as a stone's shadow. He suddenly wasn't sure if it was the same raven he'd seen on the morning of the hunt. They all looked the same. They were like the lesser birds, not like gryfons who each had their own coloring, their own special place in Tyr's eyes. All ravens were black. All had the same clattering call. All were equally frustrating and useless.

Or maybe not useless. It had been a raven that led the she-wolf to him before, after all. *More or less,* Shard thought, and then the raven spoke.

"Me? You," the black bird called from the trees. "Do you expect a wolf to come to your call, mighty gryfon?" He sidled one way across the tree branch, then another, then stopped and cocked his head. "Do you expect she has nothing better to do?"

"What do you know of wolves?"

"Songs songs!" The raven called, then *awked* into the forest, the call echoing even farther than Shard's voice had done. A shiver thrilled down Shard's spine. *What word was that? What message, if any at all?*

"I don't expect that she has nothing better to do. I just need to speak with her."

"Ha!" But the raven flew to the ground, a talon's reach in front of Shard, unafraid. "Why?"

"Why should I tell you?" Shard ruffed the hackle feathers of his neck.

"I can call her. Or take you to her, if you're brave. I know the wolf song. Oh yes, I know. I know. Tell me what an arrogant, bumbling wind brother wants with an earth sister, a singer."

He spoke too fast, too many words, too many of them riddling. But if what he said was true, Shard had to listen. Out of grudging respect, he lowered himself to the ground, on his belly to speak level with the black bird. Kjorn would die of shame. "The day of the hunt. She gave me words to say to Lapu. I need to know what they meant."

"Words, words!" The raven bobbled his head, then peered at Shard with one black, star-bright eye. "So inquisitive. Why? It worked. It worked. Why bother to know what they mean?"

"Because I said them!" His tail snapped back and forth once. "It's important to me."

"Mh. Mh. Mh." The raven paced six steps one way, three steps back, stopped in front of Shard again and made a little *quork*ing sound. "Foolish to come here. But brave. A little. And wise. Most speak many words. Even when they know the meaning, they don't know what they're saying. Or care."

"All right," said Shard, wearying. "Can you take me to the wolves?"

"No need! I can tell you what the words mean. Speak them to me."

Shard blinked once. "You know wolf language?"

"Earth language, wolf language, rock, stone, tree, memory, yes, I know them all. You should too. You have earth paws. It is half your birthright. Half your heart and soul, son of Tyr and Tor. You spoke to Lapu. He spoke to you."

The bird chortled with delight at his unintended rhyme.

Shard shifted his weight, uncertain. He didn't know the name Tor. "You're not going to take me to her, then?"

"To her?" The raven ruffled his feathers and cackled, marching in a circle in front of Shard. "Her, her, red Catori? Or to the wolves? Any wolf? Any who can speak earth words? I can tell you. But you don't want to just know, you don't want to chat with a lonely old bird? Her? Afraid another wolf will attack you? Hm? You are wise to ask for her. A dreamer. Are you a dreamer, young Vanir?"

The black bird *awked* again to the sky and laughed.

Impatience sizzled at the roots of Shard's feathers and he stood. "Never mind, *bird*. I'll find them on my own."

"Never mind! Never mind! Too late." The raven flapped into the air. "They found you."

Shard whirled, ears back, hissing as the wind shifted and brought him the heavy scent of wolf. *Stupid raven!* He shouldn't have trusted it. Two wolves padded toward him, boldly across the open meadow. It was in league with wolves, it fed off their kills and led them to prey. He should have known its babbling was only a trap, that it had called a warning into the woods.

The wolves' shoulders were even with Shard's, sloped and thick with muscle. Ears forward, gold eyes intent, Shard thought at first he was being unobservant and couldn't tell them apart. But the closer he looked as they approached, tails up, hackles smooth, he realized that wasn't it. Both had pale gold eyes. Both had ghostly white faces that mottled into heavy neck fur of russet and gray and black that glinted indigo in the sunlight. They were identical.

"Stay back!" Shard opened his wings, muscles tensing to leap into the air. The wolf brothers paused, then looked at each other.

"But you called," one said.

"You called," the other agreed, and licked his muzzle.

Shard rumbled a warning growl at the gesture. "I called Catori. Or tried to. Who are you?"

"I am Ahote," said the first, "I am Ahanu," said the second, and Shard knew that if they moved around, he wouldn't be able to tell one from the other. The first, Ahote, stepped forward, lowering his head, tail low, though he didn't cringe and cower. He was trying to show respect, Shard thought.

Hoped.

"You think our little sister would meet a gryfon alone?"

"Alone?" echoed the other, Ahanu. "Our poor little sister, without protection?"

"No, *thief.*" That word again! Lapu had called him the same. "She would not." Ahote took another step forward, lifting his head proudly. "But we will take you to her."

"If you're brave." Ahanu showed his fangs, long, yellowing, sharp. Both wolf brothers looked ragged and fierce, with winter fur hanging in dregs from their coats, the way Shard's own feathers must look. He twitched a hind-paw to back away, then stopped himself, flexing claws into the ground.

"Are you *brave?*" the other taunted. Shard lifted his head, flared his wings and fanned his tail feathers.

"Take me to her." He hesitated, and met both sets of golden eyes. "And thank you."

The wolf brothers paused, blinked at each other, then raised twin howls of amusement. *Or is it approval?* And without a word of warning, they bounded across the meadow.

With no time for second thoughts, Shard snapped his wings to his sides, glanced once at the raven who bobbed its head, and leaped after them into the forest.

7
BETRAYAL

THEY PLUNGED THROUGH TWISTING JUNIPER and pines that sang with wind in their needles. The first time they darted under a grove of rowan Shard thought again of red Catori, and tried to remember the place. At first Shard tried to mark their trail, to remember which way they came, then he realized that they often doubled back, that the wolf brothers led him purposefully in circles to confuse him. Shard wondered if they meant to take him to Catori at all.

The land rose. They climbed a slope broken by black rocks adorned with pale, drying winter moss and crawling white lichen.

"So slow!" yipped Ahanu. Or Ahote. Shard had lost track and he didn't care. He kept pace when they ran. His hind paws were well suited to the earth once he found a good rhythm, but the wolves allowed him no time.

"Maybe if you led me true," Shard snapped. He let his tail lash. Let them see his anger, let them know he wasn't foolishly following blind. But both wolves only loosed warbling laughs to see him struggling up the rock hill, dark and chilly from the shade.

He raised his face to the breeze, which was still warm. They climbed in the lee of a starward-facing slope, where cool winds shuddered. It would be a good place to cool down in high summer, he thought. Not that he planned to return, except to hunt.

"Do you plan to take me to your sister at all, or just lead me in circles until I collapse?"

Ashamed of his weariness on foot, he sat down for a moment on a broad slab of rock just below where the wolves stood. Kjorn would have clawed his ear off for such stupidity. One brother showed his teeth.

"Why do you want to see her?"

Shard's muscles tightened and he looked around. The wolves lowered their heads, ears perked. He heard the sea. They were near the shore; waves swirled and crashed against rock somewhere close. It sounded as if they had climbed a rise that dropped straight down into the sea.

He stood, feathers sleeking tight against his body with unease. "I wish to speak to her. That's all."

"Ha."

The wolf brothers crossed each other, pacing once. Shard thought it was Ahote who bared his fangs and spoke. "Gryfons don't speak to wolves. They steal. They kill."

"They kill," echoed the other.

Maybe I could tell them apart, Shard thought, pinning his ears back. *One always follows, always laughs. One is the leader, stronger. Ahote?*

"No," he said firmly, digging his talons against the rock. "She helped me. She helped all of us to kill the boar. I want to learn more. I owe her my thanks."

"Your thanks."

"We owe you something too." Ahote bared his long sharp teeth, dark hackles rising.

Shard tensed, half crouching. "I came here peacefully."

"We lived here peacefully," snarled Ahanu. "Until you winged thieves came and stole and killed. You and your kings, red with dragon's blood."

Fighting instinct flared. Shard's gaze darted around. Trees closed them in. The tumbled rocks made footing awkward for him, but suited the wolves, with their long legs and four solid paws. They had chosen their ground, and he walked right into it.

"I should have known better than to trust wolves. What have I done to—"

They leaped. Shard flared his wings halfway and scrabbled to the side, which brought him directly under Ahanu's belly as the wolf landed. Pale and russet fur writhed above Shard and he rolled to his back, clawing upward. He caught only matted, un-shed winter fur.

"Stop!" Shard squirmed free and scrabbled away from them, loosing an eagle shriek that deepened to a lion snarl. The voice that rumbled from his chest barely sounded his own. "I have no quarrel with—"

"This is vengeance," rumbled Ahote, stalking forward. Shard backed away awkwardly over the rock, realizing too late that they were driving him backwards up the slope. Toward a cliff? *Fine, I will fly away.*

"For our brother," yipped Ahanu. "Our nephews—"

"All our kin," growled Ahote. "All who have died and suffered at the claws of your thieving, murdering red kings!"

Shard didn't realize he'd moved until the wolf slammed into him and they wrestled, talon to claw in a tangled struggle up the slope. Ahanu nipped at Shard's tail but then skittered away when Shard slashed talons or snapped his beak.

He felt Ahote drawing back more often, shoving his weight, clawing less, and thought he was winning at last, and saw the blood he'd left in the russet fur.

"For them," the big wolf snarled, snapping his jaws toward Shard's throat. Shard shoved back to dodge—and fell into open air.

He flared his wings with a yelp of fear. One wing knocked against a tree, his hind paw caught in two rocks and he shrieked. Both wolves leaped forward, snapping and snarling, to shove him backwards down the jagged rock face toward the sea.

A low howl rang far off. The brothers perked their ears, ducked their heads and loped away. Shard lost his footing and fell, rolling and scrabbling down the rock face. The weak shale crumbled under his claws. His wings struck trees and boulders. He snapped them shut to avoid breaking bones, clawing madly for purchase on the crumbling ground.

Rocks and shale slid down with him. Shard bumped against a slab of stone, flipped and skidded head-first toward the edge of the cliff. Trees lunged at him. He thrust out talons and snagged a root, but his momentum flung him in a sideways arc to knock his head against a neighboring tree.

Crashing seawater strewn with rocks filled his vision before his daylight flashed to black.

KJORN GLIDED LOW TOWARD his father on the topmost slab of rock on Copper Cliff. The king gazed far off, windward toward the home of his fathers. Kjorn's shadow slipped over Sverin and he looked up, keening once as Kjorn lighted beside him on the rock.

"Caj said you wanted to see me?"

The king, as red as his father, kept his ears perked toward the windward horizon and did not speak.

"Father," Kjorn went on, checking himself when one red ear slanted his way. Then he straightened, lifting his head, filling his chest with a breath. "Father, it's been so many days since the hunt. Everyone is afraid of your decisions. When will you tell them who can remain?"

Sverin turned his golden eyes on Kjorn at last. "Tell Thyra and her hunters to bring extra kills. Birds, if they can. Hares. Delicacies. We will have a feast at sunset. I have great things to tell our pride."

Kjorn's heart quickened. "Will you tell me first, Father? Will you tell me—at least tell me of Shard. My wingbrother. You won't banish him? We wouldn't have taken the boar without him."

The son of Per looked at him, golden eyes fierce. Then he blinked once, as if he'd been looking at something far away and only just saw Kjorn. His expression softened, as it always did, for Kjorn knew he had his mother's coloring and face. Kjorn's mother had carried him over the Windland Sea to the Silver Isles, and died the first winter before she could raise him.

Sverin tilted his head, one ear flicking back. "Not yet. No. Forgive me, my son. But even you must wait."

Kjorn ruffled, then smoothed his feathers and mantled, dignified. "Of course. I trust your will."

"Sunset," Sverin said as he sat down, now facing the dawnward sky. His tail swept the rocks restlessly, feathers flaring to a fan and closing again. "Here at my rocks. Spread the word, everyone is to attend to hear what I have to say."

"Yes, Father." Kjorn dove from the high rocks and glided across Sun Isle to spread the will of the king and to tell Thyra what she and her hunters must do. He told warriors, fledges, and even mothers to bring their littlest kits. There was only one gryfon he couldn't find.

SHARD WATCHED A PALE gray gryfon plunge alone into the sea. Red clouded out around him when he struck the water.

A bolt of skyfire split the blue sky, arcing above a vast foreign plain toward jagged white mountains. A roar shook the mountains and huge herds of deer on the plain turned and fled from the sound. In the distance, he thought he saw gryfons flying.

The water rose around him, filling his eyes, his throat, dragging his wings, and he had no more strength to fly out or swim free—

Icy salt water seeped under Shard's feathers to shock the skin around his eyes. He gasped to awareness and tried to flare his wings. They hung heavy as stones from his shoulders. He shook his head once, flinging away water, taking slow breaths.

An ache pierced his head. Unease and fear clung to him. He tried to remember if he dreamed, and couldn't, but a fear lingered in him, so heavy it almost didn't feel his own. *I must have had a nightmare.*

Shard looked around slowly, wary of his pulsing head. He'd fallen from the cliff into the sea. Ahote and Ahanu had tried to kill him.

I'm lucky I didn't drown. Thank bright Tyr. The waves had dragged him nearly a league out into the broken rocks in the long shoals off Star Island. As Shard shifted he felt one hind leg, pinned between two jagged rocks.

Maybe that saved me from washing out to deep water.

The sea stretched out around him. Shard fought a sense of rising panic that also sent pain trotting through his skull. Wedged in the rocks, he was trapped in the sea, his wings waterlogged.

A gryfon could fly in heavy rain for a time, but Sverin warned so heavily against the sea. Shard didn't know if he could fly with seawater in his wings. They felt so heavy. He had to have been pinned out in the water for several sunmarks.

Tide was out, but if he didn't free himself soon, the rocks that had saved him from deeper water would hold him until he drowned.

Sverin's low voice rolled in his head. *The sea brings only cold and death.* Fighting a burst of panic, Shard let out one gasping yowl.

But the sun still shone, and he could move. He could fight. He could escape the chill grip of the tugging waves.

Muttering, panting against numbness, he dragged his wings closed from their useless splay. *Not broken, please don't be broken.* He felt twinges, bruises, but no restrictions. Relief swelled and burst to anger inside him. He had been so stupid, trusting wolves, then falling.

Gryfons don't fall.

He fell, broken, dying, into the sea.

The image leaped to him. Shard sucked a breath and shook his head. *A nightmare.* He had dreamed, unconscious in the water. *It doesn't matter now. It was a dream, and I have enough trouble.*

He forced one hind leg to move, to lift under the water, working the life back into it as he looked around. Carefully, he flexed the muscles of the leg pinned by the rock, and when there was no pain, continued flexing lightly, feeling for a safe way to tug free without scraping or straining. Heartened, Shard knew that once his muscles relaxed, he could push himself free.

Don't panic like a kit, rolled out of its nest. Grimly, Caj's advice from long ago came back to Shard, when he was still learning to fly. *Panic makes kits wander off cliffs, and grown warriors make stupid mistakes.*

He could drag himself out if he stayed calm. If he did it soon, he could climb the higher rocks, let the sun dry his wings and his headache subside. He ground his beak and then swept his free hind foot against the rock, seeking a firm place to push. Pain darted up his hind paw and he remembered feeling it twist as he fell, and went still again.

Little silver fish darted by, unafraid. Their motion kept catching his attention and he perked his ears, then shut his eyes as the light on the water dazzled like Sverin's gems.

His belly clawed as insistently as a gryfon kit yowling for food. And he was thirsty.

"I am a warrior," he muttered to the rocks around him. "A proven warrior and hunter of the Silver Isles. I am not afraid of you," he snarled at the glimmering water. The little fish continued to flicker around him.

This was a minor trial. He could almost feel his foot now, but shivers trembled uncontrollably through his body. Despite the warm sun, the sea around the Silver Isles remained cold in all seasons.

The sea is death.

He panted against the sun's heat on his face, coupled with the ice of the water. Squirming, he rested his free hind paw against a rock under the water, then lifted his forelegs to grasp the faces of rock that poked above the water. He pulled, straining against heavy wings, exhaustion and the aching bruises that needled to life under every muscle. Saltwater stung like nettles in the scrapes from his fight with the wolf brothers.

The rocks that pinned his hind leg seemed to squeeze tighter the harder he struggled.

"Great, golden *Tyr,*" he gasped, blinking toward the nightward horizon. The sun stalked too close to the edge. Soon the tide would rise.

"Make me strong," Shard whispered, clicking his beak once softly. Bracing himself for pain, he pinned his ears back, gripped the rocks harder with his talons, and heaved. His wings weighted him down. The rock tugged his hind leg. Forelegs trembling, Shard forced a firm, steady haul from his muscles, shutting his eyes, and with a roiling snarl, felt his hind leg pull free.

Legs quivering, wings throwing his balance when he tried to move, Shard clung to the small bits of rock that stuck above the water and looked toward the shore. Free now, he could wade through rock and sea. His hind paw throbbed and ached, but he saw no blood.

He took a short, slow jump toward a larger rock, but his wings dragged him short. He clawed at the rock and his hind legs collapsed under him. A surprised squawk escaped his throat and he dug his talons against the rock, shuddering as waves lapped against his hind paws. He let his wings hang low, too tired to hold them at his sides. Thirst burned his throat and belly. The high wind tossed salt spray into his eyes. At last out of the water, he rested a moment.

Only a moment, he thought, dizziness and ache twirling his head.

A wave splashed his face. He twitched awake.

"You're nothing," he growled at the rocks. "I faced down a boar."

Ravens circled overhead now, thinking he might soon become their meal. He wondered if he knew any of them and stifled a hysterical chuckle.

This time he moved slower, carefully feeling the weight of his damp wings, the bruises and trembling of his limbs, pausing on each rock to rest and catch a breath. The sandy shore rippled in front of his eyes.

"Almost there," he growled. The little silver fishes seemed to follow him, as if his progress amused them. He wondered how large they were, and if they were good for eating. He thrust his talons into the water and they scattered. Relief at missing filled him when he realized what he'd done. It was forbidden to hunt from the deadly sea.

Shard huffed and turned his gaze toward land again. Before being pinned, it appeared he'd drifted a good dozen leaps from the cliff where Ahote and Ahanu attacked. A narrow, rocky strip of beach stretched in front of him now, only a few paces deep before surging up into another hulking cliff face. Shard realized water would swallow that little beach when the tide rose. He couldn't rest there; he would have to climb.

The last distance was the hardest, crawling through sharp, slick rocks, the wind soaring along the cliff face and trying to batter him down.

With one last short, weak jump Shard landed in a heap of feather and fur on the rocky shore. For a moment he lay quivering and digging his talons in the gravel, but he couldn't stay. Sun hung nightward and the moon crept up, nudging the tide higher. He forced himself to his feet and limped along the narrow beach to find high ground. Thirsty, hungry, pain from bruises lancing with each step, and an ache from salt in his blood wounds, he moved forward on blank instinct.

Is this how the witless creatures move?

With the thought, he became aware of himself again. The water slipped against the rocks below.

Below? Waves crashed, the sea was dark with evening, and the tide crept up the cliff. But it was below Shard. Without realizing, he'd found a break in the cliff and climbed up to a grassy deer trail and wide ledge.

Trembling, he dropped to the yellow grass, splayed his wings to let the wind and sinking sun dry his feathers, and then he remembered no more.

Above him on an outcropping of rock, a raven *quork*ed a message into the forest and hopped from the cliff to circle once and fly away.

8
THE EXILE

SVERIN PACED ON HIS ROCK, ears perked toward his pride. Kjorn watched him warily for a moment from below, then glanced to the pride. The last lances of sunlight made every gryfon shine like the gems he wore that evening, the dragon gems Kjorn's great-grandfather had stolen. Drawing a breath, Kjorn padded up the rocks to his father. Sverin spoke without looking at him.

"Is everyone here? Every hunter, warrior, and kit with its eyes open?"

Kjorn bowed his head. "Yes, Father." He could tell Shard what his father said, later. Surely his wingbrother was on one of his long flights. *No need to draw Father's attention to his absence.*

Sverin glanced at him, eyes narrowed to glowing gold slits in the orange wash of sun. "Is something wrong?"

"No." Kjorn looked up, fluffing his wings, though his gaze strayed nightward. "No. All are ready to hear your words."

"Good," said Sverin, and Kjorn began to climb down from the rocks. "No," Sverin murmured, his low voice almost a purr. "Stay here with me."

Kjorn perked his ears, fluffed with pride, and sat beside his father. Worries about Shard left his mind; he would solve that when necessary.

"Gryfons of the Sun Isle!" Sverin's lion voice boomed and rolled over those assembled, and all fell silent. Ears perked his way. Even kits squirming in their mother's claws heeded that voice.

The Red King stopped pacing and faced his pride, opening his wings to let the sunset fire catch them. "After the last hunt for the great boar, we saw new, fine warriors come into their own. Never have I or my fathers seen such prowess. Or such bravery, and loyalty."

Kjorn watched his father curiously, shifting his front feet. Tonight would have been the night he announced which young males could stay with the pride. Sometimes the exiles left quietly, in humiliation and fear. Sometimes they fought. It was never a happy occasion. This was an odd way to begin such a somber moment. But surely, his father knew best. Sverin glanced to him, eyes glinting, then out again over the assembled.

"It has given me a vision." He climbed to the next level of rock as he spoke, then up to the top of the rocks, so all had to look up to him as they would the sun. "A vision, of a great future for all of us."

He flared his wings, giving a piercing call to the darkening sky before lowering his fierce gaze to the pride. "It is known that affairs of gryfons are best handled under the light of day or the rising sun when bright Tyr is mighty. But a change is coming, and so I have brought you here." The sunset rained fire through his open wings and Kjorn stared, knowing he would never be such a king. "Here," Sverin called across rock and plain, "under Tyr's reddest light," his voice dipped and all shifted in to hear, "to share my vision with you."

A TALON MOON HUNG low in the nightward sky. Shard didn't move, taking a moment to remember where he was. Waves washed below him. There was no wind. He sat up, stiff and crusty from salt water.

Star Island.

Wolves.

He shoved to his feet and ruffled his feathers, relieved to find his wings dry, and tucked them at his sides. Blood rushed his head when he stood too fast; the dark and stars spun and tilted before his eyes and he shut them. His tongue felt stuck to his beak. Dizziness prowled at the edge of his vision. He needed water before he could fly.

"Tyr," he whispered, his voice a rasp, "guide me. Make me strong."

"I thought you'd sleep 'til dawn," remarked a low, coarse, male voice.

Shard whirled, peering through the dark, and at first saw nothing. He squinted and a shadow moved, defining itself higher on the deer trail. He'd thought it was a rock. His intended roar came out as a weak, dry hiss. Gryfons could see a gull three leagues off, a bird in a branch, or a rabbit in the woods—but they could not see well in the dark.

"Who are you? Name yourself!"

"Well, I'm not Tyr, that's certain. But maybe I'll do for now, young gryfon."

Shard's hackle feathers lifted indignantly. "I am a warrior of the Sun Isle.

"Of course." He sounded too amused. "I see that now." The voice, low and deep, had the eagle edge of a gryfon voice, not a wolf. But it was not a voice he knew. "I'll take you to fresh water. Come."

"Who are you?"

"You asked for help," the stranger rumbled. "Here I am."

In the gloom and faint silver moonlight, Shard saw the figure turn and climb up the trail. He stood for a moment, beak open, feathers sleeked, wondering what choice he had. He couldn't fumble around in the dark searching for water. Wolves could find him. He could get lost, or run into another boar.

"Wait!" Shard stepped forward. An ache shot up his hind leg and he hobbled another few steps. "Tell me your name. I followed wolves into the woods, trusting them, and this is what happened." He drew a deep breath, raising his head to a proud angle, even though it was dark. "Tell me who you are."

Tell me how you see in the dark, Shard wanted to demand, but other things were more important, first.

The dark figure turned and the moon and stars picked out the edge of feathers, the bend of a wing, the thick muscle of a feline haunch. His feathered tail twitched once, and he gusted a sigh.

"My name is Stigr."

"I don't know you."

"I know you. Trust me, warrior of the Sun Isle, and I'll bring you to water."

"How is it so many creatures I've never met know me?" Shard muttered. But, he felt more secure knowing it was another gryfon, that he had a name, that he seemed respectful. Thirst scraped his throat and his questions dried up. Stigr turned and Shard, reluctantly, his senses tuned for danger, followed him up the cliff and into the forest.

His foot snagged in a crawling tangle of brush and he yelped as he yanked loose, then gnawed at the tangle. "Slow down, my foot's injured."

"You've got three others. Keep up, *warrior* of the Sun Isle."

Heat bloomed across Shard's skin. Ahead, Stigr stopped but didn't offer help as Shard caught up. He had no idea how far they walked and he couldn't yet smell water. Stars peeked through the pine.

"How do you avoid the tangles?" he snapped.

"Go around."

"I can't see them. Can you see in the dark?"

"There are other ways of seeing than just your eyes," the older stranger rumbled, and Shard heard him turn and continue on. "Use them."

Shard limped after him. "What ways? What do you mean? Is it magic?"

A dry chuckle. "Oh yes, very old magic. The first. Your ears to hear. Your sense of smell. You'll notice the pines have a scent. Feathers to feel, talons to part the tangles. Use them. You don't have to bash through the woods like a boar, as if your hide was made of stone. Which it isn't. You'll learn that the first time you spar off with a nettle brush, warrior."

Shard bristled and then forced himself to walk forward without arguing. His mind swam in the dark and around the stranger's words. More than anything, he wanted water. But he tried to slow, to see without his eyes. In the dark, he heard when Stigr shifted, edging around tougher brush. He perked his ears. He reached his talons in longer, slower steps and lowered his body to the ground like a lesser wild cat, fluffed his feathers to feel the brush around him. When the tangy scent of pine drifted his way, he slipped around and avoided bumping into any more trunks. Elation at this new skill rippled under his feathers but he clamped his beak against comment, wary of the stranger's mockery.

It wasn't exactly like seeing, but he avoided anymore tangles. Then, as his legs trembled with weariness and he couldn't speak for the dryness in his throat, the trickle of water whispered ahead. In the still air the scent came to him sweetly. His new night-movement forgotten, Shard plunged forward, snapping underbrush and tangling his tail feathers. His talons splashed in the trickle and he thrust his beak down to drink.

As he tilted his head back, Stigr spoke. "Drink slowly. Or your belly will ache."

Shard growled in acknowledgement but heeded. The old stranger had given him water as promised and helped him to move in the dark. There was no reason to stop listening to his advice.

"There is a meadow three leaps dawnward," Stigr murmured as Shard drank. "You can fly out from there." Shard lifted his head and shuddered.

"Tyr forbids gryfons to fly at night."

"Does he now?" Stigr's tail flicked through the brush. "Then I'm sure he'll protect you from the wolves when you sleep here tonight."

A small creature darted through the brush. Shard startled and Stigr chuckled.

Shard fluffed indignantly. "It is forbidden—"

"The *red kings,*" Stigr snapped, "forbid flying at night. In all my years I have never seen bright Tyr himself strike down a gryfon for opening his wings in the moonlight."

Shard shifted, muscles twitching to jump and flee. He forced a deep breath. Clearly, this gryfon was not part of Sverin's pride. No one spoke of the king in that way. No one spoke so lightly of flying at night.

But I can't stay on Star Isle, either. Maybe once, if no one knows I flew. Surely bright Tyr can forgive me. Rather than argue, he said evenly, "I've never flown at night. I don't know how."

"It's easier than walking the woods, which you've just done. Orient yourself by the Day Star. But I think you'll see the islands clearly when you get high enough. There's more light in the dark than you know."

Shard sat down to rest, taking a moment to preen salt from his feathers and think. He didn't want to sprint away and risk a bellyache, and he felt exhausted after the trek through the forest. He supposed it was perfect terrain for wolves, but he hated it.

Stigr sat silently while Shard preened and became aware of the night sounds; small creatures scuffling through the roots and ferns, and far off, an owl called but received no answer.

Abruptly, Shard raised his head, ears twitching to the sides with mild embarrassment. "Thank you, by the way. Thank you, for your help." For all they might disagree, he did owe that.

A soft rumble of acknowledgement was his answer. Or had the old stranger purred? "It was an honor, of course, to help a warrior of the Sun Isle."

Shard sleeked, eyes narrowing at the edge in Stigr's voice. "Stop mocking me."

"I'm not," the old gryfon murmured. "I wouldn't. But tread carefully in life, young warrior. You think everyone has your sense of honor. That, mixed with your blinding pride, will cause more problems like this day, if you let it."

"I came here peacefully."

Stigr made a soft noise. "There is no peace between wolves and gryfons now. Why did you come?"

"To…" Shard sighed, flexing his talons, and briefly told the tale of the hunt to this stranger. *What harm can it do?*

"I see." Stigr made another low, curious sound, an 'mh, hm' like a raven that was thinking.

"Were the words magic? What would make a boar lay down his head?"

The older gryfon chuckled, a half purr. "What makes you think I know? I've never hunted boar."

Shard blinked twice, and stood again. *I think he does know. I think he knows much more than he says. How else can he walk about fearlessly at night on the wolves' island?*

"Please. Who are you?"

"I told you."

He wished he could see the stranger's face and coloring. "You're an exile. You must be. You show no respect to the king and I don't know the name Stigr."

"Exile?" A growl sharpened his voice. "I am of the Vanir and always will be. I follow the old ways. I swear no loyalty to the red conquerors from the windward land." Shard had the strong sense that the older gryfon stared hard at him through the dark. "If that's what you mean by exile, then yes, I am."

"The Vanir," Shard whispered, skin prickling, making his feathers ruffle. "A raven asked me—"

Wolves howled in the night, close. Shard tensed, half crouching, and even Stigr shifted weight and lifted his head. That much he could tell, in the dark. "You should go back to Sun Isle."

Without thinking, Shard reached out to catch the older gryfon's wing in his talons. "Wait, I have questions—"

"There's a time for questions. This isn't it." Wolves sang under his words. They were hunting, calling to each other. Stigr seemed to hesitate, then added in a softer tone, "If you want to know more of the Vanir, if you want to see *real* magic, meet me again, young warrior. Meet me on the Black Rock Isle, middle mark of the full moon."

"I won't fly at night twice."

Stigr made a low noise. "Well. If you're too frightened, I understand."

Shard ruffled, not releasing his grip on Stigr's wing. "I'm not frightened. You're an exile. I could be cast out too, for even speaking to you, even when I've just done so well on the great hunt."

"But not alone," the older gryfon said, soft as a wind in the grass. "You've just told me. You had help, but there's no shame in that. The Aesir of Severin's pride have great gifts. But the Vanir had gifts too." He flexed his wing against Shard's talons. "You should think about that. Think about what's expected of you now, and what you have to offer the pride. If you don't know your own strengths, how will you keep up? I can show you where you came from."

"What—"

"What harm could it do, in the service of your king?" The old gryfon's voice fell sly as a raven's. Shard's talons flexed against his wing.

"But—"

"Midnight of the full moon."

It was madness. Shard tried not to listen. Either way, he owed this stranger one more thing. Stigr tried to turn and Shard tightened his hold, catching skin without clawing or tearing.

"Wait! Who is your family? I could send word, tell them that you're alive, at least."

"That would be dangerous, Shard." But his voice was soft, tempted. Shard didn't recall telling the exile his name.

"I owe it to you. Tell me what your place was, in the pride before Per the Red." Shard loosened his talons and perked his ears. The old stranger took a slow breath.

"I'll tell you, if you promise only to tell one gryfon of my presence here."

"I promise," Shard whispered, stepping forward. "I won't betray you."

In the brief moment of silence, a high pitched howl cut the air. "You may tell my sister that I live."

"Who is she?"

Another silence, another howl farther off. "Your mother."

Shard's beak opened and before he could shut it, Stigr left him, disappearing in the brush as quick as a wolf. Shard blinked, flattened his ears and whirled to run. He crashed through the underbrush to the meadow the older gryfon had told him existed. *My uncle.* With a leap, he shoved himself into the black, starlit sky while wolf howls rose around him.

STIGR STOPPED AND TURNED to watch Shard go, ears perked. The wolf howls drew closer, singing back and forth the location of their prey. They must have scented Stigr, but he didn't fear them. The wolves wouldn't hassle him, for he had never hunted on the Star Isle.

"His blood runs *red,*" observed a voice from above and to his left.

"I know," Stigr murmured. Peering hard, he saw Shard's outline against the stars, correctly oriented. *Good.*

The raven croaked, fluttering down to the bushy forest floor. "Too much fondness for your *dead* wingbrother's son blinds you." A wing smacked Stigr's face. On purpose, he thought. "He would only use your knowledge to gain strength for the king."

"If that's what it takes," Stigr said quietly, and stood. "We must do whatever it takes."

"We, indeed," chuffed the raven. "He won't replace what you've lost."

"No," Stigr murmured, peering through the dark. He'd lost sight of Shard, but felt confident he'd find his way. He was Vanir. "But he may redeem it."

9
THE KING'S VISION

"I STILL DON'T UNDERSTAND WHAT YOU were doing on Star Island," Sigrun huffed as she examined Shard's hind paw. Dawn light warmed her empty cave.

Shard winced when her gentle talons found a tender spot. "I told you. I wanted to try hunting on my own."

Her ears flattened in disbelief and annoyance. "And you decided not to fly when you saw wolves coming?"

That time, Shard didn't answer. He took a deep breath, smelling all the scents of his kithood. The herbs, dry rock and soft musk of his mother's feathers comforted him. "I thought—"

"You proved your bravery on the hunt," Sigrun snapped, turning his paw gently. "A gryfon who doesn't have to hunt alone, shouldn't."

"Yes, Mother," Shard muttered. He thought of the exile, Stigr, who had to hunt alone. Why had he stayed on the islands at all? As far as Shard knew, all other exiles had fled. *Or died,* he thought.

"Well," she said, standing. "This is only a strain and a bruise. If it was broken, you would know. Be easy on it for awhile. If it's hurting you too much, eat willowherb with your meat."

"It doesn't hurt," Shard lied, and stood carefully. Sigrun fluffed.

"Suit yourself."

You may tell one gryfon of my presence here. He heard Stigr's voice again. *If I don't tell her now, then I have to keep lying.* He had lied about the hunt, about his reason for flying to Star Island, and now another voice came into his mind, and it was not Stigr.

Sigrun cannot speak of this. He remembered the Widow Queen. Maybe he could lead in to the exile another way.

"Mother," he began softly. She tilted her head at him, ears perked, as late dawn light slipped into the cave. "After the hunt, a gryfess approached me."

"Oh?" Her voice grew sly and Shard ducked his head.

"No, nothing like that. It was Lady Ragna."

Sigrun's eyes widened and her ears slipped back, fierce as if he'd challenged her to a fight. "What did she want?"

Shard blinked and stepped back, wincing when he absently put weight on his hind paw. "She only congratulated me. She said that I'm like my father. She said you would have told me that if you could."

"Hush now," she rasped, ears swiveling to the cave entrance. "We don't speak of it. *I* raised you. *Caj* has raised you."

"But am I like—"

"*Rashard,*" she snapped. "We don't speak of things past. We are Sverin's pride."

Shard stared at her, thought of the difference between her and Stigr. Rather than confirm his fears, her anger pushed him toward the other side. Toward curiosity. *Has she hidden things from me all these years? Do the Vanir possess powers that Sverin forbade, out of fear?* He had survived his night flight with nothing more than a rough landing, and great Tyr had not struck him down. He had spoken with wolves. He had spoken words that made a boar lay down its head. Shard wondered what else had the red kings told them all that might not be true.

Feeling less afraid and more rebellious, he lashed his tail. "I met another gryfon, too. An exile. On Star Island."

"Shard," she whispered, looking breathless, eyes glazed with panic. "What are you trying to do? You've just proven your loyalty to Sverin, to your wingbrother the prince. But that means nothing if you disobey the king. Do you crave exile?"

"He helped me," Shard said quietly. "He helped me and asked nothing in return. But I offered to tell his family he was alive, and he asked that I only tell one."

"Who? Don't claw anyone else into this madness. Did you actually fly home at sunrise this morning as you told me, or did you fly at night—"

"His name was Stigr."

All breath and fight seemed to leave her at the name. Shard watched her expression soften, then grow cold and fierce. She opened her wings, stepping toward him. "You will *not* fly to Star Island again alone. You will not speak of Stigr or your dead father or any other of this nonsense. You are here now, my son, here safe, friend to the prince, a proven warrior, and with the king's eye on you."

He knew she spoke the truth. But he had spoken with wolves. He had spoken to the great boar, walked at night, flown at night, spoken to an exile, and come back whole. Shard had decided that he had to learn his strengths if he was going to have anything to offer Sverin and Kjorn.

"You can't forbid me anything. I'm not a kit."

"You are my son!" Sigrun snapped her beak, flashing her wings wide as she advanced on him a step. Shard crouched back, reminded that the healer was also a warrior, a huntress and once, long ago, had also fought against Per the Red.

"Just tell me," he whispered, forgetting that he had once told the king he didn't care, "if I really am like my father."

"Tyr help us if you are," she snarled. "Be content."

I was! Shard stared at her in the growing light. He had never been restless before he spoke to the wolves, before he flew at night or spoke with the exile. "I just want to know—"

"Let it rest." Sigrun folded her wings, her expression flickering back to calm. Perhaps she saw that in her rage, she was pushing him away. "It is all past."

A draft at the cave entrance drew their attention. Caj landed roughly and trotted three steps into the cave. He paused, ears swiveling to both of them.

"My mate," Sigrun breathed, too relieved at the interruption.

"My mate," he murmured in return, though his gaze was on Shard. "Forgive me missing the dawn with you. The king needed me. Shard."

"Caj." Shard shifted his wings a little, but Caj saved him any further niceties.

"The prince is looking for you."

Exhausted of words, relieved for the excuse to leave, Shard dipped his head and plunged out the cave mouth into the winds of dawn. Other gryfons stirred, calling greetings to him as they stretched or took off on their own morning flights. Shard sucked a deep breath of the morning air, thinking how strange it had all looked at night–dark, unidentifiable humps and looming shadows in the starlight. With his eyes nearly blind, his ears had felt sharper and he'd heard every whistle of wind in grass and through trees. After a tumbled landing, he'd slept where he touched ground.

He didn't see Kjorn at the Copper Cliff. If the prince wasn't out hunting for breakfast, Shard knew only one other place he might go, so he angled his flight toward the birch wood that sprawled on the far side of the nesting cliffs. A river split the land there, springing up trees and brush all along the lowland to the high, broken hills and mountains beyond. Called the Nightrun, it plunged from the gryfons' hilly plain in a great waterfall over the steep cliffs to the sea. It was a good place to hunt small meals, for fledges to practice stalking and, closer to the waterfall, to be alone.

Below him, kits and fledges tumbled around on the grass; young males of his own year mock-battled while females looked on, lazy before their round of hunting. Shard perked his ears. *Why does everyone seem so jubilant?* It had to be more than the warming weather.

A flicker of gold in the woods drew his eye and he stooped, ready to crash through the trees to pounce his friend.

"*Don't,*" Kjorn called from below. "I see you."

Shard laughed and changed angle, wheeling in a tight circle to slow before dropping to earth. This time he remembered to favor his hind paw before it pained him, and trotted into the woods. The dawn light filtered golden and green through the bright birch buds, and the thought of spring leaped with joy through Shard's body. Nearby, the Nightrun splashed and rolled, swollen and ice-cold with mountain run-off.

Kjorn watched him land and padded forward, eyes narrowed. "Where were you? What happened to you? What's this?" His face darted in before Shard could answer even the first question, preening at the faint scrapes of wolf claws on his ribs. Shard backed up, surprised at Kjorn's irritation.

"I…tried to go hunting."

"On Star Island? Alone?" Kjorn stood with wings half open, sleeked and wide-eyed. "Not even a gryfess hunts on that land alone. Why?"

"I…" Shard shifted his wings to his sides.

"I had to lie for you. I lied to my *father* for you." Kjorn ruffled his feathers in displeasure and sleeked again. "Now listen, I have a lot to tell you."

Kjorn turned to walk and Shard followed, out of the wood and up the slope toward the Copper Cliff. The sweet morning wind rustled their feathers and Shard felt his gnawing hunger return from the day before.

"He announced that all the males who attended the hunt could remain on Sun Isle, and the younger ones who haven't yet hunted will have a chance again even before next year."

Shard perked his ears, his hunger forgotten. "*All* of us can stay?"

"Yes. He means to settle gryfons on every isle, beginning with the Star Island, for the good hunting." Kjorn drew a breath, and Shard watched excitement grow in the prince's face as he told Shard all Sverin had said.

The king wanted to spread out the pride. Rather than exile, he planned to keep families and friends together and grow them across the islands, until they really did claim the Silver Isles as one land, all under gryfon rule.

Shard opened his wings, restless with excitement. The wolves, the sea, even mysterious Stigr brushed aside with the thought of it.

All he could muster in response was, "Oh."

Kjorn laughed. "Yes, exactly! I knew you would understand his vision. He's confident that our pride is honorable and loyal and that, with time, we could grow to be the greatest in all the history of the Aesir."

Shard considered that, his heart starting a lope, and began to speak, but Kjorn went on.

"That wasn't all. Because we will need numbers, he said you may stay, *and* take a mate."

Shard stopped walking and stared at Kjorn. In the dawn light the prince's feathers gleamed like true gold. "A mate?"

"Yes, Shard. That's what it takes to grow a pride. Mates. Kits. Surely your mother the healer didn't skip over all that."

Shard swiveled his head, looking toward the nesting cliffs. He'd never considered a mate. He had never thought he would be allowed one even if he did stay. Most bachelor males stayed only as guardians–brothers, sons, friends, but only those nearest and dear to the king's kin were allowed a mate.

"I never thought…"

"I know. Don't worry," the prince laughed, "I'm sure Thyra has many friends who would love to meet my wingbrother."

Rather than make him hopeful, the words slapped Shard's pride. *Wingbrother to the prince.*

They wouldn't just want to meet 'Shard, who had helped kill the boar.' He was wingbrother to the prince. They wouldn't be interested in Shard, the only Vanir kit to survive the Conquering, constantly under the Red King's gaze. They saw him as a Vanir, cursed with the losers' blood of the Silver Isles. Shard wondered what female would choose that. Who was he, Shard realized, to be worthy of anything more than to be valued because of his friends? *Because of Kjorn. Even the king let me hunt only because of Kjorn.*

Kjorn picked up his pace to a trot and Shard realized he'd stopped walking altogether. He pushed into a lope to catch up.

"So when you see my father, be sure to thank him and pretend you were there the whole time."

"I don't like lying." Though, he realized, he would have to lie about Stigr. He had already lied about the boar hunt. Now he would have to lie about this. That made three lies. *I am a liar,* he realized with a twist of his belly.

"Well you'll have to, or admit that my father bestowed honors on an idiot."

Shard paused when he realized where they were walking. "Did you say, *when* I see your father?"

"Yes." Kjorn shook his head. "We have to tell him of the wolves who attacked you. The wolves who attacked you when you went off for adventure without me, *wingbrother.*"

Shard chuckled in spite of his new worries, realizing Kjorn's anger was as much worry as being upset over being left out. Kjorn so badly wanted a wolf hide. In that moment, Shard thought the pelt of Ahote might be especially cozy in the prince's den. A pang lanced up his paw and he twitched it.

"Why? Then he'll know I was gone, and you just said—"

"No." Kjorn nodded once, decisively. "I was wrong. We can't hide it from him. We'll tell him you weren't at the meet, and we'll pretend it was you being brave, after the success at the hunt." The prince narrowed his eyes. "Brave, but foolhardy. He'll want to know of the wolves. Come with me."

Shard, ears flat, tail low, followed the prince.

"So." THE RED KING lay sprawled across a slab of coppery stone on his cliffs, ears perked toward Shard and Kjorn, stretched on their bellies in respect before him.

"Wolves attacked you, unprovoked, left you to die in the sea, and you remained the night on the Star Isle. I thought I missed your faced at the last meet." He glanced sidelong at Kjorn, for it was Kjorn who was supposed to have gathered everyone to Sverin's call, and Kjorn who told the king everyone was there. Shard shifted nervously as the prince spoke.

"Forgive me, Father. I didn't want Shard in trouble because I didn't know where to find him. The fault was mine."

"No," Shard said quickly, "I should have told him where I was going. It's my fault."

"Yes." Sverin seemed to agree with both of them. At length he continued. "You could have told me, my son. You mustn't keep things from me." He looked between them and relief that he didn't seem angry relaxed Shard's chest. "Or from each other. Wingbrothers should never have to wonder where the other has gone."

"Yes, Father," Kjorn whispered, as Shard said, "yes, your Highness."

He is my king. And a just king. Maybe he doesn't always trust me, but that is the fault of the old Vanir who fought him. Shard meant to prove himself different, and loyal.

Sverin looked back to him. "Back to this adventure of yours. You escaped. First the wolves, then the sea." His long, feathered tail brushed into a coil and back down. "I suppose that's your Vanir blood. Good for something, anyway."

"Yes, Sire." Shard remained with his belly low to the ground. No gryfon was to stand higher than the king. Sverin stared hard at him, gaze flickering here and there, as if to determine if the deadly sea transformed him, somehow, into an enemy.

"I know it was foolish to hunt alone, but…" he glanced sideways at Kjorn, who tilted his head slightly to encourage him on. "But I was still feeling brave after the boar hunt." That much was true.

"Too brave," the king murmured. His golden eyes didn't leave Shard's face. Shard hadn't been so close to the king since the day of the hunt, and forgot again how massive he was. He wore no gold and looked wild and fierce, red as war in the dawn light. "There are worse faults." He stood and stretched, as comfortable in Shard's presence, it seemed, as Kjorn's. "I trust that my son has brought you up on the most recent news."

"Yes, my Lord." A moment of silence settled, Sverin watching him expectantly, before Kjorn tapped Shard with his tail. Face hot, Shard rose to his feet so that he could bow. "Thank you. Thank you, for the great honor and for your trust in me, my king."

Satisfied, Sverin climbed higher on his rocks. "You know I only wish the best for you, Rashard. For my pride."

His full name in the king's voice shot like twin bolts of skyfire. Terror, and pride. "I–I wish the same."

Gold eyes pierced through him. For a moment, Shard felt the king could see everything, just like the sun, could see his doubts and his lies and his wings opening under the moon. He had never known a mightier gryfon his whole life, or heard of one in a song, one more worthy of serving.

"How could I not trust the one my son chose as his wingbrother?"

Wingbrother to the prince. But Shard met eyes with Sverin, and knew the Red King didn't unintentionally use the phrase. It was a reminder of what stood between him and exile. Shard had no answer for that, so he remained silent. Beside him, Kjorn puffed his chest proudly, and nudged a wing against Shard's in encouragement.

"In fact you proved your worth so fully on the great hunt that I have decided you will be instrumental in our upcoming settlement on Star Isle."

Kjorn tensed beside him and Shard's muscles locked.

"My father spared your life at the Conquering," murmured Sverin. "And twice you have met with wolves on Star Island and escaped with only a tale to tell. Whether that is your Vanir blood or some cleverness of your own, I will not ignore the signs of great Tyr. You are meant for a special purpose."

Shard's throat ached from holding his breath. He let it out, hollow but for his ramming heart. "My Lord?"

Sverin looked pleased as a mountain cat. "I mean to settle a colony on Star Island, Shard." He flexed his black talons luxuriously and his next words were a boon, a command, and a dismissal all in one. "As honored wingbrother to the prince, and one who seems to have a knack for survival, I mean for you to lead that settlement."

KJORN WAITED UNTIL SHARD was out of sight.

"You didn't tell me this!"

"The last time I checked," Sverin said, "I was king of Sun Isle, not you."

"You would tear my wingbrother from me?"

"Star Island is a mere flight away. You may see him any time you wish."

"Or I'll go with him, and help the settlement."

"You will not," the king said easily, as if Kjorn was still a fledge declaring that he would leap from the Copper Cliff.

"You did it on purpose," Kjorn growled, rebellion stalking through him. He had promised Shard safety from exile, a place in the pride, a mate, a real future, and his father dashed it all with a single blow.

"This is a great opportunity for Shard. Do you lack confidence in his ability?" Sverin watched him, talons flexing, and Kjorn ruffled.

"Of course not. But it's an unnecessary risk. What does Shard know of leadership? Or settling? There are others with more experience."

"I know this. I have personally selected the very best to advise him."

"But not to lead. Not to succeed or fail or *die* magnificently." Kjorn huffed, unsatisfied. "You may speak of honor and glory and special purpose, but I know why you've done this."

"There are so many who are more worthy of your friendship, my son."

"None," Kjorn said fiercely. "You never bothered to see him as I do."

Sverin paced away, hopping casually to a higher rock as if they only chatted about whether it would rain. "And you have never bothered to understand what I do. Let us hope he proves himself on Star Island."

"Proves himself? Again? How many times must he prove himself, Father?" Kjorn flared his wings, ears flat, ready to leap and prove his point through violence. It would end poorly, but he was ready all the same.

Until his father rounded on him, head high, tail lashing and talons splayed.

"*Always.* He must *always* prove himself, until my heart runs dry and I fly with Tyr in the Sunlit Land. The blood of the Silver Isles is in him and I will never trust it. I will not lose you as I lost her."

Kjorn tried to find words, argument or courage, but could only lock stare with his father and see the depth of anger and sorrow that still burned in his golden eyes.

"Father—"

"Never forget," the king's words cut high, "what became of your mother when she trusted the Vanir."

10
WINDWATER

S HARD FLEW HIGH, AT POINT. The first wave of gryfess hunters and initiated males followed in a wedge behind. He had never led a flight before, and felt as if every sharp eye behind him watched each nervous twitch in his feathers.

He huffed at himself. *Me, nervous of flying.* Sigrun often said Shard was born to fly, if nothing else. He fledged early, flew, could fly nearly any trick in the air that anyone dared him to.

If everything else about the settlement business failed, Shard decided, it would not be his flying.

Clear, cool morning air lifted him and he stretched into it, letting his wings relax and roll against every gust and updraft. Kjorn had once compared him to an arctic tern, small but swift. Longing to tilt into a roll and dive, spinning toward the gulls far below, he checked himself and glanced back and around to make sure the others kept up. Halvden and Einarr, also chosen by the king, proudly flew at the first points behind him, keeping pace better than the other full-blooded Aesir with their broader, slower wings.

Star Island loomed, enormous and bursting with green spring. A fortnight of scouting, squabbling, and snap decisions had led them to a suitable nesting place on the windward face of the isle, mirroring nesting cliffs on the Sun Isle.

Shard keened a call to descend into the wind and stooped to dive toward the chosen gray face of rock far below.

The winds calmed the lower he flew, and were still by the time he touched paw to earth. Einarr lighted closer, and Halvden in a rolling lope farther off. The gryfess hunters landed and remained in a rough wedge, awaiting command with the other warrior males. Last to land was Hallr, a stocky, lumbering, gravel-voiced warrior of blue-green coloring. Halvden's father.

"All well then?" Hallr called across the flight. Murmurs of agreement. Ears perked toward the forest, a safe ten leaps off, now in bud and even deeper and gloomier than when they had hunted the boar. As everyone answered, Shard mentally reviewed his plans. He and Kjorn had exhausted each other with lessons on leadership over the last days. His wingbrother would see him succeed or kill them both trying.

The first order of business ought to be seeing to the dens, he thought, cleaning and digging them out deeper. His ear twitched toward the forest, though. A raven shifted in the trees and Shard raised his wings for attention.

"I think—"

"You lot," Hallr addressed the young female hunters, who perked, "find provisions for the night. The rest—"

"I think," Shard said, louder, voice catching against his heart in his throat, "that we'd be best off all scouting the field and forest for the next sunmark before we settle in. Wolves can appear without warning."

Ears swiveled his way. Hallr looked as if Shard had told him he was a flying mouse. Hallr was almost twice his size, shorter but wider even than Caj. But somehow, Shard had survived wolves twice, alone, and the king had appointed him to this position for a reason. He met Hallr's stare.

"You can begin in the woods."

"There's plenty of space between us and the woods," Hallr said. Shard could see where the easy edge of arrogance in Halvden's voice had come from. "A wolf who tries to ambush us by crossing that field will be sorry for it."

"There are other creatures than wolves," Shard said evenly. "And they know secrets of the Star Isle that we have yet to learn."

The older warrior's ear twitched and he looked away.

"Whatever you think is best. Of course." Laughter edged his voice and Shard was almost there with him. *Who am I, to tell an experienced Aesir conqueror what to do?* Shard hated to question the king, but he wasn't sure his appointment was the best idea.

But then, the Aesir hadn't conquered the Star Island.

"Lead a group to the woods," Shard ordered, more boldly than he felt. "Explore at least a league in, on foot. Find the best trail to the streams."

Be sure of yourself, Kjorn had taught him. *Or at least pretend to be. If you don't trust yourself, no one else will.*

Shard raised his voice. "Einarr, take a group along the cliff edge." He glanced to the female hunters and picked the one who looked least doubtful. "And you…"

"Kenna." She straightened, looking more attentive, her feathers rich blue-violet in the midmorning.

"Kenna," he said, dipping his head. "Take a third group to the shore below the cliffs. Be sure there is no way for mudding paws to sneak up on us in the night."

A few rough chuckles at his language filled Shard with relief. Tails twitched, gazes wandered. "Well? Go on," Shard said, trying to summon up the way Kjorn sounded when he gave firm orders. "Back in a sunmark. The rest with me to the dens."

To his relief and amazement, they went. Halvden followed his father and five others into the woods, Einarr chose four to patrol the long edge of the cliff, Kenna flew down with her group to the shore, and Shard led the others into the dens. There was digging, cleaning, and exploring to do.

For the first time since Sverin's surprising appointment, excitement, not dread, winged in Shard's chest.

THE DAYS SLIPPED INTO lashing spring winds and pelting rain. What time the gryfons didn't spend huddled in their caves, they spent hunting and sparring. The wolves didn't show themselves, but Shard was sure they watched. Ravens flew over the nesting cliffs, which the settling group had collectively decided to call Windwater. That was all there was to their new colony, it seemed. Wind, water, and the forest crouched at their backs.

On visits to Sun Isle, Shard didn't speak to Sigrun about Stigr again, or ask any questions that might mean he was anything but thrilled about the thought of conquering Star Island. Truthfully, the more days they went without trouble, growing fit with the warm weather and easy hunting, the more he thought Sverin's vision was greater than any of them could know.

And, Shard decided, why shouldn't gryfons have a home on Star Island? As Shard relaxed, so did the others. Their patrols became shorter. Their wanderings into the woods less alert. They ranged farther and farther starward into wolf territory to find prey.

The sliver of moon grew to a fat egg moon that hovered in the day and night sky. Shard watched it rise from his den, but always turned his face from it before he fell asleep.

"SHAAA-AARD." KJORN FLARED A wing in Shard's face to get his attention. Kjorn, Caj, and others from the Sun Isle flew to Star Island every other day or so to practice fighting. "What's the matter with you today?"

The full moon. The moon tonight. Shard shook his head and faced off from Kjorn again, assuming a crouched, fighting stance. He hadn't decided whether or not to fly to Stigr, and the indecision drove him to distraction.

"I didn't sleep well. That's all." That much was true. Ever since coming to Star Isle he suffered restless nights with vivid dreams that he forgot on waking. He was sure most of them involved wolf teeth and ravens, feeding.

The golden prince swiveled his head, studying him closely, blue eyes keen. "You aren't getting off so easy. You need more help than most of the fledges." He snapped his beak and trilled, amused with himself. Shard gave a weak huff and chuckle, wishing it wasn't true.

Around them, gryfons sparred. Furrows and claw marks bruised the field of high yellow grass and brave spring flowers. For once, the wind was still and the day warm and dry. At the far end of the field, Caj demonstrated movements to fend off up to three attacking wolves.

Hallr and Halvden stood off to the side, muttering. Shard perked his ears. Watching them, he thought of the father he didn't remember. Sigrun never allowed Shard to ask if his father had been a warrior, or a great flyer, like Shard. Shard wondered about the exile Stigr. *My uncle.*

Though the settling seemed to be going easily, Shard felt unease grow with each warming day. Why, seemed the silent question among all the gryfons, hadn't the wolves attacked them?

Kjorn was watching him, and Shard pretended fascination with Caj's fighting technique.

"He's amazing," Shard murmured. Kjorn ruffled beside him.

"He taught my father to fight, and me. While you were off flying, he taught fighting, that's all. You just need practice. You should ask him for help."

Shard's ears flattened and he swiveled away. It was almost middle mark and the horizon was crisp, pale blue. "He would laugh."

"Why? He's your mother's mate. Your nest-father, if not your true father." Kjorn sat, seeming to accept that Shard wouldn't be sparring more at that moment. "And my father's wingbrother. And you're my wingbrother."

"That doesn't amount to him owing me any special treatment." Shard clawed loose a root of grass, and yelped when Kjorn nipped his shoulder to keep his attention.

"He's training everyone. If all of our warriors are prepared, then skirmishes here will be no trouble. I'm sure he'd even be pleased if you asked for his help."

Shard looked across the field at Caj again. The gryfon whirled and fought like cobalt skyfire, fast and wily for his age. His younger foes were quick and numerous, but he seemed to know how they would attack even before they did.

"He leaves himself open," Kjorn muttered. "He knows what they'll do because he makes them do it. See, there, to draw them in, then—"

They both winced when one of the young "wolves" took the bait of Caj's exposed flank to lunge. The blue gryfon whipped about, swiping talons inches from the younger one's eye. He often went for the eyes, the only sure weakness of any creature.

"I'll never fight like that," Shard whispered, fanning his tail.

"Well." Kjorn stood again, looking intent on joining that group. "Caj will never fly like you. But you'd better do your best." He peered at Shard, ears perked. "I don't plan on losing my wingbrother on this cursed island."

Far afield, Halvden and Hallr turned and lunged into flight toward the forest. Shard shifted, but decided against speaking up. If they wanted to patrol, he didn't need to stop them. The father and son were the best fighters of their little settlement, so he certainly couldn't demand that they stay to spar. They flew nightward.

Shard narrowed his eyes, and Kjorn nudged him.

"Shard, I said, why don't you go sort yourself out," the prince murmured, and his next words were amused, but worried. "You're useless today."

Shard forced a chuckle. "I know. I'm…going to fly a patrol. Make sure Caj doesn't bruise Einarr too badly for me. I think he's the only one here who takes me at all seriously."

Before Kjorn could answer, Shard sprang from sitting into flight, wings beating hard in the still air. He followed the cliff face, soaring low along the coast until the cliff dwindled into broken rock and a long grassy beach that built itself back into forest farther inland.

Shard glided around the rocky coast to the gryfess settlers' favorite spot for hunting. The silvery gravel-strewn beach led to sloping lowland, bursting with yellow and violet flowers. Thanks to his mother, Shard knew their names and what they were good for, besides sheltering rabbits. Spring runoff found its way to the sea in a hundred broken streams, which Shard supposed sourced somewhere in the heart of the isle.

Keeping his flight low, he peered along the coast and into the woods. It hunched, dark and still. He saw scattered deer, birds quarreling over nesting materials, and even once, what he thought was the shadow of a young boar.

Thank you for my good death, brother.

Shard took a deep breath, angling higher to regain the height he'd lost on his long turn around the edge of the island. On his right stood the Star Island, and to his left, Sun Isle, where he could see motes of color flying about their business. The other smaller islands spread in a neat line before him, Black Rock last among them on the nightward edge of the scattering of isles.

Glancing toward Star Isle, Shard pushed back a flicker of guilt for lying to Kjorn about where was going. But he had to scout Black Rock in the day if he ever planned to fly there at night, and pretending to patrol was the only way.

The king's words floated through his mind. *Wingbrothers should never have to wonder where the other has gone.* But Shard couldn't explain to his wingbrother why he wanted to see Black Rock Isle, after so long, not caring about it. *No. For now, it has to be secret.*

It took a whole sunmark to fly there, hugging the chilly northern coast of the Sun Isle. It would have been warmer, but slower, to fly the windward route, and he might attract attention from gryfons in the nesting cliffs. He didn't need any more attention. Shard rose higher as he drew near, better to see the lay of the island.

It appeared to be nothing more than its namesake: black rock. Shard fidgeted his talons together as he peered down. There was no feature to it, no woods, just some stunted grass and a clump of stubborn juniper here and there but otherwise bare as the tumbled rocks of its neighboring isle, Pebble's Throw.

The surface had an odd gray tint and roughness to it like shale. Was the island active with earthfire, like Pebble's Throw? Shard had never seen an eruption, only some slow red trickles of liquid fire that ran themselves cold into the sea.

Shard didn't fly too low, in case Stigr was there, or some other beast. Circling once, he figured a gryfon could walk across the whole island in less than a day. Tiny, compared to Sun Isle, which had reaches Shard hadn't even explored; the great hills beyond their nesting cliffs, rivers, the stark White Mountains and the barren coast beyond.

Having made his circuit, Shard decided the windward side of Black Rock, in the lee of the Sun isle, would be more habitable for a gryfon.

If he went at all that night, he would start there.

With the island scouted, Shard turned into the wind, stroking the air to gain height. They would be wondering about him. *Maybe.* Shard suspected that no one particularly noticed when he wasn't there, since they scarcely listened to him when he was. Young Einarr made an effort, and violet Kenna, but both were easily swayed by louder words from Hallr.

Shard narrowed his eyes, letting the cold, higher air give him energy. The king had appointed him this post. He would see it succeed.

As he arrived again over Windwater he saw a large knot of gryfons gathered near the cliff edge. Caj and Kjorn were not in sight; it looked like sparring was over for the day. He would have no support from them if something was wrong. Shard tried to imagine himself as strong, sharp ice, and stooped in a quick descent to see what was happening.

"Aside." He shouldered a young female and another male, who blinked at his tone and shuffled away. Others parted for him. "What's going on here? We have patrols, and hunting—"

Hallr stood over the bloody carcass of a young wolf. Shard tensed, wings lifting, and disturbing relief washed him when he found he didn't recognize the fierce, lifeless face. He snapped a look to Halvden.

"We were attacked?"

To his surprise, Halvden's gaze flickered to Hallr, and the older gryfon answered for him. "In the woods. My son and I were hunting, and this one had at us."

Shard tried to lock a stare on Hallr that would rival Sverin's. The turquoise gryfon met his eye calmly until Shard had to look away, back to the dead wolf. It was large, no doubt, fur silvery blue, hinting at violet where the wind flickered through it.

Maybe it did attack them, Shard thought, anger crawling up his spine as he remembered Ahote and Ahanu attacking him. Another, odd irritation crept through that thought. *But Hallr ranges too far into wolf territory.*

Every gryfon stared at him, waiting for his response.

"A mighty kill," Shard finally said, his gaze traveling the length of the wolf body, down lanky forelegs that ended in paws yet too large for them. A young wolf. Foolish, maybe, thinking to drive gryfons off his hunting ground.

What do I care? Shard thought wildly. *Young, old, a wolf is a wolf and our enemy.*

We lived here peacefully, Ahote and Ahanu had told him. But Shard didn't know if that was the truth.

This is vengeance.

For our brother, Ahanu had said. *Our nephews, all our kin—*

Shard shut out the memory, tore his gaze from the dead wolf and reformed himself as strong ice.

He lifted his head, addressing all. "We will restrict our hunting to the windward banks of the river."

Hallr chuffed. "Because of one wolf? Are you afraid of them, son-of-Sigrun?"

"There is no reason," Shard ground out, "to go so deep into wolf territory. Spring is here. The forest overflows with game in every direction."

"Shard," Halvden began, and Shard snapped his beak, opening his wings as anger lunged like an alien creature through his body.

"You will bring them down on us!" The voice felt not his own, roiling deep from his chest, as it had when he faced Lapu. Tall, bright Halvden crouched back, ears perked in surprised attentiveness. "There is no reason," Shard repeated, struggling at the anger in him that felt almost not his own, as if another claimed his voice and muscles. "No reason. When they've left our settlement alone."

"Shard," Hallr rumbled.

Shard whirled on him, ramping up to his hind legs. "Hallr," he snapped. "The king chose me. Heed. Restrict your hunting windward."

"The king will hear of your cowardice," growled the old warrior.

"Then the dishonor will be mine. Not yours." He looked around at the assembled and saw that most of the young gryfons had backed out of their semicircle, some closer to Hallr, and some to Shard. "All of you. This is my post by Sverin the king. Heed my decisions, or face the consequences."

Bold words, a nattering voice in him mocked, sounding almost like the raven. *How will you back them up, when insolence comes to call? Who are you, to order this warrior around as if he were a fledge?*

Shard didn't know. He met Hallr's stare one last time, then turned and stalked away as Halvden stepped forward to claim the wolf meat and pelt.

He didn't know at all how to back up his words without running to the king, and that would not do. He needed skills of his own. He needed something Hallr didn't have, things Hallr didn't know. He needed strength.

He needed to fly to the Black Rock Isle that night, and meet with Stigr again.

11

BLACK ROCK

THE LAST PINK LIGHT OF sunset faded. Shard watched it from his den, stretched out on his belly. He'd meant to sleep to be alert when night fell, but sleep was a hare he couldn't catch. Ears lifted, he listened to the gryfons of Windwater settling for the night. Stars pricked the darkness. The moon had already risen above his vantage point, but he noted the glow that turned the black sky to velvet blue.

Midnight of the full moon. Tail flicking back in forth in time with his breath, Shard waited, wondering if the night was always so long.

He may have slept, for the next thing he remembered he couldn't see but he heard every sound. The crawling waves stalked and crashed into the rocks. Wind in the grass five leaps above him, rooted hard in the rock. Somewhere, a gryfon snored. Shard's ear twitched and he opened his eyes.

Wolf howls sang across Star Isle. They had woken Shard before. Hunting howls.

To me, brother. To me, sister. Here, here. Shard flattened his ears. Surely, he imagined the words. *Mudding earth words.* He pushed himself up and crouched at the edge of the cave, peering out. Away from the horizon, the white moon perched like a queen gryfon high in the dark, white, bright as a false day. Shard could even see the shadows of sea wheat whipping farther down the shore, and remembered Stigr's words.

I have never seen bright Tyr strike a gryfon down for opening his wings in the moonlight.

In this darkness, Shard wondered if Tyr saw at all. *Will he see my second flight in the dark, when my life isn't at stake, and turn his light from me?* The alternative chilled Shard in a way, that Stigr might be right and it was only the law of the red kings that forbade flying at night.

"Only one way to know," Shard whispered to the breeze, and lunged out, flaring his wings to catch the first draft and soar high. A wolf howl cut the air, triumphant. The hunt was done. Shard banked, leaving Star Island behind him.

Son of the Nightwing, he had been thrice called. His father had flown at night, often enough to bear a nickname. Something flickered in Shard, something warmed, an ember.

My father.

He had come from somewhere. He had a legacy.

He stroked the wind and rose until the islands were dark, slumbering humps in a silver sea. Feeling a little homesick, he took the longer route, windward of the Sun Isle. He flew high, over the nesting cliffs, and looked down at his home. No one would be awake to see him.

The moon shone bright on him, cold silver light completely unlike sunlight, light without heat, only showing him the way. No other his age had seen this. Kjorn had never seen this. Kjorn couldn't see in the dark. Hallr, Halvden and all the other mighty Aesir would never know the sight that Shard saw.

Something shivered through him and broke out as laughter.

What are they afraid of? Wheeling, he folded his wings and dove, spinning through the air like a pinecone before flaring to glide again. It felt as if the whole night belonged to him.

Night wind battered and tossed him, challenging, lifting and then sinking him without the heat of thermals from rocks warmed by the sun.

As Shard came around starward of the Sun Isle, he saw Black Rock. It looked huge in the dark. Everything looked larger and he couldn't fathom it. Shard squinted, trying to determine if it was a trick of the dark and moon. The silver edges of the waves seemed farther back than a normal tide. He had never seen it so far out before. Disoriented for a moment, Shard cast his gaze up to the Day Star, and turned his flight accordingly.

Black Rock loomed huge in the moonlight, seeming bigger than he remembered. Not knowing the surface of it well, he chose to glide low and land on the sand beach where the tide was out. Wind whispered between the rocks. Shard's talons crunched in the wet, pebbly sand. The night shuddered through him still, excitement banishing nerves as he caught his breath.

He perked his ears. "Hello?"

With tide so far out, the broken rocks and jagged edges of the little island formed a wet, black maze in the night. He felt foolish. The strange old gryfon could be anywhere, or nowhere at all. *A cowardly exile playing games with me.*

"Stigr! I've come!"

A step shuffled in the sand, but rocks blocked the wind and Shard couldn't catch a scent. A shadow in the dark lee of a rock stopped, then bounded away. Not like gryfon movement.

"Wait—"

Shard snarled and sprang after it. Tripping over rocks and threatened by tiny crabs underfoot, he finally shoved into the air, flying swift, narrow swoops through a maze of wet rock. The challenge warmed his blood and he almost laughed. The shadowed creature kept just ahead, and almost seemed to pause a few times so Shard could keep up. *It can't be some witless creature.*

"Might as well stop now!" Shard called.

At last his quarry sprang into open ground, onto a trail that led up the face of Black Rock to the surface. Shard swooped down to catch it, talons splayed—but it sprang, too quick, to a lower ledge of rock. With no time to pull up, Shard landed hard, breathless with the thrill of the hunt.

The ground crunched under his feet, brittle shale or dead timber. He didn't bother wondering about it as he turned, ready for a fight.

His quarry padded back up to the top of the rock, and in the white wash of light he clearly, but impossibly, saw Catori, the she-wolf of Star Island. Shard caught a sharp breath.

"You. What are you doing here? How did you come here?" A wolf couldn't swim so far.

"I always come to Stigr on the full moon," the she-wolf answered evenly. "And I was about to say that it's good to see you again."

"Your brothers tried to kill me!"

She perked her ears as if surprised, then shook herself and lowered her head, ears forward. Her voice remained soft as if they were still talking in the woods under the sun. "I didn't know. You must believe that."

"I've never killed or attacked a wolf and they would have killed me that day." But he thought of how he gladly would have fought her in the woods if she'd accepted his challenge. He thought of the dead young wolf at Hallr's feet. "They would've had their vengeance on me for the acts of others."

"The anger is old, and growing," she said quietly, as if she didn't notice his crouch and lashing tail. "Now your king has pushed even beyond the boundary of the gryfon's isle. We were content on the starward side of the river."

Her words, like a freak wind, tossed him. "You…left us alone on purpose?"

"Of course." She lifted her nose to the wind. "It is high spring. No reason to fight over food when food abounds. But if you bring the fight to us, don't think my family will not fight back."

"You already have. One of your young hunters attacked members of my pride."

Catori perked her ears, then lowered her head. "So. You believe that arrogant Hallr. No. None of my hunters attacked you. They came upon us by surprise to steal a fresh kill."

Shard laid his ears back. "I don't believe you. Gryfons don't steal their food."

"You may never think of stealing food, but you are a better hunter than Hallr and his son." She paced and Shard shifted, checked by her words.

Shard hesitated, not sure if that was true. A part of him believed that Hallr would seek out trouble, kill out of spite and not defense.

But what am I thinking, to believe the word of a conniving she-wolf over a gryfon?

But, Shard thought, growing irritated in his uncertainty, Catori had helped him once. *What has Hallr ever done but question me?*

"I don't hold you to blame, Shard." Her eyes glinted in the shifting dark, the eerie, reflected green of a creature who saw through the black. "Not this time. But choose your path well. My family will seek vengeance if given the chance."

"That sounds like a threat," Shard snarled. Part of him cried out, wanting to say that he had admonished Hallr, that he tried to restrict the gryfon's hunting, that he, too, thought there was enough for everyone.

But meeting an exile and treating with wolves would make me a full-fledged traitor to Sverin's law.

"It's a warning." She tilted her head. "That young wolf's name was Kwahu."

"I don't care." Shard's hackle feathers lifted as Catori circled him, like a teasing wind or a raven.

"He was named after the eagles. He admired gryfons, once."

"Stop! I don't care! He interfered with a hunt and that is the price."

She stood beneath a rock now, in shadow. "I just wanted you to know. To know that he had a name. You were willing enough to learn Lapu's, before you killed him. What has changed?"

"I've been given duties by the king." He straightened. "And I won't see his efforts fail. You speak winding words all around me, trying to confuse me, trying to make me see him as a villain, but even you should know that only the strong endure."

"Yet there is balance. We are not the Nameless, witless beasts at the mercy of hunger and fear." The wind stirred her coat, the black feathers matted into her fur flickered. Light slivered and diffused as clouds gusted over the moon. "Has she taught you nothing?"

"Who?" Shard loosed a frustrated, witless shriek. "How did you come here? Why do you bother me? How do you know Stigr?"

She laughed at him. "I walked. I think we can be friends, you and I. I see confusion in you, not arrogance. Stigr is my friend since he helped me once, as a cub. What else do you want to know? You don't know the joy I feel seeing you out in the night, son-of-the-Nightwing."

The breath left him. "I think you're toying with me. And I'm through with it. Your brothers would've killed me for the acts of others. Why should I believe that young wolf didn't attack Hallr for the same reason?"

She flashed her long white teeth. "You'll fall back on the way of the Aesir, then? Or the witless beasts? You're stronger. My brothers are weary and angry and have run dry of forgiveness. Have you?"

"Forgiveness? They attacked *me*. What should they forgive?"

"The crimes of your king! Once, wolves and gryfons shared these isles in peace but now, after so much death…Rashard, *which came first?*"

"No!" His shout cracked off the stone and then fell dead in the night. "No more riddles, no more songs, leave me in peace!"

"Which came first?" Along with her voice, in his head he heard the gryfon in his memory, strong and gravelly. Shard lunged and she darted away, her voice quick and sing-song.

"The mountain, or the sea? Not even the eldest could say—" she leaped away from his snapping beak and he tripped, stumbling across the strange, dusty ground. "—whether first came wave or tree."

Shard paused and she stopped with him, ears perking, then skittered away when he leaped. She laughed as if it were a game.

"Which came first? The silence, or the song? Not even the rowan could say–"

"Be silent!" The lion roar shook his voice. Catori spun to face him, crouched and ready.

"…had it a voice," she intoned, calm as a summer night, "and lived so long."

Shard crouched to spring, wings tense, when a rumbling voice cut through the air between them, a barrier as real as stone. It echoed what Shard knew, in some dark forgotten place of his kithood, was the rest of Catori's song.

> *"Only in stillness the wind*
> *Only from ice the flame.*
> *When all were Nameless, the wise will tell*
> *It was only by knowing the other*
> *That they came to know themselves."*

Shard looked up to see Stigr lounged on a slab of rock above them. Clouds drifted free of the moon and revealed the exile's color, the same dusty black as the volcanic rock. Shard realized at once that those weren't *raven* feathers braided into Catori's fur. Stigr's tail coiled and uncoiled in lazy sweeps as if he'd been lying there watching the whole time.

"Children," he greeted both. "Welcome. Shard, show respect. This is hallow ground."

Shard glanced back to Catori, then to his uncle. Something in the exile's face made him look slowly around, now that the moon shadows had cleared and sharp light shone down. There, under the pale, bright moon, he at last truly noticed the ground on which he stood.

Across the entire surface of the isle, from where his talon touched to the farthest edges falling into the sea, were scattered the bones and skulls of gryfon dead.

12
UNDER TOR'S LIGHT

"WHAT IS THIS?" ICE CLAWED Shard's heart as he lifted his feet, stepping up and around gingerly. There was nowhere to step that wasn't bone. He shifted in place and then leaped onto Stigr's rock, scrambling away from the ground.

"Your forebears," Stigr said, watching him. In the bright moonlight, Shard could at last see some of his features, and he swallowed a squawk. A slashing scar gnarled the place where Stigr's left eye should have been, and he was as lean and wiry as a gull.

This is what becomes of an exile. Catori remained on the ground. Magically, her paws seemed not to disturb anything.

"A cursed place," Shard breathed. "Why did you ask me here?"

"Cursed?" Stigr tilted his head, then stood. He was taller than Shard by a head, giving Shard distracted hope that he might yet grow taller himself. "This is hallow ground, nephew. The place where Vanir lay down their last, and go back into the earth. We are not just lords of the sky. We are of the earth, and must return there. What do Aesir do with their dead? Eat them, I suppose? Wear their feathers as remembrances?"

"*Don't* mock them." Shard absently shuffled his talons against the rock to brush off the dust of bones. "They fly the dead to the fire hills of Pebble's Throw."

Shard recalled in sudden blazing memory the funeral flight of Per the Red. Gryfons had filled the sky, every gryfon old enough to fly, and some mothers with kits in their claws. He'd barely fledged then, but he remembered seeing the old king catch and burn, red feather becoming red flame. He shook himself.

"That way, in flame, they can join bright Tyr—"

"As if it is this feather and bone that flies to the Sunlit Land."

"They burn the flesh to be free of it." Shard supposed the old exile would have found a way to mock any answer. He fluffed and then shook himself, standing proud. "You asked me here. Why? What will you show me?"

Wind shifted uneasily between them. "This alone means nothing?" Stigr extended a black wing to encompass the burial ground. "All who came before you? Who died before and during the Conquering? Your past means nothing to you? This place that you've never seen before, a place sacred to your bloodline, your ancestors…it means nothing?"

At Stigr's words a shivering chill raced across Shard's skin, and the wind sang through the hollow bones, lending whispers to the dead.

Shard swiveled one ear back, listening to the whistles through bone. *Before and during the Conquering.* Despite his promise to Sverin that he didn't care about his father, Shard couldn't help but wonder if, somewhere, on this ground, his father's bones were turning to dust.

Catori perked her ears as if the dead might actually speak words to her, but otherwise remained silent, letting Shard and Stigr speak.

"It's not *my* past," Shard finally managed.

"Then you are an Aesir in the skin of the last-born Vanir," Stigr growled. "I should have seen it when I rescued you."

"Rescued? You helped, and I'm grateful, but—"

"You'd seemed interested in learning something," Stigr said quietly. "But I see now I was mistaken, since you already know everything."

"You should have warned me what I was coming to. Where I would be walking. I don't–I've never…"

Stigr studied him quietly. "Then you do, at least, feel something."

"Of course!" Shard stared around at the bones, his feathers laying sleek and tight with anxiety. He doubted Stigr would share his knowledge if Shard confessed *what* he was feeling.

"Good." Stigr turned to climb higher on the rock. "Then follow me."

Catori snuffed against the ground and sprang up to follow them. Shard paused, letting her pass him, not willing to let her walk at his back. She hesitated, giving him a rueful look, as if she knew why he let her go first. Before Shard could say something, she bounded past to walk shoulder-to-shoulder with Stigr.

It looked bizarre, Shard thought, a wolf and a gryfon standing as close as wingbrother and sister. Hallr's bloody wolf blazed again in his mind. Distracted from the climb, he slipped and stumbled when rock broke under his claws, wondering why they didn't just fly. But he climbed dutifully to humor Stigr.

"Behold," Stigr boomed, startling Shard from his thoughts. They reached the crest of the rock pile and Shard stifled a sigh, wondering what other sacred horrors lay in store on the exile's island.

His wings drooped from his shoulders when he saw, feathers thumping on the ground.

From this height under the white moon and with his eyes more adjusted to the dark, Shard saw why the islands had looked strange and large during his flight.

From the coast of Black Rock all along the sea channel between the smaller islands and the Sun Isle, the sea had pulled away, leaving solid beach between. It looked like a massive, mountainous single land broken by cliffs and canyons. The waterfalls of the Sun Isle crashed down to empty beach and the wet sand gleamed silver between all the islands.

"This night," Stigr's voice thrummed, "once a turn when bright Tor is at her fullest, she pulls away the tides to show us that the Silver Isles are one isle. That we are bound together."

Shard realized his own beak hung open, panting. It was beautiful. Shocking. He never would have thought the tide could pull away so far. Leagues away, he saw the hulk of Star Island and realized Catori hadn't mocked him. She had, truly, walked to Black Rock between the islands.

It took Shard a moment to find his voice and in the quiet, the gryfon bones whispered, the waves washed, and he couldn't remember why he'd been angry before.

At last he turned again to Stigr. "Who is Tor?"

Stigr stepped back, wings lifting. "Who indeed. It is Tor who commands the sea, she who brings the thunder when Tyr brings the wind and rain, she who guides a gryfess in her season. Tyr's mate, Shard. She is Tor."

He lifted his face and it turned silver in the moonlight. Shard swiveled hesitantly to follow his gaze up to the moon. Perched as a queen in the sky. Tor.

He wanted to argue, to laugh, to say that there was nothing at all anywhere to rival the power of bright Tyr in the heavens, but there she flew. *And she did this to the sea. As there is light, there is shadow. As there is stillness, wind. As there is Tyr...*

"It was only by knowing the other," Shard whispered, "that they came to know themselves." Memory and understanding and confusion sparred in his head.

"That is called the Song of First Light," Catori said quietly. "And it is known by the same name among wolves and gryfons alike. It is to remind us that we can only see who we are by first understanding who we are not."

"Who will you be, Shard?" Stigr watched him. Shard grasped for his anger, and his purpose. He had come here to learn what powers lay in him, but he would have to be careful. Stigr seemed intent on turning him against Sverin and the Aesir. The old exile and the wolf witch knew tricks and words and songs, and ways of tangling thoughts in his head. He would have to guard himself and be strong in order not to betray his king, or Kjorn. Or himself. He drew a slow breath.

"I want to learn from you."

"Learn what, exactly?" Stigr cocked his head, as if Shard were an imploring kit, as if he'd begged to come here instead of Stigr asking him.

"Of the Vanir. The old ways. I want to learn…" he paused, phrasing carefully. *What do I want to learn?* "I want to learn what I can be."

"You're nearly ten." Stigr paced away, wind ruffling up his feathers the wrong way. "That is old to start learning the way of the Vanir. And I understand you now have a settlement to oversee."

Shard slanted an ear to Catori, wondering if she and Stigr spoke often, or if ravens passed between them, bearing news. Shard shifted his feet. "I'll come at night. I'll come every night and meet you here, and learn as much as I can."

Stigr stopped and faced him and Shard stared at the black gryfon's missing eye. *How did he lose it?* Maybe Shard would learn that, too.

"Then we have a bargain."

Clouds muddied the moon. Wind sifted through their feathers and Catori's fur and Shard dipped his head.

"You haven't asked me about your sister."

Stigr's ears perked, then he glanced away. "Not this night. I don't know how much more my old bones can handle."

Shard wasn't sure what that meant. Stigr seemed somehow disappointed. Inwardly, Shard huffed.

He has no right to be disappointed by me. All I do is for Kjorn and the king. Stigr's opinion didn't *really* matter to Shard, not the opinion of an exile who lived on a dead island.

"Fine then," Shard said. "I'll see you tomorrow at midnight."

"Fair winds, nephew."

Shard lifted his wings, pausing to glance at Catori. He had absolutely no idea what to say to her. She was unlike her brothers. She had been willing to defend herself if he attacked her, but, Shard realized, he had been the one to start the fight.

"I would like if we could be friends," she said softly.

Shard backed away a step. "I'm sorry," he whispered. "I can't."

He shoved into the sky before she could respond. He'd meant to say that it wouldn't work at all, that he had to be loyal to Sverin and follow his laws, but he had no personal grudge with her. *I'm already meeting with an exile, a Vanir, a traitor, all in one. Friends with a wolf?*

For Shard, it was too much. He hoped she wasn't there the next time he flew to Stigr.

It was only when he reached his den that Shard realized he never asked her what words he had said to Lapu.

STIGR WATCHED SHARD'S FLIGHT. He noticed that the young gryfon took the longer route. Pleasure fluffed his feathers. Despite his bravado and his pride in serving the Aesir, at least Shard truly took pleasure in flying at night, in seeing what mysteries lay under the full moon. There might be hope.

"His blood is red. Through and through." Catori pressed her shoulder to his and all the scents of Star Island came to him in her fur. She had skipped hunting with her pack to come visit him, though Stigr wondered if she'd known Shard would be there too.

"Funny you should say that," he murmured, thinking of the raven. "What else have you seen, in your dreams? Do you think he'll come around?"

"Too many choices and others involved to say." She dipped her head and snuffled the ground, distracted. "But you were right when you said that ten is old to learn the way of the Vanir. It isn't a thing you learn. It's a way from birth."

"He learned some from birth." Together they glanced toward the Sun Isle. "But it has all been forgotten. Burned away by red glory and gold and greed."

Catori huffed and thrust her cold nose behind his ear to shock him from his gloom. She kept him young, that was sure enough. "You should've been born in a wolf skin. Speaking fatalistically of balance and doom."

"And you, a gryfon's wings," Stigr muttered back. "Perhaps he would listen to you then."

"How I wish."

"Tide is returning."

She perked her ears and showed her teeth in what he'd come to learn was a gesture of affection. "Is that my dismissal, old wing?"

"Unless you wish to take the longer way, in the dark." He looked around at the bones. "Or stay here, among the dead Vanir."

"I don't mind the long way, or the dark. And the dead aren't always bad company." After a moment she perked her ears and stepped forward, watching him. A breeze stirred the black feathers in her fur. "I would stay if you asked me, my friend."

Stigr considered her earnest face, then looked away toward the silver sea. Another moment of silence stretched between them.

"Go," Stigr said, since she wouldn't take the hint. Her ears laid back in disappointment. "Go feast and sing with your pack, live, be a proper young wolf. All this company is too much for an old outcast."

"You aren't that old."

"And you are that young." He stretched his wings, letting one nearly bump her from the rock. "I'll see you again."

She nipped his wing. "Fair winds then, Stigr."

"Good hunting to you, Catori." Without needing further words, she bounded away into the moonlit night.

13
CHANGING WINDS

H E STOOD IN THE BONES *of the dead. Silver moonlight shone at the edge of the earth, and sunlight on the other, both in the sky. Daynight. Under this light the dead rose and the light and wind flickered together to make their colors. The wind sang through their bones and they told him their names as he walked among them.*

"I am Ivar," said a hulking warrior of pale mossy color.

"And I, Freja." Dusty yellow and rose. "I was queen." Shard saw a flash of her life, and her death, drowned in a flooded river to save a kit. More names whispered to him, all who came before: Ingra, Kor, and Jaarl, a pale blue king who spoke with whales and, at the end of his life, flew to the top of the world with them.

"Don't forget us. Don't forget us. Don't forget yourself. The winds are changing."

He picked up to a trot as their names brushed his feathers up like winds. "Where is he? Where is my father?"

"He does not lie here," sang the dead. "He is not here. He fell. He fell and his spirit is trapped there in sorrow and fear."

He shoved from the island but the dead reared to catch him, and it was like dragging his wings through water again. "Don't forget us." He broke free of their silvery talons and thrust into the air. Storm gathered. Dark.

A bolt of red skyfire struck him and he fell. Fell to the sea. His face hit a salt wave and red fire spread like blood.

SHARD ROLLED, STAGGERED TO his feet, and crashed into the rock wall of his den.

Since spending more nights with Stigr, more dreams had come to him, vivid and pressing like flocks of starlings, clamoring for his attention. The dream of dead gryfons slipped from him and he stood, panting.

The last few nights, when Shard confessed his dreams to Stigr, the exile told him to try to remember them, that sometimes the Vanir dreamed truths. But Shard could never recall them in detail. This one, he wasn't sure he wanted to.

Shard stretched, shook himself, took a moment to sharpen his talons against the thick vein of lime near the front of his den, and dove into the morning.

A LONG AND WINDY spring soared through the isles. Caj and Kjorn continued to train the young male gryfons. As hunting became easier in the warm season, the females joined to learn what skills they could that they hadn't learned while hunting.

Shard struggled to focus, to learn and grow stronger. Even Stigr said it was wise that he learn to fight in the way of the Aesir, so he worked, sparring each night with Stigr as well, to learn what advantages could be found in being smaller, lither, quicker. Never had he thought he might be able to beat any of the full-blooded Aesir in a spar. Now, hope grew that he might have strengths that, though they were different, were equal to Kjorn's.

"There are as many ways to fight and defend as there are creatures who walk and fly," Stigr instructed. He taught Shard graceful, flight-like movements of evasion from the ground that led into roundabout attacks. Old secrets of the Vanir. Shard had no trouble focusing on those nights, though he was weary.

"Think of the sparrow," Stigr said, one dark night of the moon. "It seems small, weak, helpless?"

He swept talons at Shard's face. Shard swiveled in a graceful ramp, hind paws firmly on earth with talons in the air, and flared his wings to draw Stigr's attention.

"Fast as skyfire," snapped the old exile. "Agile, invisible in the tree, and by all winds, impossible to catch if it goes for your eyes.

Shard twisted and lunged, threw Stigr to the ground, and pressed talons to his throat.

"Good," Stigr crowed. "Again! Observe and learn from all crea-tures, nephew. Think of the fox."

Shard lost that round, and decided to continue thinking of the sparrow. Every night they learned and sparred. Catori didn't show herself on the next full moons, but Shard had the sense of being watched every time he took off from Windwater at night.

Every sunset Shard napped until dark. Sometimes he caught sleep in the afternoon when the females hunted. He had begun to wake at sunset, and waited until true, quiet dark, when the others would be well asleep, before walking to the edge of his den. If any gryfon woke, or saw him standing at the entrance, ready to fly, he said only that he heard a sound, but didn't think it was a wolf. That was usually enough to send a weary gryfon back to their nest. Shard could wait as long as he needed to for all to be asleep.

Then he flew out to Black Rock.

Stigr taught him to fish from rocks in the shallows and Shard ate well, feeling more energy with the extra meals, more strength. There was a new sheen to his feathers that Stigr said was oil from the fish, and would help him if he ever again fell into the sea.

The first night, Stigr had dashed his argument that hunting from the sea was forbidden. Shard eventually decided he must be right. *Bright Tyr hasn't struck me down, after all, or Stigr, who has fished all his life.*

In fact, Shard felt healthier and stronger than ever before. The Aesir forbade fishing. Sverin, who lost his mate in the sea, forbade fishing. Shard accepted that. Sverin didn't want to lose any more of his pride to the sea. But that didn't make the sea itself evil. Shard didn't like to doubt the king, but he began to wonder if Sverin could be wrong.

"Besides," Stigr had said gruffly, "it wasn't the sea or the fish that had killed Sverin's mate. It was lack of skill, a crash, and bitter winter."

Stigr said he would die before he saw Shard afraid of the sea.

"You are the last full-blood Vanir born in the Silver Isles," Stigr reminded him one night. They met every night from midnight until the gray of dawn glowed. "If you forget yourself, we will truly be conquered."

Stigr taught him to look to Tor's gentle light for guidance in his dreams and fears, just as he looked to Tyr for strength and courage. He showed him the spirits in the sky formed together by the stars, great points of light arcing across the starswept expanse that could help him remember history and songs, and guide his flight if he ever left the Silver Isles. His favorite was the Dragon, a long and coiling constellation that extended along the rim of the windward sea almost from one horizon to the other.

"The star dragon is called Midragur," Stigr told him. "It is from the myth of the dragons themselves. They who believe the earth was born from Tyr and Tor, and that a great dragon of stars still coils around it, protecting it as a mother dragon would her egg. That egg will still hatch one day, and that day will be the glorious end of the world."

He flicked some fish gut off his claws. Shard stared up at the dragon of stars. Stigr could speak in the rhythm of great songs, but an ironic edge in his voice always hinted that it was probably best to leave songs in their place and continue with the daily fishing, rather than plan for the hatching of the world.

"How do you know a dragon song?" Shard looked back to him, eyes wide as a kit in awe. He'd grown fond of Stigr's rough voice, his gruff teaching, even the cuff of his talon when Shard said something stupid. Even the familiar, frightening sight of his mutilated eye. If there hadn't been the Conquering, Shard thought, he could imagine there would've been many starlit nights like this, lounged on the edge of a cliff with the wind in their ears, bellies full, and stories to last until dawn.

"The migrating cranes have told me some. An albatross. The whales."

"You speak to whales?" Shard stared. Dreams flickered up and clawed his mind. Stigr chuckled.

"Not well. Their voices are long and slow and they take a good deal of time to say anything. But they live the longest of any creature on the earth or in the sea. If one of them speaks to you, you take the time to listen."

"Like Jaarl?"

Stigr swiveled to focus his eye on Shard. "Where did you hear that name?"

Shard hadn't meant to say it. He ground his beak. "I don't remember. Just, once. Maybe someone told a story."

"Sverin allows stories of the old Vanir?"

Shard saw the gryfon's ghost emblazoned in his mind as the dream winged back to him. The ghost's feathers were a rich, dull blue, shifty like the ocean under cloud, and he knew the gryfon had been real, and so had the dream. "I don't–I don't remember. Did he really speak to whales?"

Stigr stared at him and Shard began to feel like a mouse. Then his uncle looked away. "Yes. He was a great king of the Second Age, when the Vanir first came to the Silver Isles. One of the founders of our ways and our life here. He spoke to all."

"Oh," Shard whispered. He wanted to ask of the other names that rushed up from his dreams, but didn't dare, in case Stigr asked about his dreams, encouraged them. Shard wasn't sure he liked this part of learning his history. "Will you tell me stories of Vanir?"

"The kings?"

"Any of them," Shard whispered, and perked his ears as his uncle laughed.

"The Vanir are as old as the sea," Stigr taught him. "We are not like the Aesir prides of the windward lands. The Vanir know of balance, of harmony and humility. We learn from our past. We take guidance from our ancestors.

"The Aesir plod ahead and let the past die," Stigr said. "Vanir are made of our past. All that came before, and all that will come after."

Every night, Stigr taught Shard to see himself, his father, and his father's father and all those who came before in every blade of grass, in the rolling waves and brush of wind and falling rain.

Through all that, Shard managed never to ask his father's name, or where his bones might lie. Stigr's silence on the topic told Shard with frightening certainty that they weren't on Black Rock with the others. He told himself that he still didn't care.

"The Vanir never die," Stigr sang to him in an old, old song. "We live on in each other."

Dreams flickered at the edge of Shard's waking mind and he became less able to outfly them.

They were things his father would have taught him, Shard mused as he flew under the stars, as he feasted on his catches from the sea. Or his mother if she was able.

He kept his promise to himself and never asked about his father, his name, or whether he had been a fighter, or great in flight like Shard. That much he could do to keep his promise to the king. Still, as the days wore closer to summer, even an outsider would have said he had become as much a Vanir as any could under the talon of a Red King.

14
OMENS

SIX RED DEER RACED ALONG the shore. Shard flanked them in the air, and across from him flew coppery Einarr. The deer had walked right below the cliffs of Windwater, and Kenna, the violet gryfess who had supported Shard, called an impromptu hunt. She had risen to a leading female at their little colony, and shouted at the males to join and learn.

They would need to know how to hunt in winter, when most of the hunting females would be carrying kits in their bellies.

She flew point, high and far ahead, showing them the way. A tawny yellow female flew with Shard, and one of pearly white flew with Einarr.

"Not to the forest!" Kenna shouted at Halvden, who seemed bent on driving the deer to the woods.

"They can't maneuver in the trees!" snapped Halvden.

"Neither can we," snarled the tawny female near Shard.

"Halvden!" Shard wheeled up and around to face Halvden as he closed in toward Shard. "Heed them."

The yellow female tossed Shard an admiring look and dove forward to continue driving the panicked herd of deer. Shard fell back, flapping in place to meet Halvden in the air. The larger green gryfon snapped his beak and slashed frustrated talons through the air. For a heart-tightened moment, Shard thought he wouldn't duck around, that he meant to attack. He forced himself to remain aloft, to hold his air. He had faced down a charging boar. Halvden was no different.

At the last moment, so close his wing slapped Shard's face, Halvden banked.

"Only because they wish it," he snarled, and shot past.

Shard hurtled down to gain speed and catch up. His heart still thundered. Halvden had looked ready to attack him. Shard never thought their rivalry was that harsh.

Shard worried that his nights with Stigr were finally breaking his focus. Everyone on Windwater seemed happy. Bellies full, feathers and coats gleaming.

With plenty of land to explore and forests full of prey, how could anyone be so angry?

Shard flicked the worries off his wingtips. Halvden was just hunt-mad, and showing off for the females. He had too much else to think about to dwell on it.

They herded the deer up the seaside cliff, snapping and grazing them with talons. It was too hard to catch them near the shore, caught between water and cliff. Better to herd them to an open field, the gryfess hunters taught them, narrow in and swoop.

Hunt-thrill lanced through Shard's muscles. Stigr had warned him of hunting on Star Island. It belonged to the wolves. Gryfons were meant to hunt from the sea. But even that first night on Black Rock, Catori had said there was enough for everyone. *She has to know I'm not really a thief. I try to respect the boundary of the river.*

The deer burst from the cliff trails out into the open field on top. Violet Kenna keened a command. The other two huntresses swooped forward to form a wedge with her, narrowing in on a single target.

Shard and Einarr glanced at each other and closed in next to Halvden to form a wedge of their own. Soon, there would be meat. Shard's blood pulsed.

Motions caught his eye. He turned his head. A wolf sprinted from the trees and Shard nearly smashed into Einarr, who squawked and swerved. The wolf's tawny fur glimmered with gold under the sunlight. Shard didn't know him. A trespasser. Hunt-anger burned at the edge of his reason.

His name was Kwahu, Catori's voice whispered. *He was named after the eagles.*

Shard couldn't fathom why a wolf would sprint into territory that gryfons claimed.

And alone? Something's not right.

Teal flashed in the trees. Hallr burst from the forest, splitting the air with a killing shriek.

Choose your path well, Catori's warning echoed, *my family will seek vengeance.*

Without thinking, Shard broke from the hunters and spun into a dive toward Hallr.

"Stop!"

Hallr slowed, checked by the unexpected command. He saw Shard, snapped his beak, and turned back to the fleeing wolf who crossed toward the trees.

"Hallr! Leave it!"

But instead, Hallr called for his son. Halvden turned immediately and streaked toward the trees to fence the wolf in.

Shard screamed in eagle's fury and closed his wings to plummet hard to the earth. He slammed into the ground between Hallr, Halvden and the wolf, and flashed his wings wide.

"I said *stop.*" The word bellowed as a lion's roar.

Halvden veered and Hallr broke short, flaring and flapping hard to keep from smashing into Shard, and landed in front of him.

"How dare you!" Hallr ramped to his hind legs and fell again to pace once in front of him. Shard heard the wolf rasp a word of gratitude before darting back into the forest. His heart pounded wildly in his chest. Hallr fumed and paced and Halvden stood two leaps off, panting, watching, as if waiting to choose a side.

"How dare *you*," Shard growled, fear of Hallr's anger needling up through him. But surely the big gryfon wouldn't attack him. The king had appointed him. "I don't believe a wolf came alone into our territory again. You sought him out and chased him down."

Hallr stopped pacing and stared at Shard. In the bright afternoon light his eyes looked pale as flame. "And if I did?"

Einarr and the gryfess hunters landed and crept forward, ears perked toward the argument.

"I told you not to hunt them. Sverin said nothing of hunting wolves, only of making the colony a success. If you bring them down on us, we'll fail."

"You're a coward." Hallr folded his wings and raised his head, huge and bright.

"And you're close to becoming an oath-breaker." Shard forced the words out, forced himself to stand his ground. If only he had Kjorn with him.

If only he had anyone.

At the edge of his vision, he saw Einarr and the huntresses edge forward, muttering to each other. "The king appointed you here to help me—"

"To help the leader of Windwater." Hallr glanced to the approaching hunting party and raised his voice. "Witness, all of you. Shard has stopped me from hunting a trespasser. I honor my vow to the king to follow good leadership." Blazing eyes turned back to Shard. Dry wind whipped the grass between them and sang high notes in the trees. "Not this. Not this weak, watery, rabbiting brand of conquering."

"Enough," Shard whispered, his resolve crumbling like shale under rain. He laid his ears back. "The king will hear of this."

"I hope so, son-of-Sigrun." Hallr stepped forward. "Son of a nameless, coward, bloodless—"

"I hope you're all pleased," snapped a silken female voice. Shard's breath caught and he lifted his wings, turning to stare. Hallr, stunned at the interruption, blinked around.

Bright violet under the sun, feathers ruffed up the wrong way in the wind, Kenna stepped forward and, with all eyes on her, lifted her head high.

"None of this nattering has gotten us a meal. The deer are gone. The wolves are gone. My sisters and I won't hunt to fill the bellies of boasting, foolish males."

Shard's breath left him and relief swelled so great at her brave interruption that he could have laughed.

The tawny female raised her head, with a quick glance at Einarr, then Shard, and finally looked haughtily to the sky. "Yes. Go on stretching your wings to see whose span is widest. You can hunt rabbits on your own and brag later that it was boar."

With that, the three females turned and launched into the windy sky. Shard released a breath. Hallr loosed a growl and didn't speak before turning to lope into the grass. Halvden hesitated, then narrowed his eyes at Shard and turned to follow his father.

For a moment, Shard stood in silence.

"Why did you do it?"

Shard blinked at Einarr. The younger gryfon still stood with him, copper against the grass. Brave enough to stand with Shard, to ask his reasons honestly.

"Why did you stop Hallr?"

Shard couldn't trust him with the answer. He tried to think of clever half-truths, something to give Einarr information he deserved. But there was only one answer that came to him that was still true.

"Because Hallr is wrong. Go on now, best you start hunting if you don't want to go hungry tonight." Shard turned and walked toward the forest. His belly rumbled and he thought of easy fishing in the tide pools. But fishing was forbidden. It would give him away. After the fight with Hallr, the thought of flying to Black Rock to work with Stigr made him want to faint from exhaustion.

Copper moved on his left. Shard paused, looking back. Einarr trotted up to him with a set expression, eyes narrowed.

"Shard," he said, firmly, as if he'd made a decision. "I'll hunt with you."

Shard blinked as surprise and gratitude glowed in him. "Well. All right. Come on, I smell quail."

ALL I DO IS *to become stronger for the pride. For the king.*

Shard told himself that as the days wore on.

Stigr told him that he would never be in his full power if he pretended to be an Aesir. As a favored child of Tor he must accept her gifts, or live a half life and never come into his strength.

With Einarr's support and the unspoken but steady support of about half the gryfess hunters, Shard let Windwater mostly run its course from day to day without meddling in everyone's affairs. He didn't go to the king about Hallr as he had threatened. But neither did Hallr see the king about him.

We're both bluffing, Shard thought grimly. But Hallr didn't make a show of herding wolves to Windwater again, and Shard let it rest.

Happy, confident, but weary during the day and attention slipping, he didn't make an issue as much when Hallr went hunting on his own. He didn't think much about the younger gryfons huddled with Halvden, muttering, or when Halvden and Hallr returned from hunting trips with not even a rabbit to show, and didn't bother with excuses. There were no dead wolves, and so Shard let that rest too.

He had secrets of his own that he was busy protecting.

No one discovered his night journeys. They probably attributed his improved plumage to the hot weather and final molting, suffering through falling feathers and prickling down like all the other gryfons of his year. Like everyone else, he looked happy because of the successful settlement and bounty of late spring.

Stigr said it was because he finally knew his heritage. Maybe that was true, a little. But Shard knew better. It was his success at Windwater, his improved hunting and fighting skill and all he had to offer the king.

He still told himself that, every time he disobeyed the king's laws by flying at night. He told himself that each time he pulled a fish from the sea. Each time he thought of the wolf whose life he saved.

Everything I do is for the pride and the king.

That was how it looked to everyone, and Shard still knew it was true. Nothing would change that.

15
SKY AND EARTH

WIND TOSSED THE NIGHT, AND clouds raced over the stars. Shard nearly smashed into the cliff face taking off from his den, but even through the wild, bowing grass, he perceived motion at the edge of the woods. The days grew longer, the nights lighter as Tyr remained not far below the rim of the world, and dull blue coated the night.

Shard banked and landed in the grass. Hesitant, ears perked, he trotted toward the woods, not wanting to shout and alert the others of Windwater.

"Show yourself." The wind grabbed his words and threw them into the night. The she-wolf padded forward out of the gloom, her fur ruffled. "Why do you watch me go, each night?"

She perked her ears. "So you did know I was here."

"I'm not blind."

She laughed softly, and the moonlight caught a green glow in her eyes before the clouds took it again. "No. Not anymore."

"Answer me." The grass whipped his hindquarters. "Please," he added more softly.

"I watch to be sure no one else is."

He choked on a laugh. "You're protecting me?"

"I don't know if I could. But I watch. It makes me glad to see another Vanir flying at night."

"Like Stigr?" He tried to keep the talon edge from his voice, but she drew it out. *I shouldn't be speaking to a wolf!* "Like my father? You speak as if you know and see all. But Stigr told me you're no older than I am. You never saw my father fly anymore than I did."

"I did," she whispered, "once, when I was a cub. His last flight."

Frustration sizzled under his skin, more at himself than at her. *I could learn from her, but I can't betray my king more than I already have. She knows that, and mocks me.*

"You don't know as much as you pretend to. Stop telling me mysterious songs and riddles."

"This is the first time I've seen you in three turns." Her voice was so gentle it grated, like Sigrun when she gave advice. "What riddles have I given you? Or have you thought of your own?"

It was too close to the truth. The dreams clawed for his attention, rallying for him to determine their meaning. "I want to know what I said to Lapu. What was it that made him lay down and die."

"His wounds made him lay down and die."

"You know what I mean!" Shard checked his voice and she flattened one ear as if confused.

"I thought you would have perceived, by now."

"I haven't."

"Listen," she whispered. So used to taking instruction from Stigr, from Caj, even Kjorn's advice, Shard absently obeyed.

The grass sang. An owl called. Far below, waves washed the shore. Little voices came to him and he shucked them off, not wanting to think of his dreams. Somewhere in the nearby woods, a rabbit scuffled and then froze.

"*You fought well, brother,*" Catori whispered. "*Be at peace.*"

Shard blinked at her. "What do you mean by that?" There was something strange about the words, the way she spoke, the soft growling undertone.

"See, you can understand. So we say to all those who die to fill our bellies."

"That's what I said to Lapu?"

"Yes." She shook herself and trotted closer, but when Shard tensed, she stopped. "I spoke the words just now in my own tongue, just as you heard them the first time in the woods, just as you said them to Lapu. It isn't a matter of learning words, but listening. You've learned to hear, truly, and if you wish, to speak the language of the earth. It is half your birthright. Son of Tyr and Tor, lord of sky and earth. All you have to do is listen, and you won't even realize the difference."

"Listen. That's what the raven said, before it led me into a trap."

"Which raven?"

Shard stared at her. "How should I know? They're all the same."

She snuffled the grass and yipped lightly. "Are all gryfons the same? All wolves? Every paw print? There are two ravens of the Silver Isles who bother to speak with gryfons and wolves. One is honorable, and one...has his own ideas. The first is Hugin, the second—"

"I don't need to know the names of ravens," Shard huffed.

"Oh? But shouldn't you? Shouldn't you always know who you're talking to, and what you're saying?" She had caught him again in words, almost his own words. He had wanted to know what he'd said to Lapu, after all.

Echoing his thoughts she said, "Those words you said to Lapu are the words we say to all those about to die, so they remember themselves, so they go with their honor and name into their next life."

Shard shifted, the wind teasing him. He had thought the words were some spell, to make Lapu die. "Then it isn't any special power. Thanking a dying beast doesn't make me stronger than I was before."

Her eyes, dark in the night, glinted. "But it does, Shard. You returned Lapu's name and honor to him, at the end. There is another song—"

"No more songs," he cut in, stepping away. "No more of this."

Her ears flattened. "You seemed eager enough to understand. Are you learning nothing from Stigr? Or are you just too afraid of your friends to really learn more?"

"I'm learning enough. You can stop watching me. I don't need help, and I'm not afraid of my own pride. If they learn of this, I—" he stopped himself. He had almost told her that all he did was for Sverin the king. But surely she would tell Stigr, or a raven, and that would end his lessons. "I don't need help."

Clouds closed over, the night grew deep, and the sudden winter in her voice told Shard he had come to the end of what seemed to be mystical patience. "I see. No doubt you've told Kjorn, your wingbrother, of your efforts? Since you aren't afraid?" The wind clawed between them. "Or your mother? Your nest-sister, beautiful Thyra? No?"

"Leave me alone," Shard growled. "This night, and every one after."

"As you wish," she whispered, and whirled to bound into the woods. Even on the long flight to Black Rock, Shard couldn't conceive of why she was angry. *I never pretended to want her friendship. I told her the first night that it couldn't be.*

Don't forget us, the dreams whispered as he flew back from his lessons with Stigr.

This time there were dead wolves, too. An ancient king, gnarled and scarred, with fur as dark as a rowan trunk, loped alongside him on a road of stars. The young wolf slain by Hallr, all his wounds still fresh and open, stalked him through the night.

Don't forget yourself.

Where is he? Shard cried at the ghosts, at the sky, at the earth, but none of them knew, and when he asked, they all fell silent. All except the littlest gryfon kit, who had never said her name but who Shard knew had been killed in the Conquering. Eyes still blind, she curled up around Shard's claws as he dreamed, whispering *war, war, war…*

16
THE SPAR

"Yes," boomed Caj, striding down the line of young males who preened and bragged as they waited to be paired up for spars. "You're all a fine lot of pretty faces."

The molting at last seemed done and Shard, at the end of the line nearest the woods, was not the only one relieved. No more constant itching or feathers floating off in the middle of conversation. The relief distracted him from the gathering.

Fledges as young as two years had joined them, thinking it more a romp than anything, bounding tirelessly around each other while the grown hunters chattered distractedly.

Caj went on, his voice wry.

"Mm. I imagine you'll all win strong beautiful mates and have dozens of fat fluffy kits. And what will you do in winter, make your pregnant mate go out and hunt and fight off wolves while you lounge in your cave?"

They laughed. Caj ramped with a roar, wings harsh cobalt against a shale gray sky. "Pay. Attention!"

Silence. Shard pressed his beak tight against amusement. He had seen that coming. Unbidden, the thought fluttered up that Caj reminded him a bit of Stigr. Or maybe it was the other way around. Off a ways, a few of the young females who didn't need sparring work, Thyra included, lounged and listened to Hallr who told tales of the windlands beyond the sea.

"Shard and Halvden," Caj said, naming partners, and Shard flattened his ears. "Shard, you're the wolf."

That only meant he kept wings closed to his sides. He hadn't sparred with Halvden since they had come to Windwater in spring.

The bigger gryfon padded up, his feathers molted to an even brighter emerald, while Shard's had done nothing but turn a deeper, roiling blue-gray like a storm cloud, his prime feathers lighter as a sunlit edge. The other males had gained an inch of height and girth while he remained short, wiry and toughened from his nights with Stigr.

Shard managed not to sigh. *At least it will be swift.*

"You will pay now," Halvden growled under his breath, "for the disrespect you show my father."

A hundred retorts snapped up and Halvden reminded him suddenly of the vengeful wolf brothers, Ahote and Ahanu. Rebellion swelled in Shard's chest. He had learned so much. *I can't just hand Halvden this fight. Not if he's going to make it about Hallr and Windwater.*

Think of the fox, Stigr's voice said in his mind. *Small and quick, who lays false trails.*

Shard drew a breath, locking eyes with Halvden, and spoke as evenly as he could. "I have no quarrel with you, Halvden." As planned, his calm response made Halvden blink. "I wish we could get along better." At least that was true. One green ear flattened. "So fight well, friend," Shard went on quietly as they circled each other. "Kenna is watching."

When Halvden's gaze flickered for one second to the violet gryfess, Shard lunged. He nearly swiped talons through Halvden's green ear before Halvden leaped away in surprise.

Think of the sparrow.

No, his mind muttered, oddly in Stigr's voice. *No wings for this spar.* Unbidden, a thought rose, even as he ducked and whirled to evade Halvden's rebound lunge of attack.

Think of the wolf.

Shard kept his wings tight to his sides, trotting a few steps back. He thought of Ahote and Ahanu and movements they had made during their attack.

Halvden huffed, ruffled his wings and laughed too loudly, to make sure he had everyone's attention. "Still quick to run, son-of-Sigrun."

"Still heavy and slow, son-of-Hallr."

Halvden's angry shriek and the surprised trills of laughter from some of the onlookers gave Shard a burst of energy and hope. *Maybe this won't end as quickly as everyone thought.*

Halvden shoved up, wings flapping hard to take flight, a gryfon's advantage. Shard darted in, talons splayed and beak open to catch the fan of Halvden's tail. Feathers crunched satisfyingly in his beak and Shard yanked, shoving forward in a hard run to drag Halvden from the air.

Pain and shock filled Halvden's voice and he closed his wings to drop on Shard. Shard lunged sharp to one side, jerking Halvden off course by the tail. The big gryfon hit the ground shoulder-first. Shard leaped in before Halvden could right himself and the green warrior snarled curses as he flung up talons up to defend his neck.

I'm faster! Shard realized with crazy, stupid glee.

Halvden caught him by the wing joint and flung him away. Shard rolled to his feet and darted in again, bruised but determined to use his strongest advantage. Always, the size and muscle of his Aesir peers had cowed him, and he lost his fights.

But sparrows drive hawks from the sky, and two wolves got the best of me.

His training with Stigr made Shard aware of his own speed, agility and advantage more than anyone ever had. He crouched, pretending to catch a breath, and when Halvden lumbered forward, he burst into a run.

"Stop!" Halvden bellowed. "Filthy cheat!" But the jeers of other gryfons drove Halvden on. *I'm only acting as a wolf would,* Shard thought. Halvden loped forward and took to the air again. His damaged tail altered his flight and Shard took advantage, zigzagging to keep Halvden faltering. The treeline loomed ahead.

"Don't you dare!" Halvden warned. Shard slowed his run now, letting Halvden narrow in to dive.

"A wolf would run!"

"Coward, fight!"

"If you like," Shard muttered, stopped, and spun to face him. The nightmare of Halvden in a full, killing dive blocked Shard's sky. Talons splayed, beak open in a triumphant shriek. Shard pictured him as Lapu the boar. *I've made him charge.*

He planted his feet, raised his head. It almost looked as if Halvden truly meant to kill him.

It's only a spar! He met the blazing gold eyes and roared a challenge—then with Halvden's talons close enough to gouge his eye, Shard dropped to his belly and shoved forward across the grass.

Halvden smashed into the ground in a tumbling, swearing heap behind him. Shard turned neatly and leaped up on Halvden's writhing bulk again, clawing a green wing aside and planting talons against his throat. Everyone fell quiet.

"I submit!" Halvden tucked his head with a snarl. "Enough of this."

A sound washed them that Shard realized was a quick murmur of surprise from those watching.

And all had been watching. Spars halted, fledges stared, even Hallr had stopped his story.

"Stay there, Shard." Caj actually sounded pleased as he stood and walked to them, ears perked. Shard couldn't remember the last time his nest-father sounded pleased with him. When he spoke again his voice was neutral, trying not to show favor.

"Halvden. Think. Submission is death."

"This was a mockery of a spar!" Halvden's words gurgled against Shard's talons and Shard loosened them, a little. "He ran."

Caj hissed softly. "If I were a wolf, I'd run from you too. If Shard were a wolf, you would be dead now. There is no rematch. What would you do here, if you were fighting for your life?"

Shard held his pose, taking some satisfaction at holding his talons to Halvden's neck. Halvden shifted, his muscles flexing with rage. "I could flare my wing, knock him back."

"You could flare," Caj said. "Or?"

Halvden twitched a hind leg. "Or…kick. I should have attacked from above in the first place."

"Except he pulled you down!" a helpful fledge hollered. Halvden's gaze snapped around and the onlookers fell silent again.

"You might not be able to anyway," Shard said, glancing briefly to Caj, who inclined his head in agreement. "The wolves would draw you into the woods if they could, to ground that's better for them. It's good to think what you'd do in a close fight."

"Such the expert," Halvden growled.

Other gryfons gathered around them, surprised by Shard's win. In the corner of his gaze he saw Thyra and Kjorn, heads high with pride. Shard's feathers ruffed proudly at the thought that they had seen the fight. Caj tilted his head, then fanned his tail feathers in approval.

"What else?"

Halvden mumbled a few other ideas and then, "I panicked, that's all. I didn't expect him to fight that way."

"You mean you didn't expect me to fight that well," Shard said quietly. "You can say it. I didn't either."

A few snickers and trills rippled through the gathered gryfons.

Caj looked up at the gathering, snapping his beak to silence laughter. "You must always expect that your next fight could be your last. Always. Or it might be. Never underestimate an opponent whether it's a wolf, a she-wolf or even a cub." Shard discerned the rare gleam of approval in Caj's eyes. "Or another gryfon. Let him up, Shard."

Shard bowed his head and stepped off. Halvden rolled away, ruffled, and stalked off.

Caj stepped up to him as the others wandered off, losing interest. "Well done, Shard. You're learning after all. If you keep improving, you'll be one of the king's best."

"Thank you." Shard stretched his wings. The compliment should have felt like sunlight in his heart, but somehow he felt nothing at all. He wished Stigr could have seen the fight. Distracted, he saw Hallr rise and go to meet his son, where the two argued with snaps and growls.

"You may have earned more than Halvden's respect today," Caj murmured. Blinking, Shard looked around and saw the gryfess hunters still lounging. Kenna hadn't gone after Halvden, after all. The violet gryfess watched Shard, and perked her ears when he looked her way.

"Oh," he mumbled.

Kjorn knocked into him from the side, bowling him over. "Well done, wingbrother!"

Shard shrieked and they wrestled through the grass, a tangle of gold and gray. Caj barked at those staring to return to their own spars, unless they wanted Shard for the next match, or Halvden, who was hungry for a win.

Thyra joined their tumble and moments later Kjorn, Shard, and Thyra lay heaped together near the edge of the cliff, breathless and laughing into the wind. The smell of rain gusted against their faces.

"I can almost claim you as my brother now," Thyra chirruped, then preened behind Shard's ear.

A sudden longing for his kithood swept Shard, for the day before the hunt, before he began lying to everyone. The fight against Halvden proved that it was worth it, to Shard. As he'd hoped, he was growing stronger. But he didn't know how much longer he could keep meeting with Stigr. Thyra chuckled at his silence, which Shard supposed she mistook for embarassment.

"Running the settlement here, beating humility into Halvden. What's next, I wonder?" Her ear turned toward her gathered friends, the gryfess hunters nearer the woods. Shard heaved a happy breath, then grunted and shoved Kjorn off him.

"And since we know you fly even better than you fight," the gold prince said, "it would be impossible for you not to win a mate."

"A mate?" Shard laid back one ear, confused. Kjorn stretched his wings and laughed.

"Shard, where have you been? Tomorrow is the Daynight. We will have songs and feasting, pledges and flights."

The Daynight. Of course he'd known it was coming. The days stretched longer and warmer, the sky never quite going black. Tomorrow night the sun wouldn't set at all, but hover along the horizon from dawn until night, bright Tyr watching them the long day and night as they made their pledges.

No, Shard thought with blazing clarity. *He doesn't stay to watch us. He seeks his mate. Tor will share the sky with him for an entire day and night.*

That must be the way the Vanir see it, not the way of the Red Kings. They saw that Tyr oversaw the pledges, the long day celebration that began summer, but Shard realized he must only be hunting his bright silver mate.

Kjorn nipped at his wing and Shard refocused. "Did you say something?"

"Ha!" Thyra bounded away laughing, and flared her wings. "You see, he's been too busy studying under you and Caj to think of it. Shard." She trotted back and he lowered his head a little, oddly uncomfortable. "There's no rush. If there isn't a female who's caught your eye—"

"Well, there is some rush," Kjorn cut in, blue eyes glinting. "If you don't mate now, it must be next year. An out-of-season mating wouldn't be wise. Not with the uncertainty of the settlement."

Shard shook his head, thinking of his uncle Stigr, thinking of Thyra and Kjorn. *Where did the spring go?* "Then it will be next year."

Kjorn looked unhappy. He ruffled his feathers and looked toward the horizon. "Whatever suits you, Shard."

But with that, he leaped twice away and pushed into the air. Shard jumped to follow, but Thyra caught his tail in her claws. He stopped, turning his head. "What's the matter with him? What does he care if I mate, or not?"

"You're his wingbrother. You learned to fly together, to fight together, to hunt together. Together, you killed the boar." His nest-sister's bright eyes studied him closely. "He thought you would do all things together."

"We can't mate together," Shard huffed, but his ears flattened. She was right. He should have matched Kjorn's progress, should have been looking for a mate. But his nights learning from Stigr left him exhausted and barely able to focus on fighting with Caj during the day. He had to watch Hallr. He had to be alert for wolves. He had forgotten. It wasn't important, not right now.

Maybe I will be like Stigr, he thought, and felt a little better before realizing he didn't know if Stigr was bachelor on purpose or not.

Thyra was watching him. "A lot of things are happening quickly, I know."

Shard studied her, and realized just how much he hadn't noticed. "You've chosen each other already, haven't you?"

She blinked twice, ducked her head, and ruffled her feathers. "Yes. Of course."

The sound of sparring gryfons filled the moment of silence between them. "That's good. That makes me happy." It was true, though a little part of Shard wriggled with regret that he wouldn't be sharing his own mating celebration at the same time.

"You'll find someone. If you like, I could help you get to know some of—"

"No," Shard murmured, lifting his head. "No, thank you. Next year. When it's right."

"All right." She began to turn and paused, studying him. "You'll always be my big brother. No matter what."

Shard tilted his head. Those words sent sunlight into his heart. "No matter what?"

She bobbed her head. Shard crouched to pounce but she braced talons on his shoulder. "I should go talk to him." She lifted her beak to the gray sky, where they could see Kjorn wheeling like a mote of sunlight.

"Of course," Shard murmured. She bumped his shoulder and pushed into the sky. He watched her go.

"Shard."

He leaped forward, feathers sleeking tight in surprise. As he turned, he had to force a laugh at his own jumpiness. The laugh shriveled when he saw violet Kenna, shiny even under the gray sky, her eyes bright with amusement.

"I just wanted to say I admired your spar."

"Oh," said Shard, noticing for the first time that her eyes were gray, like a falcon. "Thank you." He shifted one foot, glancing around. He'd expected Caj to keep him working, but the blue gryfon seemed not to see him anymore, weaving between the other fights, calling instruction. In fact, no one was looking at them, and Shard thought it purposeful. He thought of Thyra and Kjorn, and his wingbrother's disappointment, and lifted his head a little as Kenna spoke.

"I was just going to the stream. To cool off. If you're also warm. That is, if you'd…"

"Thank you," Shard said quickly, feeling foolish. *I should have been the one to invite her.* "I'll come."

Kenna's feathers fluffed up with pleasure, though, to Shard, she also looked amused. He wasn't sure if that was good or not.

They walked through the long grass and humor left them as they stepped under the shadow of the trees, heavy with spring growth. They remained alert for wolves and other dangers that might stalk from the shadows. The scent of the woods always took Shard back to the day of the hunt, and he looked hard into the trees and ferns, half-expecting to see Catori's red shadow disappearing from the corner of his eye.

Kenna was speaking. "…hold the celebration on the Sun Isle, since the new-whelped kits are too young to fly, and it would be too much of a risk, all gathering here."

"Yes," Shard agreed, distracted. He forgot about drinking once they reached the stream, still peering around the woods. Listening. Little voices whispered from the trees. *No, it's only wind.*

"Shard."

He blinked and looked at her, and realized they were standing so close he could see that her violet feathers gleamed iridescent blue when she shifted. He wondered if her Aesir mother was somehow related to Caj. Then he ruffled and banished the thought of Caj from this moment. The blue gryfon had never given him any advice about choosing a mate beyond, "Don't fall for beauty alone," and that had ended the conversation because Sigrun had asked what he meant by that, and it stretched into an argument that lasted days and resulted with Caj doing his own hunting more often than not, for a fortnight.

"Where did you go?" Kenna murmured when Shard snapped his attention back. The wind was calmer here, but the scent of rain thickened.

"Sorry," Shard mumbled. "There's so much—"

"I know," she said simply. "A lot to think about. I see it in you all the time. Drifting off. Thinking ahead. Thinking back. Thinking too much." She tapped him with her tail, as Thyra might do, but in a way that was altogether different. "I think it's a Vanir habit."

The warmth that had surprised him at her playful touch cooled. "A Vanir habit?"

Her gray eyes remained playful, but her tone was serious. "You are full-blooded Vanir. I think it makes you more thoughtful than others. It's what I like about you."

"It is?" He tried to catch up, to think of when he had seen her paying attention to him at all. *Was she at the initiation hunt?* Stupidly, he couldn't remember. He remembered the first day of settling, and the day he had talked Hallr down after he'd killed the young wolf. Both times, Kenna had spoken up, and he'd barely noticed.

"Maybe…" She hesitated, then drew herself up. She was smaller, and Shard realized she must be at least four years his junior. Barely old enough to mate. Made older seeming by the hunting, the responsibility. "Maybe we can speak of it sometime."

"Of what?" His wings twitched, wanting to escape, even into the rising storm wind.

"Of being Vanir. It's half my blood, anyway. My father has spoken of it to my mother and she didn't stop him."

"It's forbidden," Shard whispered, staring at her. She stepped back, glancing around. This was not how he'd expected the conversation to go. If he'd been stronger, maybe they could have been speaking of something else.

"I've seen you." She perked her ears and stepped forward again, tensing. "Leaving at night. I've seen you fly out and return at dawn."

Her words hollowed him. Ice lumped in his belly. "Kenna, please…"

"You shouldn't. It's dangerous, but I haven't told anyone."

"Why?"

She laughed, a breathless trill. "I thought you knew."

"Knew?"

She bumped her head in and nuzzled under his ear, and whatever he was going to say winged off into the wind.

Then worry rose again. *If she was watching me, was anyone else? Anyone more dangerous?* But, Shard thought, surely, anyone else would have told the king by now.

Kenna spoke quietly, and her tone had shifted so completely that Shard couldn't keep up with what she wanted from him. "No one else knows, Shard."

He dragged himself back to the moment, and tried to think what a more experienced male might say, like Kjorn. "I just—"

"Don't worry." She laughed at him and flopped by the streambed, batting at his wingtip, inviting him to play just the way Thyra might. Shard hesitated, then crouched, tail lashing. She blinked and watched him, then her eyes grew keen and she started to speak, but Shard leaped. She laughed and they rolled together, wrestling. They tumbled into the stream once, both shrieking at the cold. It wasn't like a spar, for Shard couldn't see trying to gain the upper claw. They just wrestled, throwing the other, beating wings, until they ran out of ground and bumped into a juniper trunk.

Shard laughed, warmth flushing under his feathers. Kenna, smaller but strong from hunting, pinned him against the trunk. She perked her ears and Shard struggled dazedly to think what he was supposed to say. *Should I ask her to fly with me on the Daynight?*

"Do you think," she murmured close to his feathered ear, "that once the settlement is strong, we will have to stay here?"

"I don't know," Shard murmured, distracted by the smell of her feathers. *Flowers? From her hunts in the field? Or does she purposefully rub flowers on them, as Thyra used to?* As a healer's son, Shard could pick out the separate scents of rosemary blossom and wild rose, but the third was elusive. Feeling bold, he nuzzled behind her ear, determined to figure out the third flower. Then she spoke again.

"But surely as wingbrother to the prince, you might choose where—"

"Kjorn?" Suddenly, the flowery scent of her feathers turned his stomach. Shard heaved, pushing her off. She slid back and blinked, sitting.

"I only mean, as his wingbrother—"

"I heard you." The warmth in him heated to frustration. *Wingbrother to the prince.* "I thought you liked *me.*"

"I do, Shard."

"Why mention Kjorn, then?" He stood and shook himself free of bark and pine needles.

"I was only curious." Her voice grew an edge. "If you and your mate might get to choose—"

"Are we mated now? That was fast." He heard his uncle in his voice and paced away, stretching his wings. "Or were you just checking what I might have to offer?"

"That isn't what I meant."

"Then what did you?"

But she never got to tell him. Another voice entered the argument.

"Well if it isn't Shard, master of flight *and* fight, and the mysteries of Star Island." Halvden strode green and flawless through the trees.

Kenna rolled to her belly and perked her ears, looking between both of them. Shard sensed, unhappily, that she was hoping for another fight. She wouldn't be satisfied, though, for Shard no longer felt like fighting for her or anyone else's affection. It didn't feel at all as he thought it would, any of it. He'd thought a female might be more like Thyra. More like the way Kjorn and Thyra seemed to just know that no one else would do, that they fit.

"Kenna," Halvden changed his attention when Shard didn't respond. "I was going to hunt before the storm hits. Join me? I still need help with that dive technique for catching a running deer."

Kenna flattened one ear, then looked expectantly at Shard. *Am I supposed to fight for her now?* He ground his beak and tightened claws into the pine needles, suddenly wanting to be alone. Surely his future mate could choose her own company without making them fight. But then, Kenna was young.

Too young.

"You should go." He dipped his head to them both. "Halvden needs all the help he can get."

Her ears flattened and she pushed stiffly to all fours again, her pretty gray eyes more like the cool sky. "Then I will."

"Good."

Her hackles ruffled, then she padded to Halvden. Together, they bound to the edge of the woods and took off. Shard whirled around and slashed his talons against the juniper trunk. *I shouldn't even care!*

"Ah," croaked a voice above him. "Young love."

"Shut up," Shard muttered, and the raven glided away laughing into the trees.

17
STIGR'S LAST LESSON

"**B**E WARY OF A GRYFESS thwarted," Stigr called to Shard over the night wind. They flew over the tossing sea, farther out than they had ever gone. Shard stared down at the roiling waves that heaved pale, salty spray toward the sky. Stigr didn't seem worried. "There isn't a power more dangerous on the earth or sky." Stigr laughed. Shard hadn't told his uncle all of it. He doubted Stigr would've laughed then.

The storm brewing earlier had mostly hit the northern edge of the isles and had blown off by the quarter mark of the night. Perfect conditions, Stigr said, to practice the master maneuver of Vanir flight, but hadn't yet told Shard what that was.

Shard hadn't told him that Kenna knew of his night flights. That worry, paired with the sight of endless black ocean stretching before him, the Silver Isles tiny lumps at his back, was enough to weigh his wings like logs. But Stigr either ignored, or didn't notice, his mood. Shard suspected the former.

"Either way, don't wait too long to mate if you want one, nephew. That's my advice. I did, and the Daynight I would have asked my chosen was the very hour the Aesir came raiding. Doesn't it figure, but I trust bright Tyr guides all. Now then."

Shard snapped his beak in frustration at the subject change. Often Stigr would do that—hint at stories of the Conquering, of his own past and exile, and then promptly wing forward to a new subject. But Shard followed. Too much information could lead to knowing things he had promised his king he didn't need to know.

Wind nearly flung him into the water. Shard gasped and stroked up, catching himself.

The sea is death. It took my mate from me…

"That's good, nephew!" Stigr bellowed over the wind and chop of waves. "Have no fear. Your wings are built for this! You're just like your father, I can see it. The Aesir can't fly this way." He spoke of true sea flight.

Subtle drafts swirled over the water that Shard, with his long curved wings, could catch and glide on. Sometimes it took more effort, and that night his flight bumped and stuttered, his wings too tense with nerves and fear to catch a glide. At least it took enough concentration to drive all else from his mind. Stigr was still talking about the Aesir.

"Their wings are too blunt and broad. They'll breed sea flight out of the Vanir soon enough, I suppose."

Shard drew a breath, flinging other worries away. He had always flown the best of any in his year. This flight, he was determined to master. Little gusts buoyed his wings, and the tangy smell of brine, sea plant, and fish swelled in his nostrils with each wave. They flew out past the islands into the windland quarter of the sea. The rush of seeing so much water nearly drove a cry from Shard's throat, and he glanced behind him only once to make sure the Silver Isles were still there.

"If you can master this at night," Stigr called over the water, "then it will be like kit's play for you in daylight. Like this, now."

Shard swallowed a reply, clenching his talons. Stigr banked sharply while Shard wheeled to avoid a high wave, stretching his wings taut to catch every eddy of air and keep aloft.

"Why do we have to fly so low?" Or maybe they weren't low, Shard realized. The waves grew larger that far out, towering as high as pine trees at their foaming peaks.

"Tor rules the sea," Stigr called as he glided in close to Shard again. "And so the sea belongs to the Vanir also. You're ready to learn the greatest flight of all."

Shard stared as his uncle pulled up, the exile grasping currents with his wings until he found a soft draft that let him spiral high. Shard followed, his long, curved wings catching the same winds as easily as a gull.

"The trick now," Stigr called from two leaps above, "is no fear. You'll find yourself with different wings than when the wolves drove you into the sea. Behold."

Before Shard could ask what he was to learn, Stigr slipped out of the current. He stretched his talons out and his hind legs back, tucked his wings, and dove.

Shard's belly dropped in sharp terror and his shriek of surprise bumped over the waves. Stigr didn't answer the call.

Is he mad?

"Uncle!" Shard wheeled tightly before rearing back in the sky to peer down as Stigr fell. Then, as Shard held his breath, the dark exile plunged into the cold black waves.

For three heartbeats Shard was alone, the night wind rushing his feathers, the moon on the mountainous waves. Then violent splashing announced his uncle lived. Shard glided lower, wary, but Stigr shrieked in triumph and, to Shard's awe, hauled himself out of the water with hard, fast wing strokes, like a sea eagle.

"*Ha!*" Stigr called into the night, while Shard shuddered and stared. Water rained from Stigr's wings in a silver curtain, droplets flying back to the waves. "Don't fear, nephew." Stigr swooped around him in an exhilarated circle. "You were born for this. I've seen you fly and spar. Go to this with the same heart, and you won't fail."

Shard flattened his ears, whispered, "Yes, Uncle," and flapped to gain height again.

No fear. Different wings.

The sea is death.

Shard tried to quiet the memory of the king's voice. Maybe it wasn't truly blasphemous to catch fish in the shallows, for he still hadn't been struck down by Tyr, but he didn't doubt the danger of the open sea.

Stigr watched him a ways off, circling slowly. Shard flapped higher, then glided, stalling. Finally, he drew a breath, quieted his doubts and slipped as Stigr had done, folded his talons, then his wings.

The horizon tilted as the sea became his sky. A rush of salt air slapped his face. Facing the waves head on, their roar and pull filled him. They rose, rolled and sank again like mountains of salt water. Shard shut his eyes, gasping against the wind. He had dived before. Often.

This is no different.

He heard Stigr's encouraging cry, then waves—the full power of the sea filled his face and senses, and he thought of the frigid water and his salt-heavy wings, then king's voice. Terror grasped him. A fear grasped him, too large to be his, digging talons into his muscles, his heart, his thoughts. It felt as if another's fear whirled over his own, as if he lived some memory. A huge gryfon circled above him, laughing. *Stigr?* But this gryfon was red, scarred, a vicious king from a hotter land. A memory that was not his own leaped up in Shard's mind, a memory, or dream.

He was falling, falling to the sea, to his death.

"Shard!" Stigr's bellow snapped him back. "Straighten out!"

Falling to his death.

But I am alive!

The world spun round and up again as he flared, flapping, stalling, and pulled into a tight spiral to glide out of his dive, a leap from the water. His tail feathers slapped the waves. His wingtips brushed the water and he shrieked to release his fear, heart nearly bursting as he regained some height.

Gliding higher, he sucked in cold night air and perked his ears down at the waves. A shadow that was his uncle loomed near his shoulder, but Shard didn't look at him. Still gripped by the paralyzing fear that hadn't felt like his own, he gasped for calmer breath.

"Well," rumbled the old exile, watching him sideways. Disappointment weighted his voice. "Well. That's all right, Shard. It's all right. Few get it the first time. Try again."

Shard swiveled to stare at him. "I—I can't."

Stigr flexed his talons, eyes narrowed as if to argue, to push him. A black silence stretched between them. Then Stigr let out a slow breath and spoke quietly in a different tone.

"Shard. Is it because of your father?"

Shard blinked, flicking his wingtips against a ripple of wind. "Is what because of my father?"

Stigr clasped his talons, edging away as their wings bumped too close. "Diving. Are you afraid to dive because of the way your father died?"

Still catching breath, Shard raced to catch up. The vision of a mad red gryfon above him whirled so fiercely he peered up, just in case, and saw nothing but stars, the moon, and drifting clouds. *I don't know my father's name,* he had said to Sverin. To his king. *I don't wish to.*

Shard tried to grasp for his purpose again, flying out in the middle of the night, over the sea. He feared that the strange vision, the terror that took him over, might at last be the wrath of Tyr, showing him the wrongness of his actions.

Aching to ask Stigr how his father died, but the refusal to break his promise to the king cold in his gut, Shard managed to shake his head, as if he knew. As if someone, once, had told him, or he remembered.

"No. I don't know. It's just frightening." The madness of the whole thing whittled at him and tensed his muscles. He would be sore tomorrow. But he saw clearly now what he must do. If this was the last great thing Stigr had to teach him.

"Well. Next time then. We all have our fears."

"Uncle." He drew a breath as they soared higher, away from the trickier breezes over the waves. The ocean rolled out under them, a shining black plain. "I can't come again."

The early summer night was almost light enough for him to sense Stigr's blank, single-eyed stare. "Why?"

"Kenna knows." Relief washed him at the excuse. He couldn't look over at the exile again. "It's too dangerous." A surprising heat locked his throat. He had never meant to become close to Stigr. An exile.

"I see."

But an edge in his tone told Shard that Stigr had heard a different answer than the one he gave. "I want to, I just can't."

"No you don't." Stigr pushed, trying to outfly Shard, but Shard flew faster than any gryfon on the islands, and he caught up.

"Oh, I knew," Stigr continued. "I knew exactly why you came to me. So you could be a stronger, conquered minion of the Red King. But I had hope. I thought if you learned something, if you learned of the Vanir—"

"And I'm glad to know!" Shard caught a draft and flew up over his uncle, trying to see his face. "I am, please believe. But what would you have me do?"

Faster than they had flown out, they reached the edge of Star Isle and landed on a cliff a safe distance from Windwater. Stigr thumped heavily and Shard more lightly beside him. In answer the exile whirled on him, hackles raised, wings hunched up like storm clouds.

"What would you do, nephew? If you weren't busy wishing for golden wings and the grace of the conquering Aesir? Don't you see, this is your home. They are nothing but killers and thieves."

"What should I do then? They're my family and friends." Shard half crouched in defense, wary. He had expected Stigr to be upset, but more gruff and cold, not this hot anger. "Come live with you among the dead of Black Rock? Spend my days wishing for the past? If that's the way of the Vanir, then I will stand by the Red Kings until my last breath. At least they look to the future!"

"I am looking at the future," Stigr whispered, staring at Shard. "Or I thought I was. You should've been honest with me."

"You said you knew anyway. Why I came. Why I wanted to learn."

"I thought the knowledge would change you."

"Into what?" Shard paced away, tail lashing, and wanted nothing more than to leap back into the sky. Dawn approached. "Ever since I met Catori in the woods, strangers have been speaking my name and hinting about a past I cannot know!"

"Why can't you know?"

"Because…" *I made a promise.* "It isn't important. Everyone else has moved on. Everyone else is happy, Stigr! The pride is strong. Even my mother, who you won't ask about. She took a new mate. She bore me a sister."

That stopped Stigr. "She mated? Who?"

"Caj," Shard said, and suddenly, out of all the gryfons in the pride he could have named, he realized that he was proud to speak that name. Comparing blue Caj with Hallr, even Sverin, who was harsh and terrifying, made him feel better.

"An Aesir? Of all of them…"

"So. You see, it's time to move forward."

"Is it." Stigr watched him, one ear flattening ironically at Shard's tone. "Good thing you're so wise in the way of the world. I see it's gotten you far."

Shard advanced a step. "What do you mean? Sverin trusted me with the settlement here—"

"Trusted you? Nephew, I see more clearly out of one eye than you ever will with two, you're so blinded by red and gems."

"What are you talking about?

"This is exile." Stigr stretched a wing. "He may preen it up and call it an opportunity and an honor, but I see what you won't. He has torn you from your wingbrother's side, from your mother, from anyone who might support you if you need it, from anyone who would show you the truth."

"It is an honor," Shard hissed, "to do whatever my king asks of me. But you wouldn't understand that."

Stigr looked as if Shard had slashed his good eye. "You have no idea…" More words and anger flitted over his face, and then he straightened before bowing his head. "If this is what honor has come to, then no. I wouldn't understand. Goodbye, Shard. Fair winds."

"Uncle!"

Stigr shoved into the sky, slapping Shard's face with a wingtip when Shard bounded in to catch him.

Shard felt foolish. Why had he expected some jovial parting, with Stigr going back to live on Black Rock alone among his ghosts? He realized the cold truth that it never would have been possible.

I used him, he thought miserably. He'd never thought to become fond of an exile. *He knew I was using him and he still taught me, hoping… hoping what?* Shard stood on the cliff edge as the dawn turned the clouds rosy and the dark sky gray. Whatever it was, it didn't matter now. Shard had gotten what he'd gone to Stigr for. As he'd said himself, it was time to move on.

"DIDN'T I TELL YOU?" gabbled the raven, winging up on Stigr's right. "Red-blooded. A waste of time."

"Don't think I won't toss you into the sea," Stigr growled. What a fool he was. His sister had been wrong, so wrong, to want to raise him among the Aesir, to think there could be balance.

"You are short-sighted," said the second raven, drifting up more gracefully on Stigr's left. "He rages like a new kit into the world. Clinging to the past, uncertain of the unknown."

"You two speak too much in riddles," Stigr muttered.

"He awakes," the calmer raven murmured, flipping happily in the wind.

"He sees both paths," rasped the first, with a mocking edge.

"But he must choose."

"But he does not know the true choice. He doesn't truly know himself."

"He does," Stigr said stubbornly. "He must. They would have told him."

"He doesn't."

"You must tell him."

"You must be there for him when he chooses."

"You be there," Stigr snapped. "He won't have me anymore." He shoved forward, finding a tailwind to outpace his riddling advisors into the dawn.

18

THE DAYNIGHT HUNT

THE DAYNIGHT DAWNED RED.

Even from his windward-facing den, Shard saw streaks of rosy fire flaring out from the dawnward sky, sun lighting the last wisps of clouds from the night. Still half in his dreams, he lay still, letting everything come back.

Stigr was gone from his life. He'd done that much. He had chosen. The relief of it felt too much like regret for him to feel proud of all he'd learned, to feel excited at the skills he had to offer the king and Kjorn.

Vanir skills, part of his mind babbled. *Forbidden skills.* But Shard had learned them in the name of the king, to serve Sverin. No one could deny that he was already a better fighter, and that was due to Stigr. In time Shard could try to convince Kjorn, and so, Sverin, that if times were lean they could fish from the sea...

I thought the knowledge would change you, Stigr had said.

"Into what?" Shard whispered to the breeze that trickled into his den. He inched forward to peer out into the morning, and froze when he caught voices on the wind, the strong, tense voices of arguing males. He perked his ears.

"—enough of this ridiculous charade. It should have been Halvden. Everyone thinks so. This whole thing is a joke." It was Hallr, but who was he arguing with?

"I didn't come here to speak with you." Caj.

Their voices echoed down against the rock, drifting clearly to Shard. He stood and jumped from his den, caught the morning wind, and flapped up to the top of the cliff where the two older males stood. He refused to hide from Hallr, or listen to his complaints.

"There's our noble leader now," Hallr scoffed as Shard landed and trotted toward them.

"Fair morning, Hallr," Shard muttered. With Caj watching him, Shard raised his head higher, lifting his ears. "Is all well? Nest-father, welcome."

"Thank you."

"You both know," Hallr said quietly, a dangerous edge to his voice, "this colony should have been my son's appointment."

"Tell that to the king," Shard said.

"The king, the king," Hallr echoed like a raven. "Always threatening with the king, because you can't back up your own words? You couldn't challenge me, whelp."

Shard stared at Hallr, his hackle feathers lifting. But Caj spoke first.

"He could challenge you."

Shard blinked at Caj, but Hallr barked laughter and the wind swept it out to sea. "He would lose."

Heat crawled under Shard's skin, goading him to leap forward and challenge Hallr right there. "I did well enough against Halvden, last we sparred."

"A spar," Hallr said. Caj lifted his wings.

"This isn't a contest of strength, Hallr. We aren't nameless, witless beasts. Obey your king. Keep your honor. Is this the only reason you've bothered me? To complain of your duty? I came to speak with my son, not you."

My son. The words shocked down Shard's back. *Not, my adopted, nest-son. My son.*

"I wanted to warn you," Hallr snapped, "That if your nest-son crosses another line with me, or dishonors my son again, he will pay. The weight of a full-blood Vanir drags down this pride and I see it even if the king will not." Hallr turned from Caj and watched Shard, his feathers sleek as a serpent's back, bright eyes pinpointed as if to attack. "You live only because you've somehow weaseled your way into Kjorn's good grace."

"And you, who have no wingbrother?" Caj's voice grew cooler. "You wouldn't understand the love between brothers."

Shard forced his feathers from ruffled back to smooth. He marveled at Caj's calm. *How does he stay so quiet and still?*

"There is no one worthy of such trust and honor from me," growled Hallr.

"You couldn't have the king's ear," Caj rumbled, "so you'll have no friend at all, is that it?"

Shard's anger cooled as curiosity wriggled up. *Caj has the upper claw, that's why he's calm.* It was confidence, Shard saw as if in a blazing light. Caj was unafraid. Bright, unbidden admiration flared for his usually distant nest-father.

Hallr didn't answer, and turned to face Caj fully as if Shard was no longer there. "You're a disgrace. Letting the whelp of a conquered Vanir witch live just because she begged. Or did she bewitch you?"

Caj's gaze slipped sideways to Shard, then he dipped his head. "It wasn't I who let Shard live."

"She witched Red Per, then!" Hallr stamped a taloned foot and Shard could tell he wanted to fight, or fly. "He is a curse on us, and Tyr will show us before long."

"He is still of my nest." The tense crawl of anger at last cut Caj's voice. "Do harm to him, and I consider it harm to me."

"I don't fear you," Hallr snarled. "You're soft. Under the wing of your soft Vanir mate, who you didn't even properly win."

"Shard," Caj said quietly. "Go wait for me in the forest."

"No."

Caj turned on him, raising his wings higher. "I said *go*—"

"No. I'm not a kit. What does he mean, didn't properly win?"

"Most Aesir," Hallr's growl broke up their argument, "were strong enough to kill the mate of the gryfess they desired. But not gentle Caj."

Caj's eyes narrowed and he hesitated, gaze locked on Shard. When Shard didn't move, Caj turned on Hallr. "I didn't kill her mate, so I didn't properly win her, is that it?"

The breath swept out of Shard. Sigrun had never told him who killed his father. Once, she had told him it wasn't Caj to make him obey the blue gryfon, and warned him never to ask of it again. He'd always thought she was lying. That was the way. The conquerors came and won the spoils: lands, dens, and widowed gryfess mates.

"That's what I mean. *Noble Caj.* Even the conquered call you so. You didn't even fight for her. Just swept in after the fighting and scooped her up and now you're true mates and love each other, is that it?"

"Yes," murmured Caj. "That's it. Should we all have done as you, and killed our mate's Vanir warrior in front them? Then their kits?"

"At least my mate hasn't bewitched me."

"I have no time for this," Caj growled. "It is the Daynight. If you have only more windblown words to throw at me, then be off."

"Watch your nest, noble Caj," Hallr warned, his words nearly lost in a growl as his gaze pierced toward Shard. "It rots under you."

Without another word, Hallr shoved into the dawning sky. For a moment, only soft wind and the sweet, tangy scent of pine lay between Shard and Caj.

"Well," the blue gryfon huffed, not meeting Shard's eyes. "I came to speak with you this morning. To tell you to be careful. You've made enemies. But I think you've probably figured that out."

The words blurted. "You really didn't kill my father?"

"No." Caj's tail flicked slowly. "I really didn't."

"Who then?" Shard couldn't have cared less about Hallr in that moment. "Did you see him? Did you ever know him?"

Caj was silent, looking wary. Then, "I saw him. But I never knew him."

"Who killed him?"

"Shard," Caj murmured. Shard could scarcely believe the regret in his voice. Caj's gold eyes watched him steadily. "Will it help you to know?"

"I don't know," Shard whispered. Too many regrets grasped him. The fight with Stigr, knowing the truth of Caj, fear of Hallr's true hatred. "But I need to know."

"Just remember that it's in the past."

"I will."

The rising sun edged Caj's blue wings with gold, and his low, calm voice filled Shard's head, as it had, he realized, since he was a kit. Caj had tried to tell him stories of the windland, tried to teach him the way of the warrior, but Shard had preferred to learn as much as he could on his own. *He wasn't distant from me,* Shard realized in that moment. *I was distant from him.*

"Your father was the last to fight against our king," the blue warrior murmured. Shard stared at him, breath halted.

"Severin…?"

"Per himself," Caj said. "Remember, he was king before Severin. He was king during the Conquering."

Is he making it up? A grand warrior's death, to make my father seem better than he was, to appease me?

Dawn's light caught Caj's gold eyes, and Shard saw that he was telling the truth.

"Per the Red himself slew your father, and he…" he hesitated, as if thinking whether to tell Shard the rest or not. "He had been so loved by the rest of the pride, that his death ended the war. Your mother begged for your life, and Per knew that killing you would start the battle again. So you live."

Winds brushed between them, smelling of the pine forest and of the sea. "Thank you," Shard whispered, looking away.

"I also came this morning to tell you that I'm proud of you." Caj was nearly whispering. Shard had never heard his voice so quiet. Voices fluttered to them, other gryfons emerging from their dens to catch the dawn wind and stretch their wings. Some called a greeting to Caj, but he focused only on Shard.

"You've done well here, and I know it hasn't been a flight in fair weather. Kjorn told me you're not going to mate this year, and that's fine, Shard."

Shard blinked back up at him, rising from his thoughts. For some reason, he'd thought Caj wouldn't have paid attention to whether or not Shard chose to mate, that he wouldn't care.

"It's good to hear you say that."

Caj dipped his head a little. Shard shifted his feet in the grass, trying to think what else to say. He'd never spoken to Caj this way, though he knew Sigrun had always wanted them to be closer.

"I would've been a father to you," Caj said abruptly. Utter silence stooped in, and now Shard could only stare at the seedy tops of the grass. "But even as a kit you wouldn't have me. I think you already knew your father's voice."

"I was too young…" It sounded weak, even to Shard, and he didn't look up. He had been cold to Caj as fledge. So, after some years, Caj had given up, and been cold in return. Shard understood now. He held his breath, let it out, thought of his nights with Stigr, and Sigrun's insistence that he mind Caj and try to learn from him, her single denial that he had killed Shard's father. Shard perked his ears when Caj shifted, and looked up.

"I'll do my best to keep making you proud," he whispered, staring at the gold eyes that had terrified him as a kit, judged him as a fledge and now, he realized, did gleam with approval.

"Your best will always make me proud," Caj murmured. "It always has."

"I didn't know," Shard said, feeling lost. *I kept him at wing's length, not the other way around.*

"Now you do." Caj watched him, then, seeming satisfied that Shard had no words for that, backed up a pace. "Remember what else I said. Be safe. We'll see you at the feast."

"Fair winds," Shard managed, and watched him lope away and leap into the sky. *And Stigr calls all of the Aesir killers and thieves.* Shard didn't know what was right anymore.

A FLAWLESS SKY STRETCHED blue above, hazy with the high, white light of summer. Darkness would not fall tonight. All morning, gryfons soared back and forth from Windwater to the nesting cliffs on Sun Isle, restless, exchanging plans for food and games, and gossip over who might be mated with whom.

In the last quarter of the afternoon they would all settle on Sun Isle to celebrate there. Some had spoken of traveling to Windwater as a show of strength, but in the end, even Sverin declared it would be too dangerous to leave the new mothers and their kits alone, and even more so to take them to Windwater. Rogue gryfons might have at them on the Sun Isle, and it would give the wolves a perfect chance to attack if the gryfons celebrated at Windwater.

Shard wanted to argue the point. He imagined the wolves would be busy with their own celebrations. And from what he knew of Catori, he couldn't see her attacking months-old gryfon kits. Also, Stigr was the only exiled gryfon he'd ever seen in the islands, and no other exiles who might've lived in the isles had ever attacked the pride.

He supposed they might be in hiding, because he'd never seen Stigr until the exile revealed himself.

That made him wonder what became of the rest, those who weren't killed in the war. Shard had no idea where they would have gone, if not into hiding somewhere in the Silver Isles. There were so many questions he'd never asked Stigr.

When those thoughts rose in his head, he went silent for the rest of the planning. Their answer would have been laughter. Instead, he proceeded with plans for five separate hunts on Star Isle, to bring a feast to the Daynight celebration. Two groups from Windwater hunted the woods, while three bands from the Sun Isle ranged along the fields and coast. Shard hunted with a group in the woods.

Flashes of russet through the heavy green trees showed him a herd of deer and he signaled to the others. Together with Hallr, Kenna, and Einarr, he descended in a diamond around the herd and closed in.

Practiced now at landing among trees, Shard angled his wings and dove. Just above the trees, he tucked his haunches, folded his wings and dropped, hind paws hitting first. The deer roamed ahead in a scatter of pine. They hadn't noticed his landing through the shadows and wind. Brighter colors flashed, violet and teal, and then disappeared in the healthy undergrowth. Shard didn't see Einarr land, for his colors blended with the juniper. As one, the herd tensed, heads up, ears flickering. Shard crouched, waiting until they calmed, gaze darting through them to seek the weakest.

An old female picked at the edge of the herd, unconcerned, a slight hobble in her step. Kenna would have seen her first, and Einarr would follow. Shard trilled softly. The hunters had started imitating birds to call to each other through the woods. After listening to ravens imitate and tease other birds, Shard came up with the idea and he was still proud of it. The gryfess hunters loved it, the males grudgingly admired. A jay's call answered him. Einarr. Then a mourning dove. Kenna. They had seen the deer. Shard perked his ears, waiting for Hallr's call.

None came.

"A pity," rasped a voice behind him, and Shard startled, whipping around. The deer herd froze again, heads up. Hallr crouched behind Shard, tail swinging back and forth. *Why isn't he at his corner of the diamond?* Fear clenched Shard's belly and he glanced around.

"Pity?"

"That the wolves ventured so close to our hunting ground." His low, growling voice was almost a purr. "It will break my heart to give the prince the news."

The instant Shard understood, Hallr leaped. Shard rolled, fighting panic. The commotion spooked the deer and they fled, hooves tearing ferns and brush in the opposite direction. The others were too far off to see Hallr, the deer herd and thick woods in the way.

"Einarr!" Shard shouted. Hallr swung around, crouched, and lunged again. Shard was already away.

Einarr's call answered Shard distantly but he sounded farther away than before. Dread tightened Shard's heart. Einarr was moving away, thinking Shard meant him to chase the herd. Kenna would follow.

Shard sprang away from Hallr's third charge. *At least I'm still faster.* If he could get to a clearing, or find Einarr or Kenna, they would see.

But they're after the deer. Already the sound of hooves grew distant. Shard bounded through the trees and Hallr barely kept pace, swiping at his tail feathers.

"Yes, run," he snarled. "That's what your kind are best at. Just don't come back—"

Shard pivoted and slammed into the bigger gryfon. Hallr shrieked and tried to rear back, but Shard clung to his back, snapping at his ears.

He should have known. Caj had warned him.

Hallr dropped to his side, slamming Shard against the ground. The breath knocked from him, he lost his grip and Hallr staggered away.

"My son should be in your place," Hallr growled.

Shard dragged himself up and yelped when Hallr's talons caught his rump, digging into flesh. Hallr shoved forward and flung Shard back to the ground on his side. Before he could move, Hallr jumped over him, crouched on Shard's hind legs to pin them, and held Shard's free leg and wing with his talons. Shard's other wing and foreleg were smashed against the ground.

"You should've died ten years ago," Hallr hissed, trying to get a killing bite at Shard's throat.

Shard struggled against Hallr's grip, tucking his head to avoid the snapping beak, looking wildly for anything, anyone.

A raven stared at them through the trees. It hunched its wings, dancing back and forth along a pine branch.

Think of the fox, said his uncle's voice. Hallr's bulk crushed the breath from him.

Shard writhed but couldn't break Hallr's weight or hold. Root and stone jammed into his ribs. Hallr clutched his foreleg, threatening to crush bone.

Think of the mother bird, Stigr's voice said. *Who draws away with a false broken wing.*

Shard gasped against Hallr's grip, and his gaze found the raven again. Thinking of wolves, thinking of Lapu, he managed to speak from his chest, speak in the language of the earth.

"Help me...Brother."

Laughing, the raven swooped from the branch and disappeared into the deep green woods. Shard shut his eyes.

"Prepare to meet Tyr," Hallr snarled. Shard's eyes snapped open. As Hallr shoved Shard's foreleg aside from protecting his throat, Shard flung his head to the side and stared into the woods as if he'd seen something.

"Your Highness?"

A gryfon call answered him. Hallr's head whipped up and Shard jammed a hind paw into the older gryfon's gut before slashing at his eyes.

The raven, his mimicking done, flapped away. Shard wrenched free and found his feet. Hallr fell back, his rage echoing into the woods. Nothing mattered but escape. He couldn't fly. He couldn't fight Hallr.

He sprinted, strong from long nights with Stigr, who insisted he work at more than flight, that he climb, run, and leap. Brush slapped his face but he clawed as nimbly over roots and rocks as a wolf.

He rounded a tangle of nettle and slammed into Einarr, who was running just as fast, toward him. They fell in a heap and Shard scrambled up, panting.

"Shard! What—"

"Wolves," Shard snapped. Who would believe that Hallr attacked him? *They know I struggle with Hallr. They'll think I'm just trying to get rid of him.* "Where is Kenna?"

"Ahead," Einarr panted, his gaze straying to the claw marks on Shard's hindquarters, then to Hallr, who lumbered up beside them.

Shard's heart curled in his throat, but the older gryfon didn't attack again. Not in front of a witness. *I am the prince's wingbrother, after all.*

Einarr's gaze darted between them. "We injured an old doe, but she's still escaping."

They ran forward, then ranged out when Einarr signaled that the doe was ahead. Shard saw her first, the old female, hobbling her way up a steep face of rock that jutted up from the forest floor. The others had no room to fly. Without pausing, Shard clambered up the rock face after their prey, practiced from climbing Black Rock with Stigr.

When the doe saw him climbing, she stopped, quivering, and seemed to wait. Shard leaped from his spot, his earlier terror shooting energy through him, and crashed onto the doe's back. They fell. Shard wrenched her under him, flinging her as he couldn't Hallr. They slammed into the ground.

Jarred from the fall, he crouched, talons dug into her shoulders and ribs. Her breath still rose and fell though she lay broken. A messy kill. Shard took a breath, then his gaze fell on her dark eyes. She was watching him. Staring at him. As Lapu had stared at him. Hallr snarled at Shard to kill the beast and hurry; they would miss the festivities. As if he hadn't just tried to kill Shard in the woods.

"Kill it," Kenna snapped, her voice hunt-hungry and tense.

Catori's voice drifted back to him, for a moment he stood in darkness, for a moment he saw Lapu again, and heard himself telling the old boar to die in peace.

Those are the words we say to all those about to die, Catori had said. *So they remember themselves.*

"You ran well," Shard whispered to the aging doe. Her glazing eye didn't blink. *So they go with their honor and name into their next life.* "Be at peace." *So we continue with honor in ours.* "Sister."

Her head lolled. Before Shard could think where those last words came from, he bit, and felt her life go back into the earth.

It was only by knowing the other, said the song, as Shard's breaths brought him back to himself, *that they came to know themselves.*

A raven called somewhere. Wolf howls rose, on the hunt.

"Divide the meat," Shard said, his throat raw. "It's high time to fly to the Sun Isle."

As Einarr and Kenna padded forward, Shard and Hallr stared at each other over the body of the doe. Hallr's eyes narrowed and Shard raised his head, ears forward.

For the first time, Hallr looked away.

19
THE DAYNIGHT FLIGHT

THE WATERS OF THE NIGHTRUN crashed and rolled under Shard and a flock of other young males. The race along the great river was just one of the traditions of the Daynight celebrations, and Shard had raced for the last four years, even though he hadn't been flying to impress a potential mate. The low sun lanced long shadows through the trees around the river and light splashed through the water.

Shard led the race, dipping easily over the water, lower than the others and quicker, taking shortcuts around the bends. Flying higher than the trees was considered cheating. All his worries blew away in flight. The joy of working his muscles and the wind and water catching his feathers left no room for thoughts of Hallr, Stigr, or the wolves.

Einarr stooped in on his right flank and Shard laughed, banking sharp to drive the younger gryfon toward the trees. Panting, Einarr shrieked laughter and shoved up and away, just under the treetops. Kjorn and the other bigger males had fallen far behind. Feeling superior, Shard dipped low to graze his talons in the water, and flipped backward a heartbeat to fling water at the others. His tail brushed the water and drops slid off the feathers as easily they would from a duck's wing.

When Shard rounded the next river bend he lost sight of the others completely and narrowed his wings to race even faster. It was his only chance to truly show off.

A glimpse of emerald in the trees ahead was his only warning before Halvden lunged out over the river. Shard veered, one wing slapping the water before he righted, shocked. *Was he waiting there?*

"You won't win by cheating!" he shouted. But even as he shouted he thought that Halvden's narrowed eyes and stretched talons looked more like hunting than racing.

Halvden didn't answer as he flapped hard to catch up again, coming up on Shard's side. Shard chanced a look behind, but the wide bend hid the rest of the racers. If he tried to turn back to them, Halvden would catch him.

"Give up," he called brightly, as if it was still a friendly game. "I'll lose you in the narrows before the falls."

The river pinched itself ahead, throwing up jagged rocks and catches of fallen timber to create dangerous pools and rapids. Then it all opened out and fell off a cliff into the sea.

Halvden's silence frightened Shard more than threats would have. Shard tucked his wings, letting small falls give him speed, then flaring to gain height again to keep from smacking into the river.

Shard's thoughts flung wildly, wondering if Halvden had spoken to his father, where this anger had come from. *Surely he doesn't mean to attack…*

Talons snagged his tail and Shard shrieked. "Halvden! I have no fight with you!" His wings slapped the water as he tried to shove up. Halvden yanked him back and pushed, trying to throw him into the river.

"I have a fight with *you*," snarled the green gryfon. The roaring rapids drowned half the words. No other gryfons flew close. *Did they give up, seeing me so far ahead?* "Your blood shames mine. And the pride."

"What—"

"Kenna told me."

Wild, witless anger consumed his eyes. Shard stretched his wings, straining not to fall into the river, not to slam against a rock.

"You're half Vanir too!" Shard wrenched free and angled toward the waterfall. "Did you forget?" Halvden's angry snarl pierced the rapids.

"Be silent!"

"You must hate yourself!" Shard tightened his wings to angled scoops like a falcon, skimming just ahead of Halvden, who had no such precise skill in flight. He only practiced fighting.

"Take it back, filth!"

Shard's gaze narrowed to the waterfall. Stigr's last lesson stuck in his mind. If he dove down, straight down, into the sea with the falls, Halvden would either crash into the water, or give up altogether. Shard hoped he crashed. It would be quicker and easier than fighting.

"Catch me and and make me!"

Shard rolled out of the trees, off the cliff that dropped to the sea, folded his wings, and dove. Behind him, Halvden stooped to follow.

Two breaths. Shard stared at the roil of water where river met sea. Wind stung his eyes. Water from the falls pelted him like a rainstorm, but slid from his feathers. Halvden faltered.

He could do it. He clenched his talons, then his breath caught as the alien fear slithered forward. A raging gryfon above him, the sea, blood clouding out into the water. The fear slithered up through his muscles and he shoved himself through it, ready. All would become oblivion in the sea. He dove fast, a falcon, a stone.

The water lunged up and he shrieked with terror that wasn't his own.

Shard flared in panic, skimming across the waves. Failure froze his muscles and heart again. He couldn't dive. He wouldn't dive into the sea. It could kill him, or, if he survived such a plunge, it would mean he was truly a Vanir. It would mean he had betrayed his king and Kjorn.

It would mean Halvden had every reason to pursue him violently across the waves.

A quick glance back showed Halvden taking a broader, slower glide down, a safe distance from the waterfall. Shard's mind reeled with indecision. *Stop and fight? Keep flying?* He'd won a single spar against Halvden on the ground. He wasn't sure he could beat him in the air.

Shard flew.

Broken towers of rock clustered off the shore, a maze of ancient moss and stone columns from the First Age. Shard wove in and out of them, with Halvden cursing farther and farther behind him.

The thought struck him at the same time as his own stupidity. He needed witnesses. A raven flew from the rock column in front of him and he blinked. The bird soared off toward Star Island as Shard turned his flight to the nesting cliffs. They were closest to the abandoned side, where the old Vanir had kept their nests.

He winged that way and relief flooded him when he saw other gryfons. They probably thought he and Halvden only continued the race. Playing. Flying through the great rock towers for fun. *And who would believe me if I told them otherwise, and Halvden denied it, and accused me of lying?*

Kjorn might have, but then Hallr might come forward with stories of Shard defending wolves and turning against him and he would have to face Sverin.

Shard pumped his wings to gain height, and Halvden followed. When he saw the others, he abruptly broke off. Shard stared, breaths catching, as the green gryfon rose to join the others in the sky, flying good naturedly, as if nothing at all were wrong.

Instead of following, Shard soared up to the old dens and plunged into one where he crouched, hiding in the gloom. His breath crept back slowly and the scent of mold and bone drifted to him. He hunched against the rock, ears flicking, listening for signs that Halvden turned back to pursue him. He took a slow breath and rested his head against the rock wall.

Then, impossibly, through his fear, he heard his mother's voice.

"…have done all that you asked without complaint." Shard lifted his head, then pressed his ear back to the wall. Sigrun's voice murmured clearly through the rock, from the next den over. "The pride is content. Is it necessary anymore?"

"Are you content?" The second voice was naggingly familiar, but Shard couldn't place it. He held his breath and edged closer to the rock, through which the voices came to him, muffled but caught clearly in the stone.

"I am." Sigrun sounded irritated. And something else. Something Shard hadn't heard before. "Well enough. The pride is strong." *Fear*, Shard realized. Sigrun was afraid. "Happy. We have peace."

"We will never have peace or freedom as long as a red king rules."

Shard's short breath left him. It sounded as if his mother was speaking to some other gryfess of rebellion.

"Then call to him," Sigrun said, her voice ragged. "And hope the king's vision was true. Call him out. Let it be soon. Let it be soon, wingsister, or not at all."

A flurry of feathers. Sigrun had left. Shard pressed against the stone, holding his breath. Another scuffle and flight. Both of them were gone. He knew his mother's voice. The second was familiar. *But who?*

Shard remained there, heart slamming, staring at the mossy rock wall.

SHARD KEPT CLOSE TO Kjorn and Thyra on the Copper Cliff, sharing in their meal of hare and quail. Too many thoughts and arguments squabbled for his attention. Hallr and Halvden wanted him dead, that much was clear, though how much more they would pursue him, he didn't know. He thought of Stigr, but couldn't go back for advice. He thought of Caj, but couldn't admit trouble to his nest-father. Not after learning that Caj was, after all these years, proud of him. He had handled Hallr and Halvden like a grown warrior, and he wouldn't back down from that by seeking help.

He thought of what Caj had told him as he watched Kjorn purring softly to Thyra.

Sverin's father killed my father. Shard tried to taste his meal but it was like gnawing stones. *Kjorn's grandfather.* Caj had told him to remember that was all in the past.

He glanced around him at the gathered pride, the laughter, romps and feasting, the strength of seeing so many gathered.

Sverin was right. They were the strongest anywhere, the greatest, and pride flickered in Shard to see it. He looked beside him to Kjorn and Thyra, who barely had eyes for anyone but each other that evening. He couldn't hold a grudge against Kjorn for the deeds of his grandfather.

Even as he thought that, Shard felt an ember warming in his heart. It didn't feel like anger, but it made him restless. He tried to let it rest for a night. *Everything I do, I do for the king and for Kjorn.*

The words were beginning to feel hollow in his mind. *Is it really why I stayed to learn from Stigr?*

As the sky paled and turned golden with the sunset that would last all night, rippled now with rosy wisps of cloud, Sverin climbed to the top of the tumble of rocks. Shard stared at him, so powerful and strong against the sky, it secured his sense of loyalty, a little.

"This Daynight shines brightly on us, my pride. I have seen you working and growing stronger. I can see our victory in all these islands as if it has already happened. So let this night be joyous." He stretched his red wings and roared to the sky, hollowing the sound to an eagle's cry that rolled across the calm, bright sea.

Gryfons knew what those words meant. Thyra laughed and sprang up, spritely as a cub, bowled Shard over with a single leap, and jumped off the edge of the cliff into the sunset sky. Kjorn pushed to his feet, ears perked.

"I think you're going to have to be faster than that," Shard murmured. He watched as laughing gryfons of his year and younger bounded off the cliff, catching the slight breeze and forming a colorful spiral over the water. He had to let his doubts go for this night. He had to, lest Kjorn hold back, himself.

Kjorn huffed. "You're not coming?"

"Not this year," Shard said, though he stood. The final decision hadn't taken long, with all the other thoughts and doubts he faced. "I spent my life thinking I wouldn't mate. I'm not going to rush the choice. Go on, Kjorn. She's waiting for you."

"Wingbrother…"

"Yes, I am." Shard butted his head against the prince's golden shoulder. "And I always will be."

Kjorn bit at his ears, then chuckled, and turned to leap off the cliff and join the dance in the air. Shard bounded after him but stopped short, lashing his tail as he watched. It was a dance. The twelve or so young pairs wheeled, laughing, shrieking challenges to each other. Shard could just imagine it. The drafts created by one another's wings, the rush of close flying. He itched to fly, to show off, to…*win a mate?*

He closed his wings. He hadn't realized he'd opened them. *Not this year.* He watched. A young gryfess, too young for him, maybe five years old, swooped down, fluttering, laughing and trilling for him to join. Her pale, pale wings were like Sverin's diamonds or rose quartz, glittering in the sunlight. Shard called back to her, but lowered his head. He saw violet Kenna swoop by, but she didn't glance his way, happily pursued by Halvden.

She had revealed Shard's night flights. But Halvden hadn't told the king. He must have feared that his own half-blood would come into question if he revealed Shard's betrayal. Shard stood, claws locked to the earth.

If he did tell, Shard would deny it.

Because I am a liar. It was the only way.

Shaking frustration, he lifted his head, ears perked, and sought out Thyra and Kjorn. He didn't see them until he looked higher. Both had raced each other high into the clear air, specks as small as sparrows. Other gryfons gathered, murmuring and trilling happily. Shard saw older mated pairs, including Caj and Sigrun, dive off the cliff together to join the dance and to renew their own pledges.

He considered Caj briefly, watching the older blue warrior fly with Sigrun. His flight was simple, strong, straightforward, no flashy wheels and turns like the younger males.

I would have been a father to you, he had said. But Shard had never gotten to see his own father fly. He shook himself again and glanced to the Star Isle, wondering how the wolves celebrated—then wondering why he cared. He pinned his ears back and looked up to peer against the bright sky, now orange and gold, to find Kjorn and Thyra.

He saw them circling tightly. It looked as if Thyra was dodging him. Shard laughed to himself. It was all in play, but if the male couldn't catch his own mate, then what sort of mate would he be? So they mock-battled. Shard watched as Thyra soared high, gaining better distance and position. But Kjorn remained below, circling wider.

"Don't give up," Shard growled. But then he saw. A trick Shard had once taught him, to hover in place.

Thyra dove, shrieking in triumph. Shard's wings flexed open as he watched, hoping Kjorn remembered the movements.

Thyra was almost on him, talons out, when Kjorn straightened his flight, then flipped backwards out of her path. He snapped his wings shut and dropped on her as she plummeted past. Shard wouldn't have guessed his friend could manage it.

He laughed aloud and bounded once in a circle around himself. Thyra squawked in surprise and then both their eagle cries rang across the islands. Shard watched as they struggled, wings beating together, until they locked talons, half-folded their wings, and fell.

Other such pairs had already locked and fallen, declaring their trust and strength and love for all to see, but none of them matched Thyra and Kjorn. They fell gracefully, flashing their wings to catch sunlight, pivoting mid-air in a sunlit spiral.

Behold! They seemed to say with dazzling flight. *Behold your future king and queen.*

Queen! Shard thought with a dizzy rush of joy, as if he flew with them. All other thoughts left. This was Daynight. This was joy and love. *My nest-sister will be queen.* Any doubts Shard had dimmed. Sverin would not be king forever. One day it would be Kjorn and Thyra.

And then what? a deeper part of him asked.

We will never have peace or freedom as long as a red king rules.

But Shard didn't think Kjorn was as severe as his father.

More gryfons watched from the cliff. Rebellious against his thoughts, Shard leaped to the edge and roared his approval. Others joined, even Sverin, from the top of the rocks. Kjorn and Thyra dropped until they were two leaps from the waves, then broke and glided low across the water.

As the other dancers in the air broke off, flying away in pairs, the gryfons wandered from the cliff edge to clear away the bones from their meals, rest and gossip over the pairings. Some winged away in the direction of Windwater, to check their dens, patrol, or sleep. They had all agreed not to leave the settlement alone for the whole night.

Shard paced in the grass. He needed a plan, some way to address his situation with Halvden and Hallr that wouldn't make him look like a coward.

A presence as quiet as a cloud approached him from the side. He looked over and saw Ragna the Widow Queen. He blinked and bowed his head low.

"There was no gryfess who caught your eye?"

He swiveled both ears to her, showing respect. She looked older, tired, a little sad. Perhaps seeing the mating flights reminded her of her own dead mate. *The old king.* Shard looked away, tail twitching. "No. It all happened so suddenly."

"Everything in its time." She seemed to approve, which made him feel better even though it was only the second time in his life they'd spoken. For a moment it was quiet between them, until Shard glanced away to watch some gryfons drifting toward their caves to nap. Some still romped, or watched the last of the mating flights.

The sun was a glowing ball of fire in the nightward sky. Dawnward, the golden-yellow edge of the half-moon peeked over the gray sea. *Tyr and Tor,* Shard thought, *watching the mating flights.* From the Daynight began high summer and then, Shard thought, the slow descend back to autumn and winter again.

Kjorn may have a kit next year! The thought was enough to keep Shard silent for another moment. Time seemed to fly before him.

"When I was young," murmured Ragna, "our celebrations would last all through the night."

"You honored Tor," Shard said, feeling bolder. He lifted his head. Ragna perked her ears, then her gaze traveled sideways, wary.

"You shouldn't speak of such things where the king may hear."

"What things?" He stepped forward, lifting his wings a little. "Vanir things? I'm of Vanir blood. Why shouldn't I know where I came from? The king knows I serve him."

She watched him, a strange brightness in her moss-green eyes. "There's been a change in you since the spring."

He didn't answer. He had no answer. Of course there had been a change, but she considered him closely, as if waiting for some answer from him, or from the sky, or the earth or wind, to a question she hadn't spoken out loud.

"In all of us," he finally said breezily. "It is a great time for our pride."

"Yes," she said softly, though her tail twitched as if agitated. "It is. Are you content?"

"Of course," Shard said, blinking. Something snagged his mind. "Honored by the king. Happy."

"Good," she said, dipping her head and turning. "Enjoy this Daynight, Shard."

"And you," Shard whispered.

Are you content?

The voices he'd heard in the cave not hours ago. Sigrun, arguing over what sounded like rebellion with a gryfess whose voice he couldn't place. Arguing for something to be done soon, or never. Arguing with a gryfess she called wingsister. Now he knew the second voice.

Ragna, the Widow Queen.

A little shadow swooped overhead. A raven. Shard couldn't fathom why they always watched him. *Maybe Stigr sent them.*

Then a larger shadow swooped above, dark and fast.

Kenna, newly mated to Halvden, Shard realized, glided over those remaining and landed in a stumble in front of the king. She and Halvden and others had flown back to Windwater earlier. Unease slipped through Shard. *Why would she return?*

Gryfons parted for her, muttering. Her eyes gleamed wildly, her faced shocked, feathers ruffed.

"My Lord!" She tried to shout over the pride, but none heard until Sverin snapped his wings and beak for silence.

"Your Highness," she panted. "We returned to Windwater—"

"What is it?" the king rumbled.

Kenna looked around once, staring at the pride, and then the king.

"Wolves, my king. They ambushed us when we returned. Hallr is dead."

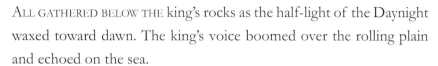

ALL GATHERED BELOW THE king's rocks as the half-light of the Daynight waxed toward dawn. The king's voice boomed over the rolling plain and echoed on the sea.

"This vile, unprovoked attack on one of our own, honored warriors will not go unpunished."

Shard had to strain his neck to watch the king, for Sverin paced on the highest rock, red sun striking him from the dawnward sky. All night gryfons had milled under the low sun and flower-yellow moon, awaiting the king's words. Now, everyone fell silent.

"Too long I have forsaken the way of my fathers, the way of the Aesir. I have worked to build our pride back after the Conquering, to learn, as we have, to become one blood again. This, we have done. We have made great plans for the future of our pride, but been too timid in seeking it. We tried to share the land with those who would see us dead." He paused, talons clenching the rock as his golden eyes pierced every face.

Shard glanced down at his feet.

"Now it is time to remember how we began."

A slow wind picked up, rustling feathers, cool enough to raise shivers. *Or is it the king's words?* Shard shifted, itching, restless.

"The Aesir," Sverin's voice avalanched over them in growing light, "are conquerors. Now that you know my desire for all of you to remain on Sun Isle, for all of you to become great hunters, great warriors, to find a true mate, to live well under my reign and that of my son, know this: we will outgrow this island as my father's pride outgrew the land across the windward sea. I will not see any of you struggle and fight all your lives. We will take what is ours, without question."

The breath of the pride went out. Shard stared, his heart thundering. All around him, the young, the newly mated, the initiated warriors, trembled with excitement and exchanged gleaming looks.

"Brave Hallr's death is a sign to me." The Red King paused again, taking a deep breath. The pride drew a breath with him. "It is a sign to continue what my father started on these isles, and we will do so without wolf interference. We won't fight and scramble for food until the end of our days."

Silence and morning breezes passed between them. Shard let his breath out.

"How?" someone raised the cry. The king laughed.

"Another great hunt. Those who wish to prove themselves, who wish for places of honor in the coming days should be the first in line. All will be rewarded. But on this hunt, our quarry is not boar or deer." His tail lashed, his gaze pierced starward as if he could see every creature on the Star Isle. "This time, we hunt wolves."

"All of them?" someone else called incredulously.

"All of them," Sverin echoed without irony. "All that there are. I mean to rid the Silver Isles of wolves forever."

Silence. In the moment when Sverin said it, the thought prickled Shard's feathers to think of having his revenge on the wolf brothers who tried to kill him.

Then he thought of Catori. *I think we could be friends, you and I.* Laughing under the moon.

He thought of what Stigr would say. *I thought the knowledge would change you.*

An ember in his heart licked up to flame and he fought against springing up into the sky to escape his own thoughts. He should have felt excited. Elated. A chance for glory. A chance to end the little skirmishes and doubts.

Only in stillness, the wind, his mind babbled.

Only from ice the flame.

The king slowly folded his wings as another timid voice called, "You speak as if it will be easy!"

"No," said the Red King in the first red light of true day. "It will not be easy." His face burned like an ember. "It will be war."

Only the wind stirred.

A murmur rippled through the assembled. Gryfons shifted, parting for someone. Shard, restless and twitching, stood, lifting his head to peer over shoulders and wings.

Slowly through the crowd, wings politely folded and every step graceful, walked Ragna the Widow Queen. She advanced all the way to the king's rocks and mantled, her pale wings shimmering.

"My Lord." Her voice carried over the pride, but with a different quality than the booming king's. Like rain. A breeze. Shard took a slow breath. No one moved, not even the king. The pale widow raised her head.

"It is still the Daynight celebration. A time for songs, and honoring bright Tyr." She swept a look over the pride, and in that glance, Shard saw what she must have been as a queen. She returned a huntress's gaze to the king.

"In light of your tremendous news, I ask your leave to sing a tale."

20
THE SONG OF THE WIDOW QUEEN

THE KING SLOWLY FOLDED HIS wings again, recovering from surprise. Ragna stood calmly, waiting. At last the king raised his head, crimson feathers shining in the morning sun. All stared, breaths held. Shard flexed his talons and released his breath only when the king spoke.

"Of course. What an…unexpected privilege. Gryfons of the Sun Isle, Lady Ragna will sing for us."

An excited, hushed trill wove through the pride. Shard glanced about and saw some bright eyes narrowed with suspicion. Aesir eyes. Older gryfons. Old Caj though, he thought, looked indifferent. Or maybe curious. At last he saw Thyra and Kjorn, up closer to the rocks. They watched with ears perked as Sverin stepped down to the lower rocks and Ragna climbed sedately higher. The dawn light edged her softly, like sun on a dove's feathers.

Moonlight would become her, Shard thought, feeling anxious. *Does this song have something to do with her conversation with Sigrun?*

"I am Ragna," the old gryfess began. "and I welcome you. We have arrived at a difficult time. This is the song I offer you now. This is a summer song, a song older than the oldest here, older than the trees on Star Isle, as old as the sea and the sky."

Her pale green eyes surveyed her audience. They were still. Her voice wove through them like spider silk, soft but infinitely strong. Gryfons didn't sing as wolves did, with long, piercing notes and melodies. They sang in the hushed, lulling tones of the waves murmuring to the shore, back and forth, the wind in the mumbling trees. Ragna remained standing.

"It is the song that Tyr and Tor sang to the world when it was as young as a fledging gryfon. As a gryfess sings to her kit of all the things to come, so they sang the world this song of hope, of fear, of love."

Older gryfons shifted uneasily; those of the old, Silver Isles blood, the Vanir. Shard watched them from the corner of his vision, saw recognition in their faces. They knew this tale. *Are they uneasy, or excited?*

He tuned into Ragna's voice, watching her soft face, wondering briefly who her mate had been, what the old king had been like. Wondering what she planned to do.

Her voice lifted from speaking into song and Shard's heart caught with it, questions brushed aside the youthful, lilting melody, sweet as spring wind, hopeful.

She sang of the beginning of the world, that Tyr forged it in fire and watched over it in the day, and Tor cooled it with the sea and watched over it in the dark. She sang of the struggles of all their children, of fear, and courage, and hate. When the tale grew darkest, a nameless one appeared to lead all back into the sunlight.

The verse wove into Shard's heart and cracked the last of his surety in decision to serve Sverin as plant roots cracked stone. *The Aesir would never sing a tale like this.*

"One will rise higher,
One will see farther,
His wing beats will part the storm.
They will call him the Summer King
And this will be his song."

He heard rustling. Whispers. Old Vanir, whispering the words as she sang them. It was like watching someone wake from a deep sleep to see the familiar world with delight. It felt as if he, too, remembered something. It felt as if his face burned. He scrambled to recall why it was so familiar. Never, not once, had he ever heard this tale clearly in his memory. But he knew it.

Ragna's voice rang like sharp wind filled with snow. Undeniable, inescapable, a single spoken line in the middle of the song.

"When seers dream of his coming, it is always the same." She opened her wings as if to encompass all of the assembled pride.

"He sees all like sky
His heart burns like the sun
He brings justice to the wronged.
They will call him the Summer King
And this will be his song."

Shard held his breath, stealing a glance around to see what others were thinking, to see what he was supposed to think. All the Vanir faces had gone carefully blanked, schooled to quiet attention. Even Sigrun lowered her eyes as Ragna sang on.

"He flies in the night
And in the day
And his wings are like light on water.
He listens to all who speak, speaks to all who hear
And his voice is the song of summer.
He comes when he is needed

He comes when he is called
He is called the Summer King, and this is his song."

Her voice floated on as if toward another verse, then checked, falling silent. Shard felt there was more to the song, but the Widow Queen lowered her head. A slow, steady wind picked up over them, brushing feathers, caressing the long grass. Far off, Shard heard the rustling of the leaves in the birch wood.

Furtively he glanced around, gauging others' reactions. He could have heard a feather fall to moss in the silence. After a moment Ragna began to step down from the rocks, then paused and mantled to the king.

Sverin rose to his feet. All were silent, watching tensely as the king climbed back to the highest rock. Shard couldn't tell if he was angry. His heart battered in his chest as if he'd been flying in high winds. *Why that song?*

Call him out, Sigrun had said to Ragna last night, when Shard overheard. *Call him out.* Call who, Shard wondered. *A nameless Summer King?*

Shard looked around, and saw that, from her spot, Sigrun was staring at Ragna. And Ragna looked straight as a falcon across the assembled to meet his eyes.

The memory crashed against him. He *had* heard the song before.

And she had sung it.

A flash of red drew his eye. Sverin opened his wings, though with less grace and subtlety than Ragna the Widow Queen.

"Thank you, Ragna. Surely your song has stirred the hearts of all here. It was needed in this time."

He's being gracious! Shard let his breath out. Ragna merely dipped again to him and walked back down among the gathered gryfons. Shard stood there panting, fighting the urge to leap up and fly. She had sung that song to him, for him, he was sure of it.

I thought the knowledge would change you.

Only in stillness the wind, only from ice the flame, Shard thought.

The king's voice cracked the dawn air and all heeded.

"I have heard this song once before. You may not have known, but I heard it when first we came to the Silver Isles. I didn't take its meaning then, but I do now."

Shard held his breath, fearful that the king sensed rebellion. Ragna couldn't possibly expect him to play some part in that. *Because I'm friend and family to both Vanir and Aesir?*

But we are already one pride!

His own thoughts betrayed him. He knew he had already planned, without truly accepting it himself, to talk to Kjorn. His wingbrother would be king one day. His nest-sister, queen. Shard realized, after hearing the song and feeling the gaze of the old Widow Queen, that he wanted more freedom for the way of the Vanir in the pride. He wanted change.

And he certainly didn't want war. Not with wolves. Not with each other. Not with anybody.

He stared as the Red King spoke.

"It may surprise you," the king declared in his purring baritone, "but I agree with the honored Widow Queen. A great time is upon us. A time to rise higher. A time to see farther. And we need great hearts to lead us there."

He climbed higher on his rocks. The red dawn darkened under storm clouds rolling in from the sea.

"I believe the Summer King is quite real." Sverin's ringing declaration silenced the murmurs.

Ears flicked. Shard stared at him, then at Ragna. Everything felt as if a storm wind had picked up, but every gryfon remained still as ice.

"I say he is real, that he is among us now!" The king's tail lashed and murmurs erupted again. "His eyes see all like the sky," he quoted from the song. "That would make him a leader among his kind. His heart burns like the sun. Wings like light. Only one among us can truly claim that." The king glanced over the pride, as if he might call out the legend from among them. "A Summer King would be one is heeded, who will be great in his time."

The pride held its breath. Sverin opened his wings in the dawn.

"I say our Summer King is my son, Kjorn, prince of the Sun Isle, of the Star Isle, and all the rest under Tyr's light that will soon be ours!"

A shock rippled through the pride. Surprised and then affirming chatter erupted, roars and calls for the prince to rise.

While the rest of the gryfons broke into eagle cries, Shard swiveled to find Kjorn. The prince looked as if the king had smacked him in the face. Then he stood, bright below Sverin on the rocks. Beside him, Thyra stood and raised her voice with the others.

Shard stood, flared his wings and raised his head—but couldn't find his voice at all.

21
THE LAST VERSE

TOWERS OF STORM CLOUDS BOILED closer, as dark as Shard's feathers with a shock of white, sunlit edge.

It was still day, but all gryfons huddled in their caves as if it were night. Except Shard. Certain that everyone else had taken shelter, he bounded up and took flight, angling his wings to shape the wind.

The first high gust almost smashed him into the cliff face. He clamped his beak against a shriek of frustration, heart thundering now. Only mad or desperate gryfons flew in a storm wind. He almost laughed at himself. Maybe he was both.

Thunder crashed. Skyfire lanced distantly through the clouds. Shard flapped away from the cliffs, choosing to chance low flight over the water rather than close to the rock. He wheeled, gliding along the coast, angling himself toward Black Rock.

Waves surged toward him and he caught the quick, hard eddies of storm gusts to carry him away. His muscles strained and cramped. After what seemed an endless, battle of a flight, Black Rock loomed up before him and relief filled him that he reached it before rain fell.

He barely recognized it in the day, being so used to landing on it at night. He tried to circle once to get his bearings, but the storm wind shoved him hard, almost ten leaps out to sea. Shrieking frustration, he dove down to land, tumbling against the black face of the island.

"Stigr!" Darkness swirled overhead. "Stigr! Uncle!"

Skyfire lanced through the clouds and a heartbeat later thunder cracked overhead. Shard scurried toward an outcropping where the rock thrust up from itself to form a short wall. A dull roar rolled toward him from the sea. Rain.

"Shard!"

He turned at his uncle's voice and saw the old gryfon down on a steep ledge, a black cliff of slick mossy stone. "Stigr, I need your help! Please!"

"Come down here!"

Shard clenched his wings and loped to the edge of the cliff. Wind shoved his feathers up the wrong way and he crouched lower. A narrow foot trail wove down. He had to get down it before rain made the edge too slippery. He pressed his claws against the rock and stalked down the trail, one wing scraping against the rock. The wind moaned past, the sea and sky thrashing like a gryfon in a rage.

Stigr reached up to catch Shard's wings in his talons and dragged him down under a rock overhang.

"Are you mad? Flying out here on a storm wind—"

"The king has declared war," he gasped. "Open war. On the wolves. I didn't know what else to do but come here."

His uncle shouldered him deeper under the ledge, and Shard saw that it wasn't merely a ledge, but the yawning mouth of a cave. The floor sloped up, and then down. Perfect for keeping water out. Stigr had never brought him there before. Black Rock held more secrets than he knew.

He followed Stigr as he blurted all that had happened, barely noticing when it grew too dark to see. "I didn't speak against it. How could I? But I–I don't think it's right. I can't just let it happen. The wolves will be taken off guard."

He spoke then of Ragna and the Song of the Summer King.

"She sang the song?" Stigr's ears perked, searching Shard's face. Shard blinked a couple of times, realizing he could see Stigr's face. He glanced around and saw soft lichens growing along the walls, shedding strange light. "And Sverin named *Kjorn?*"

Outside, the constant ring of thunder battered the island over the drumming roll of rain.

"He saw the Vanir growing restless," Shard murmured, realizing everything more clearly in his memory than he had in the moment. "He had to do something. I think Kjorn could be the Summer King."

"Don't be ridiculous," Stigr said, and Shard felt as if he were his uncle's student again, and that no argument had passed between them. They kept walking, deeper, down, and the air fell as cool as evening.

"He could be," Shard insisted. "He isn't like his father."

"He is. He will be. More than you know. The Aesir are greedy, violent conquerors, all of them—"

"They are my family." Shard stopped walking. The glowing lichens clustered thick along the walls. He could see his uncle's angry face, the ugly scar over his eye that made him look fierce and old. "You might hate all of the Aesir, but I grew up with Kjorn. He is still my wingbrother. Maybe Ragna sang that song to me. Maybe she wants me to do something, but I won't betray my brother."

He flexed his talons against the cold, dry rock. It smelled of minerals. Farther off in the still, quiet air, he smelled water too, and heard the scrabbling of rodents.

"You already have," Stigr whispered. "Don't you see? You have become a Vanir. I see it, even if you won't. You are your father's son. You know this war is wrong as he knew the Conquering was wrong.

Sverin and his kin aren't the mighty conquerors they make themselves out to be."

Shard cocked his head. Stigr had never said anything like that before. "What do you mean?"

"Don't you think it's strange that the Aesir, who claimed to be raiding and conquering, came that first summer with their kits?" Stigr paced in front of him. "Better to conquer first and then bring your family."

Shard swiveled, not meeting Stigr's eyes. Rodents scuffled away from their voices, filling the cave with little whispers. "And so?"

"And so I say they were fleeing something. Some disgrace or enemy in the windward land. They conquered here because they lost there."

Shard turned away. "That makes no difference. They're here now."

"Let yourself rise up, Shard. Even Sverin can be fought. And defeated."

"I'm not strong enough!" Shard slapped talons against the stone. "Anything I might want, I'll have when Kjorn is king. When Thyra is queen."

"I'm telling you it won't be so."

"You don't know him!"

"I know his father. I know the Aesir." Stigr tried to approach Shard and he spun, ears back and wings lifted in warning, feeling trapped and wild and half witless with confusion.

"There will be unbalance," Stigr continued. "He will continue to conquer and claim as his father did, all the while assuring you that it is the only way."

"What would you have me do? Declare myself the Summer King and challenge Sverin and my wingbrother, Kjorn, in front of all the pride? Stop the war?" Shard's breath left him with a harsh laugh. His uncle didn't laugh.

"Yes."

Somewhere, water dripped.

"You're mad," Shard whispered. *Only from ice the flame,* the song sang in his mind. "You planned all of this. You twisted my heart and now I can't see which way is up to fly."

"Only by knowing the other," Stigr replied, "did they come to know themselves."

Shard stood, breathing hard. Torn between wanting to tear out his uncle's other eye and beg him for further advice, he stood witless and still. Then, from nowhere, he said, "When Ragna sang the song, I felt there was more."

Stigr blinked, then perked his ears, fully alert. "Tell me what she sang."

For a moment Shard stood in silence, then dipped his head, whispering.

> *"One will rise higher*
> *One will see farther…"*

His own voice grew in strength and shimmered back to him from the cave walls. It sounded like another. Deeper, fuller, his voice having grown as he had come into final growth over the spring and summer. When he finished, the last echo drifted back to him and matched the memory of the voice in his mind. His father's voice. He knew it now. He had inherited it. He knew it.

"And that's all she sang?"

Shard thought Stigr looked fiercer under the pale, haunted light of the cave. "Yes."

"You're right." The old exile paced away, tail lashing. "There is another verse. Maybe she didn't want to sing where Sverin would hear. But I think in your heart you know it."

Shard's heart beat like wings against his breast. "What is it?"

Stigr turned and his low voice thrummed through the glowing cave as rain lashed outside, singing the last verse Ragna had not.

"He is borne aloft by the Silver Wind
He alone flies the highest peak,
And when they hear his song at battle's end
The Nameless shall know themselves
And the Voiceless will once again speak.
He comes when he is needed
He comes when he is called
He is called the Summer King, and this is his song."

For a moment, all stood silent but for the wash and pull of waves on the rock outside and the clatter of rain. Shard whispered, "What is the Silver Wind?"

But then they heard a scuffle on stone.

Shard whirled, heart slamming, and hissed a challenge. The light revealed a strange sight. Catori stood miraculously at the deeper edge of the cave. Stigr's laugh echoed across the walls when Shard stopped, staring at the she-wolf.

"How in four winds did you get here?" The moon wasn't full. Storm wind lashed high tides around the islands. No ordinary creature could have made it to the island in the tempest, not even a winged one.

The she-wolf blinked at Shard, but didn't laugh at him as Stigr did. Instead, she dipped her head and murmured, "The song has been sung?"

"Yes," Stigr said. Shard looked back and forth between them.

"The last time it was sung, a king fell, and the time of war came upon us."

"So it will be again, I think," murmured Stigr, and looked at Shard. "Where will you stand, Shard, when the Red King draws the lines of battle?"

Shard couldn't answer, still shocked over Catori's appearance. "What is the Silver Wind? Speak plainly. Tell me the meaning of the song."

"The song is plain," Stigr rumbled. "One will rise higher. One will see farther. Will it be you? The Silver Wind is the highest way, the way above ways, the wind that touches the stars, the breeze that bears Tyr and Tor and carries the scent of all the history and future of the world."

"Well that explains it," Shard muttered.

"The truth," murmured Catori more helpfully. "The Summer King is borne by the truth. Who will you be?"

Shard stared at them, breathless. *What is my own truth?* He didn't know if he could be this supposed Summer King, even if Stigr wanted it. Shard struggled for his own answer, whether Hallr was right or wrong and deserved his death or not, whether he could stop a war, whether he could betray Kjorn.

He shut his eyes and listened to the stillness in the air, the drumming rain. Something in him stirred. A quiet breeze. A wind. Like a voice. His own voice, his own words. *I don't think it's right. I can't just let it happen.*

He opened his eyes. "We have to tell the wolves of Sverin's plan."

Stigr's face lit as fiercely as if Shard had declared war on the Red King. Inside, Shard quailed. He still couldn't choose a true side. He was just doing what he had to do.

"Let us go to the Star Isle," Catori said, stepping forward, watching Shard closely. "And speak to my pack."

"We can't fly in this storm wind."

Stigr's laugh boomed through the cave again. "Nephew, we won't be flying."

22
THE WOLF KING

K JORN THREW ANOTHER HAPLESS FLEDGE to the ground and pressed talons to his throat.

"*Pathetic!*" Caj roared from far afield. The prospect of war gave the pride extra energy, extra everything, and war lit the Sun Isle like fire, but if anything, it looked as if the blue warrior thought everyone was getting worse at fighting.

"This isn't a spring romp with bunnies on the Nightrun."

Kjorn helped the fledge up, who peeped and scrambled as Caj stalked closer. "This is war. Every fight could be your last. Every wolf has your death marked on his teeth."

"Caj," Kjorn rumbled, glancing at the younger fledges. Uninitiated. Unable to fly and join the battle. But Sverin had given all of them leave to learn fighting with Caj. "They're too young."

His father's wingbrother stopped in front of him, wings hunched in threat as if Kjorn were a squirming fledge like any other. "No one," he rumbled, "is too young to die. Pairs!"

The warriors fell in. Kjorn stepped away to leave this one out. Einarr sparred and instructed the fledges more calmly than blue Caj.

Earlier, Halvden had sparred with a vengeance, as if each opponent were a true wolf, as if each one might be the wolf that killed his father. Now Kjorn didn't see him, and supposed he'd gone back to Windwater.

Kjorn tried to stand proud, but his wings felt heavy. Shard wasn't there either. Maybe he'd gone to patrol Star Isle and told Kjorn, but in all the commotion, he'd forgotten.

Kjorn narrowed his eyes and turned from the spar to lope away and bound off the cliff. He angled starward.

The Summer King. He didn't feel like a Summer King. He didn't feel like anything at all but what he had been before that song. He knew why his father had done it, but it felt like a lie.

Shard always helped him keep his head on. He flew for Windwater.

Gryfons already stirred there, but it didn't look like a hunting party. Surprised, Kjorn squinted, barely able to see in this half-light.

Two warriors harried a smaller gryfon. Kjorn narrowed his eyes and slipped out of a warm draft to glide lower. He made out Halvden's green feathers, but not the others'.

They bullied the smaller gryfon toward the cliff edge as if to drive him or her away from the cliff. Spying Kjorn, the warriors below called his name.

The second word Kjorn heard clearly was *traitor,* and he gave a ringing, angry cry as he dove.

THE CAVES REACHED UNDER every island. They linked into a maze of caverns and tunnels carved by all the ages of swirling sea and, in the oldest times, Stigr said, boiling flows of earthfire. In places, the pocked, black stone still looked the same as the glassy crags of the volcanic rock on Pebble's Throw. Even though the rock was cold and the volcanoes dead, they still avoided those tunnels.

Shard ran, lost in a dream of smoky lichen glow, mineral scents of underwater streams, and high columns of rock supporting vaulted stone ceilings. Some places narrowed so low he had to crawl on his belly while the rock above scraped his wings.

At first he'd laughed when Stigr told him of the network of caves that wove under the islands, but now it made sense. He already knew that the islands were really one.

"Catori," he grunted, crawling low on his belly. She whuffed softly in acknowledgement ahead. "What happened, on Daynight? What really happened? Kenna flew back and said that wolves attacked them."

Ahead, she snorted and Stigr huffed. Shard tuned his ears forward and listened, but also had to duck to avoid small thrusts of rock and deep, curling roots. *We're nearing the surface again.* At last, Catori answered him.

"Will you believe me?"

"I will," Shard promised, rueful. "I haven't been the friend to you that you've tried to be for me."

She made a quiet, soft whine. "Since the gryfons chose to celebrate the Daynight on Sun Isle, we came out of the forest with our family, the young summer pups, and the old. We stayed clear of Windwater though. We hunted, feasted, and watched your mating flights from afar."

Shard paused in surprise, then wriggled forward to catch up, only to smack his face into a low-hanging jut of stone. He muttered, "You watch the flights?"

"Of course! The dance is beautiful. We have our songs, but no such beautiful ritual when we mate in the season of red rowan. Only a great hunt and a fast run." He heard her panting through the words. The length of their journey wasn't tiring, it was the constant change of level, the duck and weave and unending dark.

She holds no anger toward us, Shard thought, full of shame. *And I've treated her as an enemy.* "What happened then?"

"We saw gryfons returning to Windwater after the mating flight, and we went to the woods. But Hallr left the nesting cliff, and hunted us. He sought out the elders and the pups. We fought him off." Her low, even voice sharpened. "And some of us were tired of running. To hunt us on a hallow day, when we'd brought no fight and not trespassed? It was too much. Half the pack pursued him back to the nesting cliff, and the other gryfons called it an attack."

Shard listened, seeing it all. The wolves and their singing. A peaceful, joyful celebration in the open sunlight. Then an attack. "Did you lose any pups?"

"No," she said softly, and Shard heard a note of surprise in her voice, as if she couldn't believe he would ask.

"Good. I'm sorry for the attack."

"So am I," she murmured, and they both went quiet again. Stigr never spoke, but crawled quietly ahead of Shard, only loosing the occasional frustrated snarl or curse if he bumped his head.

At last, in darkness, spent and aching from the unnatural crawling, he caught the scent of pine. Star Island. He perked his ears, worming forward.

Catori could go to any isle, any time. If all the isles are one, do caves stretch even to Sun Isle?

But no wolf would be so foolish.

Shard thrust his shoulders out of the crack of a cave mouth that opened halfway up the side of a sea-washed cliff. Disoriented, he swiveled to find the sun. Not quite dawn, but the paler sky told him this cliff rose on the starward-facing flank of the isle. He had never been so far beyond Windwater. Not on foot.

"This way," Catori murmured, giving them both a quick sniff before she bounded into the woods. Shard clamped his beak against a groan. He was tempted to fly part of the way, but it would be too dangerous. Others would be waking, readying to hunt. Planning war.

And here I am, with the enemy. Stigr nudged his shoulder and they ran after Catori, climbing the cliff and diving into the cool tangle of forest.

Gray light found its way through the darkest halls of the forest. Shard and Stigr followed Catori through the woods, over broken crags where little creeks ran, past meadows and even along the shore, until they ran so deep into the forest that Shard couldn't see the sky.

Catori led them to a clear, mossy space under a dark canopy of trees, and stopped in front of a face of rock that thrust up from the forest floor. A rowan tree crowned the broad slab of short cliff, one so tall and vast that Shard had to tilt his head back to see its full height. He tried to recall ever having seen it from the sky.

Holes riddled the jagged rock face but the gnarled roots of the rowan grasped it together like long, spindly talons. In some places the rock was broken just in narrow cracks, in others, the ancient rowan root had grown and twisted so it thrust the cracked stone apart to make a cave. It crouched there, solid, gripping and hunched against the rock like a beast about to leap.

Shard realized in a beat that Catori had brought them to the very heart of wolf territory. Their den. And the rowan tree guarded their home.

As he stood in awe, witless birds flittered in and out of branches, calling, laughing at his shock. A squirrel drew his eye up the trunk, so squat and broad that, had he tried, Shard wouldn't have been able to wrap both wings around it.

The trunk spiraled away in a mass of twisting, peeling gray bark, and burst into a thousand green branches to form the canopy over their heads. Now Shard knew why he couldn't remember seeing the place from the air. From above, the guardian rowan must look like a thousand different trees.

Shard lashed his tail, stepping forward to get a scent. Beside him, Stigr sniffed and peered around for signs of more wolves. Shard turned to thank Catori and found she had slipped away. His talons brushed a bump of root and the shock of knowing it snaked from the tree paused him again.

Shard peered behind him into the woods, trying to see how far the roots stretched, shook his head, and looked back to the tree itself.

Scars from wolf claws and lightning strikes lined the long trunk. Marbled browns and grays in the bark displayed its history—indeed, the history of the islands—droughts, providence, hard dry winters and short sweet summers.

"They call it the First Tree," Stigr murmured as they stepped forward. "The wolves say its roots touch the heart of the world, that it connects them to Tor, gives them dreams, protects them. Show respect."

Shard had never seen a living thing from the First Age. He had seen relics; mountains, rock, and fossil bone all told the history. So did this tree, Shard understood. The first wind had carried its seed from the Sunlit Land long before any of them, and it would remain long after they were gone.

Stigr inclined his head low, and so did Shard.

"Now what?" he whispered, feathers ruffled, anxiety tightening every muscle under his skin.

In answer, Stigr raised his head and bellowed a lion's imitation of a wolf howl. Then he called words, earth words. Shard found if he listened intently, he could interpret their meaning.

This wingbrother greets you, Stigr called toward the den. *Here to treat with the great hunter, your king.*

Wolf scent drenched them. Shard turned around once, wary as he heard faint sounds, like fur brushing leaves in the undergrowth.

"I come peacefully!" Shard called. "To speak with you."

A chorus of voices answered them. Ghostly faces peered out of the dens, between tree roots. Shard whirled again when he heard a wolf rushing behind him, but didn't see it. Then all fell silent. Shard held his breath. A sound whispered behind him. Stigr turned calmly, opening his wings, and so did Shard.

A massive wolf stood before them. He stood of a height with Sverin the Red King, and had long, strong legs, and shoulders like slabs of wind-beaten rock. His gray fur deepened to black along his back and glinted indigo when he shifted. Shard met his eyes. His old, chiseled face and muzzle were starlight pale, and his bright amber eyes as familiar as the moon.

Shard bowed before Stigr had to tell him to.

"Helaku," Stigr spoke as he straightened, folding his wings. "You honor us."

"You're bold," rumbled the old wolf, "to walk into my home. My family is not happy to see you. We hear whispers. The birds whisper. The winds whisper. There is trouble tangled on the Sun Isle and they think we can't see or hear." His amber gaze settled on Shard, taking him in critically. "You're a fool, to come back to this place. Didn't my sons run you off the last time?"

"I am a fool," Shard said, digging his talons into the earth. "But I had to speak with all of you. Catori brought us here."

"Do you think my daughter's friendship with gryfon liars and thieves pleases me? That I'm honored that you stoop to speak with her?"

"I am no thief," Stigr growled. "I've never hunted on Star Isle, and Shard knew no better until now."

"But you fail to stop them." Helaku bared his long yellow teeth. "Outcast. Exile. Beaten warrior. Your people are conquered, half bred out, too ashamed of their defeat and afraid of the Red King to speak." He lowered his head, ears perked toward Stigr. "You will all be gone within a generation. Broad-winged, afraid of the night, and blind. I have seen it."

"None of that is cast in stone. Even the stars can fall." Stigr stepped toward the wolf king, wings opening. "The time wasn't ripe. You should know that."

"And now the time has passed." The wolf lowered his head, ears perked toward them, amber eyes glinting like bright gems as he circled them slowly, sniffing, taking their measure. His voice thrummed as deep as a rockfall. "Your nephew has grown into a liar and a thief and coward, bowing to the Red King like all the others. You promised—"

"It takes time," Stigr snarled. Shard laid back his ears, grinding his beak to keep from growling at the wolf king. Stigr spoke on as wolves crept out of their dens, out of the woods. Shard had never dreamed of so many. The more they gathered, he saw that the pack rivaled Sverin's pride.

"Gryfons don't grow as quickly as wolves. His mother kept him from me. She wanted his heart to grow as well as his strength, and Sverin is too watchful. I haven't yet had time to teach him—"

"Teach him *now.*" The wolf king snapped his jaws. "Teach him. Tell him the truth. I see in him that he doesn't know."

"Of course he—"

"You are blind." Helaku lifted his head, a quick, hunter's movement. "Tell him everything now. Teach him everything now. Now. Then let him answer. And then I will pass judgment for your presence here."

"Great Helaku—"

"Tell him!" A growl almost buried the wolf king's words in his chest. Shard thought of old Lapu, the boar, and how his words had barely been discernable. *He has outlived any kind of joy,* Catori had said of him. Shard feared that Helaku was becoming the same.

He stepped forward, burning to know what Helaku hinted he didn't know, but wary of his uncle's hesitation to tell him.

"Honorable Helaku," he began, pausing when a red shadow flitted in the corner of his eye and Catori's scent shifted to him on the morning breeze. She had brought him here. Trusted him. The dawn light was rising and he was a gryfon, son of burning Tyr. The day was his. He raised his head.

"Whatever I need to know can wait. Whatever has happened in the past can wait, because I came to tell you that the whispers and rumors you've heard are true."

A disturbed rumble rippled through the wolves. Yips and growls and murmurs. Stigr lowered his head while Shard went on.

"Hallr's death angered the king beyond reason."

"That gryfon came into our woods," Helaku said. "Stole our prey without honor or repay or gratitude. Then he hunted us, hunted our new cubs on a hallow day. I killed him."

"However it happened," Shard forced his voice to stay calm, "Sverin plans to attack you before the end of summer, to drive you out." He took a breath. *No. That's not the whole truth.* He forced himself to look around, to meet every pair of harsh golden eyes, even the pups with their soft faces. "He plans to kill you. To kill all of you, and claim the Star Island."

"Why tell us?" Helaku raised his head, his expression half twitching to a snarl. "You are a proud warrior of the Sun Isle."

"And I'll fight for the Sun Isle." Shard forced himself to meet Helaku's eyes rather than bow his head. Hearing the words aloud, a shiver of terror at his own treachery slipped down his back. "But you should be prepared."

"You still support Sverin?" another male voice snarled. Shard turned to face it, and saw one of the wolf brothers, Ahote or Ahanu.

"He's my king. My family. Would you turn on your father?"

Every wolf shifted. Shard's own confidence quivered. He was almost sure it was Ahote who growled on.

"Why tell us? Why not run away to exile like your uncle? Are you hoping we'll beg for peace? Are you afraid your people will lose?"

"No!" Shard opened his wings. "No. I come because I want you to be prepared. I come because once, you helped me. You helped me earn a place among the gryfon warriors by killing the boar Lapu."

He looked around again. "I come because even when you meant me harm, Ahote and Ahanu, you made me stronger."

Shard took a breath, his nerves like skyfire through him, beak opened as he panted, and turned to speak his final words to Catori. "I come because one of you has tried to become a friend, and I should have accepted."

The wolves shifted, silent.

"And when the battle comes," thrummed Helaku's voice like crumbling stone, "where will you stand?"

"When the battle comes, I'll fight as honorably as I can, even if I must fight you. But I hope to bright Tyr it never comes to that."

Silence gathered for a heartbeat, and then a bird sang. The woods glowed gold with the dawn. Shard folded his wings. Catori bounded up to stand on an outcropping of rock.

"You see, Father? Didn't I tell you he was the very image of the Vanir, the old legends? He will bring us peace!" She lifted her face and howled as if the moon were high. Old Helaku lowered his head, turning his ears toward Shard.

"Your words are bold. Now that you've told us, what will you do to help?"

"Whatever I can," Shard whispered, for he had no plan beyond this. "I'll think of something."

Stigr walked up beside him. "Helaku. He has a true heart."

"He has ignorance. He is ignorant and he should not be," rumbled the old wolf. "I see it in him now…that he is the Nightwing's son."

Shard's feathers prickled up. He had broken every other vow. He could keep the last promise no longer.

"Who was the Nightwing?"

Stigr blinked at him, huffed a sigh. "Another name the Vanir among Sverin's pride are not allowed to speak. He was your father."

"Obviously," Shard growled, tail lashing. "But who?"

Stigr tilted his head. "Who? His name was Baldr. The Nightwing, mate to my sister—"

"Sigrun," Shard murmured.

Stigr went still. His face lit and then shadowed as if he suddenly understood many things. "Sigrun?"

His whisper cut into Shard's heart like frost. *Why does he sound like that?* The older gryfon walked around in front of him and spoke low, soft, as if they were not surrounded by wolves.

"No, Shard. My sister is Ragna." He perked his ears as a shudder chilled Shard's muscles. "Mate to Baldr, called the Nightwing. Dead king of the Sun Isle. Ragna is my sister, the white widowed queen. And you are their son." Stigr mantled and bowed his head low. "Prince of the Vanir."

Shard had no words. His breath panted out. He flattened his ears and tightened his wings to his sides.

"I thought they had told you." Stigr's voice barely caught above a whisper. "Long ago, Sigrun told Per the Red that you were her kit so that he would spare you. He would never have let Baldr's son live. Never. But I thought at least she would have told you, prepared you… surely Ragna would have told you…"

"No," Shard growled. "No one told me."

"But you know now!" Catori's strong voice cut into their words as she leaped down from the rocks to his side. "You know, son of the Nightwing, who spoke all tongues, who even my father says ruled with strength and grace and honor. And you are his heir. The true king. The Summer King."

She turned to face her pack. "Some said Baldr the Nightwing was the one that gryfons call the Summer King, and we call the Star King. Yes, we sing of him too, Shard." She yipped a laugh at his surprise. "I think all children under the sky have a song of him. *One will rise higher.* Now the birds whisper that the Red King named Kjorn the Summer King."

She left Shard's side and every wolf was silent, watching her. The daughter of the king. "But I say he has come to us now. I say he may still be learning, but he is courageous and true. I say he is learning to speak to all creatures as the song says he will. I've seen him fly in the night and the day, and his wings are like light on water."

"Daughter," growled Helaku. She ignored him and raised her face to the trees.

"I say our Star King is Rashard, son of Baldr the Nightwing and Ragna the White, prince of the Vanir, true king of the Sun Isle, and only he will bring us peace!"

A fierce rumble trembled through the wolves, through the very earth. The birds fell silent. Shard half-crouched, readying himself for attack as the wolves around him rose, even the pups. But they didn't attack.

They raised their faces to the sky and sang, laughing, long notes of agreement.

For a moment Shard crouched in shock. He looked to Stigr and old Helaku the king, who stared. Then both old warriors raised their voices with the others. The sound echoed through the vast forest of the Star Island and across the seawater and crashing waves to all the Silver Isles touched by the rising sun.

23
A Heart Like the Sun

QUICK WINDS BLEW AS SHARD flew from the wolf den. Dark clouds stalked along the nightward horizon.

Shard looked down as he gained height against the gusts, and memorized the look of the rowan tree that cradled the wolves' den. From the air it did look like many trees. No wonder they had never noticed it.

He will bring us peace, Catori had howled into the morning. Straining muscles, Shard pulled higher into the sky. Cooler air bit his face. Far off in the air over Windwater, he saw multiple gryfons wheeling and circling. He perked his ears to the sounds of sparring. *Are they aerial fights?* Caj hadn't made them practice fighting other gryfons in the air since…

"*Shard!*"

Kjorn's cry from above sounded like an eagle call. A furious eagle. Shard slipped to the side just in time to dodge Kjorn's dive. Talon caught his left wing feathers and he jerked down, pulling into a quick dive. Kjorn snapped his beak and banked to circle and gain height again.

"What was that for?" Shard peered back and saw mad light in his friend's face. Fury. Kjorn shrieked and drove forward, his flight more powerful but always clumsier than Shard's, who easily swung down and to one side to avoid him again.

"Where have you been?"

"Hunting," Shard barked into the cooling breeze. The lies came too easily now. The scent of rain flickered, though the storm would hit late in the night, he thought. Two storms in one day, and from different quarters of the sky made for a bad omen. Now his wingbrother was attacking him. He spun and dove under Kjorn, seeking a draft to rise up before he ran out of maneuverable air.

"Stop lying to me!"

"I never—"

Kjorn knocked into him from the side and Shard snarled, clawing for purchase on Kjorn's wing or talons. They locked briefly, tails lashing, wings battering as they spiraled down.

"Let go!" Kjorn shrieked, snapping his gaze to the trees rushing toward them.

"Will you listen?" Shard jerked and thrust himself back, clapping his wings together around Kjorn to throw them both head over tail toward the trees. It was a move Caj taught them. Only Shard, because of his swiftness, had ever been able to do it, to throw another gryfon over his head in flight.

As Kjorn rasped, "Yes," Shard unlocked his talons and let the gold prince spiral and thrash his way upright in the sky.

Shard tucked his wings into a controlled descent and Kjorn shoved above him, his wings powering better lifts. Before Shard could duck, the prince locked talons to his wingjoints, attacking again like a gryfon gone mad.

"Kjorn!"

The trees lunged up.

"Tell me the truth! Tell me why you fly at night, *wingbrother.*"

Kenna. She had to have told him. Or Halvden. It didn't matter. Shard thrashed and his hind paws hit the tops of towering juniper and pine. "I don't—"

Kjorn snapped Shard's ear, and they dropped lower. Pine branch slapped Shard's belly and face. Kjorn couldn't drag him aloft much longer. No gryfon was strong enough to bear another alone.

"To learn the way of the Vanir!" Branches snapped and slapped and stung against his legs and face. "To be stronger!"

Kjorn released him and Shard dropped one wing beat into the trees before he caught himself. Pounding his wings, he tangled in the pines before finding a branch to shove off from. Furious, he mounted the air and tried to snag Kjorn's tail feathers. The prince whirled with a snarl and stooped, dropping on Shard like an eagle to a hare. They crashed through the forest, snapping branches and wrestling until they hit the bed of needles on the ground. Birds scattered and small animals leaped deeper into the green.

Both gryfons lay still.

Suddenly terrified, Shard stirred, fresh scrapes and cuts pinching every part of him. "Kjorn?"

The prince's ribs rose and fell with breath. Shard fluffed his wings in relief. Then Kjorn lifted his head and stared at Shard with summer-blue eyes.

He is more a Summer King than I could ever be, Shard thought. He suddenly hated the song, the war, the wolves and himself. He waited for Kjorn to name him a traitor.

"You should've told me. Why should I hear it from someone I barely know?"

Shard blinked, staring as Kjorn, with a groan, rolled to his feet. "You're not..."

"I'm furious," Kjorn whispered, then shook himself of pine needles. "But I understand."

A strange calmness crept into Shard. He should have known his wingbrother would understand. Of course he understood. Shard let his beak open but no words came. "You won't tell your father?"

Kjorn laughed, sharp, single and harsh. "No. But you have to stop. Halvden's mother has been banished. You have to stop flying at night."

"Halvden's…"

"Mother," Kjorn said, flexing his wings to test for bruises and breaks. His face darkened. "This morning she left a fish outside my father's den as an insult. Then she flew to Windwater to tell Halvden that now she was free of his father, she wouldn't pretend to be an Aesir anymore. She said, *'The song has been sung.'*"

Shard shifted his talons against the pine needles. Catori had asked Stigr that. *The song has been sung.* Ragna the white Widow Queen, trying to call forth the Summer King.

My mother, he realized. *She was trying to tell me who I am.*

Kjorn rounded on Shard, tail ticking back and forth. "A traitor, Shard. So Caj has us practicing battle against our own kind in case there are more. And then I learn that you've been flying at night."

"To…" Shard let the lie fall to the ground and spoke the truth. "To meet an exiled Vanir who helped me learn our ways. To make myself stronger. I did it for your father," Shard whispered. *Our ways,* his mind babbled back at him, like a raven. *Am I a Vanir?* "I did it for you."

"I think," Kjorn murmured, standing close enough now that Shard remembered he would never grow as tall or strong, "that I believe you."

The breath left Shard. "Brother, I shouldn't have let things go so far." Already the wolves and their singing and his conversation with Stigr seemed a distant thing.

"No. But here you are, now. That's all that matters."

Straightening, Shard extended his wing, speaking the words of the wingbrother pledge. "Wind under me when the air is still."

"Wind over me when I fly too high," Kjorn murmured, stretching his wing to eclipse Shard's, though he didn't quite meet Shard's eyes.

"Brother by choice."

"Brother by vow."

They spoke the last words together. "By my wings, you will never fly alone."

Prompted by such sudden relief at Kjorn's grace, and a lifetime of unquestioning loyalty, Shard blurted, "I know where the wolves make their den."

Instant regret drowned his mind, amber eyes, the faces of the young wolf pups.

Where will you stand? Rumbled the wolf king's voice.

The prince's eyes lit and he searched Shard's face, then seemed to let the reason go. Unquestioning. A true wingbrother. A true prince.

And here I stand, one foot on the Sun Isle, and one in the wolf den. And traitor to both. He didn't feel right about keeping information from Kjorn or from betraying the wolves' trust.

There must be an answer. Mind awhirl, he barely heard the prince speaking.

"Come," said Kjorn, a wry edge to his voice. "We must speak with my father."

"You won't tell him?" Shard followed Kjorn as he turned to walk free of the trees. "About me flying at night?"

"No. But don't worry, Shard. Even if he ever knows, he wouldn't banish you."

Shard perked his ears, hopeful that he had finally made himself useful in the king's eyes. Severin must've seen his work at Windwater, or his new skills as a warrior and hunter. *He must see that I'm loyal.* For a moment Shard thought maybe his old doubts were foolish, and it was time to turn from wolf and Vanir ways altogether.

"He truly wouldn't?" They stepped out of the trees and a cool gust hit their faces. Kjorn laughed as he bounded forward.

"Of course not." He paused to glance back at Shard. "You're my wingbrother!"

The prince lunged from the ground into the sky to fly back to Sun Isle. Shard stood frozen, letting the wind whip his face. Wingbrother to the prince. *That's all I'll ever be.* He crouched to fly as Kjorn keened at him to hurry.

Wingbrother to the prince. Son of Baldr the Nightwing. Son of Ragna the White.

Prince of the Vanir.

The Summer King.

Who will you be, Shard? Stigr's voice asked in his head.

Somewhere in the woods a raven called, another answered, and the birds broke into chorus as Shard shoved from the grass to follow Kjorn.

A STORM HOVERED OUT to sea, checked by winds around the islands. When they reached the Sun Isle, Kjorn invited his father to fly with them to the birch wood. He told him that Shard had information to end the war quickly.

As they walked under the dappled birch, Shard told all that had happened over the spring and summer, with a twist. It wasn't a lie, but a half-truth. A riddle, a raven story. He told that the wolves hadn't attacked him on the boar hunt, but instructed him how to kill Lapu. He told the king he'd been spying, that the wolves trusted him.

He told everything he knew of them, which turned out to be very little, but it was more than any other gryfon had known of the wolves since the Vanir were conquered, and so the king was impressed and grateful.

Doubt wriggled in Shard's mind, but he had done all he could. *Haven't I been fair? I have to serve my king. I have to stand by my wingbrother.*

And yet. Even as he'd flown with Kjorn, Shard thought of a way to salvage what he'd done, and imagined himself strong as stone to see it through.

At the very end, he told the king where the wolves made their den. *Please let this work,* he thought, watching Sverin.

They stopped walking at a trickle of stream. Small animals fled their presence, leaving the wood silent and still, waiting for the next storm. Dry, cool wind brushed them, bringing the smell of the sea and rain. The king paced between two birch trees and his red feathers shocked against the pale bark and green summer grass.

"A pity you didn't take a mate. We need more clever warriors like you." He drew up in front of Shard, tail swinging.

He's so tall, Shard reflected, though oddly Sverin reminded him of no one so much as the wolf king, Helaku. His golden eyes were like the sun, and Shard feared he could see everything Shard truly was.

Staring back at the king, Shard saw in his eyes nothing but war, power, more land than they needed, and nests lined with dragon gold. *Kjorn will be different…*

"Thank you, my Lord," he whispered, lowering his head. Sverin lifted his beak slightly, measuring Shard, and paced away.

In that moment, Shard knew he had done the right thing. It had to work. He wouldn't really be betraying anyone.

"Now," murmured the king, eyes blazing in the dimming light. "Tell me, based on what you know, when will be the best time to attack them."

Shard met the king's eyes and hoped his terror didn't show. "Three days."

Three days. Surely, that would be enough time.

24

HE FLIES IN THE NIGHT

THAT NIGHT IN THE RAIN, Shard flew. All through the cloudy sunset he had sharpened his talons, sparred, made an appearance at preparing for battle. Kjorn watched him and seemed relieved, but Shard didn't speak to the prince at all, afraid Kjorn would see betrayal. As darkness fell Shard waited, waited, restless, and was grateful for the storm that drove the pride into their dens as night closed its wings around them. No one would stir that night. Not with the rain. Not with the battle so close.

The rain that was soft on the earth lashed harder in winds above the islands, doubling Shard's night blindness. Weary, wings aching from flying in bad conditions and no sleep, Shard angled himself starward, aiming toward the looming black lump that was Star Island.

He nearly dropped from the sky once after falling asleep, despite the wind shoving him. Pumping his wings hard, he peered through the murky air and drifted lower. His wingtips brushed spiky pine needles and he snapped in frustration, unable to see a meadow or even the shadows of more trees. He would have to land blind in the forest.

He flared, beating his wings to hover, and kicked his hindlegs down to feel what lay below. Three trees grew there, with little space between. Shard folded his wings and dropped, flared halfway to soften his landing, and thumped hard on wet pine needles.

He ran in a circle, bumping his wings on rocks and trees, and released a rasping, breathless laugh. *I landed in pure dark, in the rain! If only Stigr could have seen.*

For a moment there was nothing but the beat of his heart and his own breath. The rainwater rolled from his wings like a gull's. He could have flown again without trouble, but it was too dangerous. He folded his wings and crept forward, feeling his way carefully, straining to hear.

I'll never find them in this!

"Help me," Shard whispered to the night, to Tyr who was far away in his daylight temple, to Tor, hidden behind heavy clouds. He lifted his face and shouted Catori's name into the forest, his eagle's crying ringing and then falling dead in the rain. He barely knew which side of the island he was on, if he was near their den or far away, close to the sea or in the middle of the woods. He called for Helaku, for Ahote or Ahanu or the ravens.

I should have brought Stigr. He would have known what to do.

Feeling foolish and desperate, with his plan only half formed, Shard shifted his feet, and then lifted his face, forming a roar in his chest that he shaped into a kind of wolf howl, as Stigr had done. The low, strange note in his chest carried through the rain and the trees.

All fell silent in the night and rain.

Then birds twittered uncertainly. Shard strained, listening for anything, anything through the constant patter of rain on leaves and pine needles.

Voices, small, whispering, twittering voices flickered to him, soft as the rain.

"He sings!"

"He speaks."

"Is he a thief? A thief?"

"But he sings."

"Like her."

"Like she who speaks to us."

Shard straightened and turned about in a circle, peering through the dark. "Who's there? Who speaks?"

"We!"

"Us! Too small for him to see."

"He's blind."

"No, he sees."

"He hears."

"*He listens to all who speak.*"

"*He speaks to all who hear.*"

"I saw him kill Lapu." The whispers came from above, like little winds, moving about. Shard perked his ears.

"I saw him fight Ahote."

"I saw him fall—"

"I saw him fly—"

"She calls him the Star King."

"I lined my nest with his feathers."

"Your chicks will be strong!"

"Bold!"

"Then we owe him thanks."

"*Who are you?*" Shard flared his wings, bashed them against two trees, and winced.

"But he is angry—"

"He is young—"

"Be silent, fools. He is Vanir."

That last voice was lower, slower, female but cracked with age. Yet those voices all sounded more like the ravens than the wolves, more like gryfons or eagles.

Birds, Shard realized, heart leaping. *They're birds. None of them are witless. I just haven't been listening.* He remembered the first time he had seen Catori, and those voices that seemed to echo her words in the wind. Birds.

Movement ghosted in front of Shard's face and he crouched back, hissing a warning. Then he blinked twice, and through the dark, saw a rare sight.

A great winter owl landed before him on the ground, so silvery pale that her white face glowed through the gloom. Such creatures rarely flew out of the high snowy mountains on the Sun Isle before winter. She reminded him of Ragna. *My mother.* Shard lowered his forelegs in a bow and mantled his wings.

"Please. I need your help. I am Rashard, son-of-Baldr." He nearly choked on the words, the first time he'd uttered his true, full name. "Prince of the Vanir. I must find the wolves tonight."

The owl tilted her head around until she peered at him upside down, then righted her face and bobbed once. "I see the son of the Nightwing, who was my friend. Follow me."

Deliriously grateful, trembling with exhaustion, Shard forced his muscles into a lope to follow the star-pale owl through the night and rain. Far off, a low wolf's note finally answered his call, and his heart filled with dread and joy. It felt as if he ran for hours. Wet brush slapped his face, he tripped over tangles and rocks, and rose again to follow the white owl as she flew silent and low over the ground.

Then, he wasn't running alone. A shape moved alongside him, shouldering him clear of obstacles, nudging him on. Catori's breath panted with his, her familiar scent sifting faintly to him under the rain.

She led him to the wolf den. The white owl flew off into the wet sky.

Catori shouldered him out of the rain into a musty cave where he collapsed. He tried to speak but she set a paw on his wing, gently pinning. "Rest, my friend."

"No," mumbled Shard, shoving to his feet. "I must speak with your father. I know when Sverin plans to attack."

25

HE SPEAKS TO ALL WHO HEAR

"SO THIS IS YOUR GREAT plan."

Helaku the wolf king paced in front of Shard. Behind him sat Ahote and Ahanu, ears perked toward their father. The storm broken, faint moonlight glanced on them now and then between the trees and windblown clouds. Catori stood at Shard's side.

"I couldn't think of another way."

"Maybe it wasn't yours to think of," Ahote snarled.

Ahanu tossed his head. "We don't need gryfons to tell us how to fight."

"Be silent." Helaku perked his ears toward his sons, hackles lifting to make him look even larger, a huge indigo shadow. All around them rose the smell of wet earth. Thunder rumbled, the late summer storm rebuilding. Shard kept his wings folded, resisting the urge to open them so he felt larger and stronger.

"There's a cave entrance on the starward side of this island, but covered by tide during the day. On the low tide, you can lead your pack—"

"I can flee with my pack, you mean." The old wolf turned back on Shard, baring his long fangs. Shard lowered his head, wings twitching. "I don't like this plan. I don't think I like you. Stigr and my daughter spoke so highly, and had such hope, but I see that all the son of Baldr the Nightwing has amounted to is a strapling, bowing coward."

"I'm trying to avoid a war!"

"Sometimes wars must be fought. Even your father fought—"

"When he had no choice. Don't you see? They know how you fight. They know where your den is because I had to tell them. Either way, they'll come. In three days."

"So you say. Or you're deceiving all of us, and intend to lead me into a trap."

"No," Shard whispered, and heard Catori's soft growl of disgust at her father's stubbornness. "That's not what I'm trying to do. You can be safe in the caves during the day, have the run of the islands at night without gryfon interference."

"Forever? Crawling in and out of the caves at night like rats? Or do you have a plan beyond tucking tail and running?"

"I don't know," Shard whispered. The ghosts of Black Rock whispered from the corners of his mind. He realized now those dead kings and queens were truly his ancestors. His history. He had a responsibility to their legacy as well. "Yet. But I will—"

"I don't need a gryfon to help me lead my pack. It stinks of trickery and cowardice."

"Then I must be trying to trick you too, Father," snapped Catori, lifting her ears and tail. "For I believe him. I trust him. My visions—"

"Your *dreams,*" rumbled Helaku, "are fantasies planted by an old, defeated exile who is living in the past. He has been turning you to his own devices since you were a cub. I respected Stigr once too, but he has nothing left. There is no fight left in him, only wishes and dreams and the weak history of a conquered pride."

"And is that all that's left in you, Father? Fight? Will you become like Lapu, witless and violent? Let Shard lead us to safety, and fight when the time is ripe!"

"Silence." Helaku snapped his jaws. Shadows stirred. More wolves emerged from their dens. Shard stepped forward, remembering how Stigr had addressed Helaku.

"Great Hunter, if you'll only listen to me—"

"I listened to Baldr!" The wolf king's roar silenced the forest. Shard stood still in shock. "I listened when the Nightwing promised me peace, promised that the wolves had nothing to fear from the Aesir, that in summer the Vanir would rise with the strength and honor of the Aesir and the old ways blended together. Yes, he had great visions too, your father, and so I listened and bided my time." The great wolf stalked up so that his face nearly touched Shard's. "But he died before he could keep his promises." A jolt lanced down Shard's spine as he stared into the wolf king's eyes. Reflected there, he saw two gryfons battling in the sky, and saw what Helaku spoke of.

"The grandsire of the prince you call brother killed him in mid-air, and he fell into the sea. I saw it. All his visions died with him there, and this I know for sure. You are no Prince of the Vanir, no Summer King. You are nothing at all."

Shard had felt it, felt his father's death in his own skin, any time he tried to dive toward the water. He remembered knowing for certain his father's bones and spirit didn't dwell on Black Rock with the others. His body was lost in the sea. Trying to catch his breath now, Shard struggled against twin fears of the wolf king and reliving another's death.

"Don't you see," pleaded Catori, shouldering between them. "Father, Baldr wasn't speaking of that war. The Vanir have a vision of the far past and far things to come. In summer. He was speaking of now, of his own son, and the pride that lives on the Silver Isles now—"

"I will hear no more of this. No more Vanir magic, no more watery moon visions from my pups." The old king paced away and his two sons stood, ears lifting. When Helaku turned to face Shard again, he looked as solid as a mountain, his sons at his sides.

"I thank you for telling us when the Red King plans to attack. It will give me time to get the young ones to safety, and lay a trap."

"Helaku," Shard whispered. Never had he expected that the old wolf would be so unreasonable, that he wouldn't even listen to Catori. *I should have brought Stigr.* "I didn't bring you that information to use against my family—"

"But you told them where our home was? I suppose you didn't mean for them to use that information against us?"

"No!" Shard ramped, flaring his wings, feeling wild and in danger. "I had a plan—"

"I don't need your plan! I am king here!" He raised his head with a howl. Cautious growls and wolf warbles from the others rose with him.

Catori paced, circling Shard, watching her father.

"I have been king on Star Island for longer than your father was alive, and I will not run."

"You're too proud," Shard rasped, breathless with disbelief. Anger roiled under his skin. He opened his wings. "You're no different than Sverin. I only wanted to help you—"

"Take him," Helaku growled.

Shard spun, flashing his wings out in warning as Ahote and Ahanu leaped forward with twin growls.

"Hold him!"

Shard ramped to meet the first wolf, slapping his wings together to knock Ahote away.

"I won't have him telling of our trap to the Red King!"

A snarling red blur whipped past Shard to meet Ahanu. Catori fought her own brothers for him.

From Caj, Shard had learned to fight two wolves at once. Or three. But at Helaku's snarling commands more wolves came forward, taking his wings in their jaws, snapping for his ankles. Helaku himself leaped forward and clamped his jaws on Catori's scruff to drag her from the fight.

In the midst of the fight a raven winged down and Shard shrieked for help. The black bird gabbled and laughed and lighted on a branch near the wolf king.

"Stop! Stop! Greatest Hunter, Helaku, I have news! I have news of the gryfon king's plans!"

The wolf king whirled, flashing teeth, and the raven leaped up in surprise.

Shard slashed talons at the face of the nearest wolf, Ahote, he thought, and the wolf dodged back. He continued his retreat, ducking and whirling against the empty air. Shard stared at him. Then he saw the tiny sparrow.

More flew down: sparrows, starlings, two small owls.

"Go, Prince," chattered a starling. Birds clouded down from the trees, hundreds, swirling around and filling the air to confound the wolves and drive them back. They cleared a path for Shard to escape. "Go!"

What does the raven know? Shard wanted to ask. But now the air was clear around him. He caught Catori's worried gaze over the roil of wolves and birds, then turned to run free of the great rowan and leap into the air.

He winged to Sun Isle.

I failed.

He would say he'd been hunting. Patrolling. The sun sat high enough now that he could easily say he hadn't been flying at night. Exhaustion gnawed at the edge of his thoughts.

Commotion perked his ears. He circled once around the nesting cliffs, staring. Below, gryfess hunters and the newly initiated all gathered near the Copper Cliff, sparring, sharpening their talons against the wet rock. Unease closed dark wings on his heart.

On the rocks, Sverin himself stood with a half circle of young, proud-standing males. Shard glided lower and landed in a loping run. He saw Halvden hop down from the king's rocks, looking as proud as he had after the initation hunt. A pair of golden, emerald-crusted gauntlets decorated his forelegs. A gift from the king. Shard trotted up to him.

"Halvden! What's happening?"

The green warrior paused, eyeing Shard with the same expression he might give a yattering gull. "Where have you been? We're preparing for battle."

"But it won't be for days."

Halvden ruffled, swinging his tail. "Apparently," he purred, "being wingbrother to the prince doesn't mean you're up on the latest news." His eyes narrowed. Shard wondered, suddenly, if Halvden felt any remorse at all about his mother's banishment.

No, he realized. *It's a black mark against him. All he regrets is his father's death.*

"The prince believes there might be a spy among us. Maybe an old Vanir. Or birds."

The raven, Shard thought, his fear growing. *The raven who called to Helaku...*

Halvden seemed to enjoy dragging out his news.

"Or perhaps some wolf witchery in the wind. Whatever the case, he and the king have changed plans."

But I had three days! Casting around, he saw Kjorn up on the rocks. The golden prince glanced his way, met his gaze, then laid back his ears and looked away.

He doesn't trust me. Maybe I don't even deserve it. Ice lumped in Shard's belly. It had all been show. Sverin didn't trust him. Kjorn didn't trust him.

He would never, ever be a true member of the Red King's pride.

He will be like his father, Stigr had tried to warn him. *More than you know.*

We will never have peace as long as a Red King rules.

"Halvden, just tell me, how many days—"

"There are no more days," Halvden snarled. "We fly tomorrow. Tomorrow, we attack at Tyr's first light."

26
AMBUSH

"Only in stillness the wind
Only from ice the flame.
When all was nameless, the wise will tell
That only by knowing the other
Did they come to know themselves."

"DO NOT LEAVE THE SUN Isle today, Shard."

Shard lunged awake and heard only waves. Gryfon wings flashed behind his eyes, a vision of a long, grassy, rock-strewn plain of reddish earth that he didn't remember from any dreams before.

All the gryfons had slept on the Sun Isle, leaving Windwater abandoned for the night. The dream slipped from him as if he held sand in his talons.

Three times during the night he had tried to escape to warn the wolves, only to see that sentries sat atop the cliff, ears swiveling, gazes nervous but alert in the dark. He had never seen night sentries before. He guessed they watched for rebel Vanir. *Or for me.* He could only hope that the news the raven carried yesterday was of the attack, and that Helaku had at least gotten the young ones to safety.

"Do not leave the Sun Isle today, my prince."

Shard blinked and turned, peering around in the gray light. Who would address him that way? A raven perched at the mouth of the cave. "Which one are you?" Shard asked, cautious. The raven bobbed his head and mantled.

"The only one I have ever been, honored Vanir."

Shard heard no mockery in his tone, though he would've preferred a straight answer. "I know now there are two of you. Two who bother to speak with anyone. I never learned your names, and that was foolish. Please, tell me your name."

The raven looked bright-eyed and pleased. "I am Hugin. My brother Munin has no sense of honor and fair play, and he has arranged trouble this day. Do not leave the Sun Isle."

"Why?"

"Shard." Kjorn landed hard in the entrance, nearly squashing Hugin, who squalled and flapped off into the morning. The golden prince ruffled and snapped at him. "Witless thing. Wanting to follow us to take food from the battle, I'll wager." The prince stared firmly at Shard, who stared back, not speaking the words that clawed his heart.

You lied to me. You never trusted me. Not the trust of a wingbrother. Your father never trusted me and he never will. And he was blind, Shard saw. Dismissing the raven. Not realizing that Shard had been changing before his eyes all summer. *Into what?* He had asked Stigr.

Now he knew.

Prince of the Vanir.

"Don't look at me like that," Kjorn whispered. "I had to. This is war. Whether it's by your choice or if you're under some wolf or exile's spell that makes you change sides again and again, I can't risk the pride."

"I know," Shard murmured, and his voice sounded oddly deep, even to himself. It sounded like the phantom in his memory. His father. Kjorn, Shard heard sharply now, sounded like Sverin, who sounded like Per, who had killed Baldr the Nightwing.

Even if he could have been a Summer King, Shard thought, *he's let himself be blinded.* Resentment crawled forward. He'd put so much faith in Kjorn. *He put faith in me too, but I see now that the way of the Aesir isn't all right.* Shard wondered if it would have made any difference if he'd been honest with Kjorn from the beginning.

It hardly mattered now.

"I understand," Shard said quietly, when it seemed Kjorn expected more of an answer.

Kjorn took it the wrong way, and looked relieved. "Then let's go. Battle is on us, brother, and we can prove ourselves. To my father. To each other. You'll fight by my side?"

"Yes," Shard murmured as he stepped to the front of the cave. "I'll fight."

We can prove ourselves.

Sverin made no speeches and no promises and no great battle cries into the dawn. Heavy with a gleaming bronze collar and gauntlets for battle, he stood at the edge of the Copper Cliff as his warriors gathered, counting heads, looking on with silent pride. Some, adorned with gifts of gold and bronze and silver, stood out as his chosen finest. Halvden and Kenna stood among them, Caj, and others of Shard's age and older.

Shard, plain and gray, stood at Kjorn's golden side. Some were not called to fight. Sigrun stood farther off, ready for the injuries, her apprentices staring in awe. Never in their time, and perhaps never again, would they see such an assembly.

Shard tried to catch Sigrun's eye. He hadn't had the chance to confront her about what she and Ragna had done in raising him. After today, Shard had a feeling many things would be different, and he might never get the chance for closure that he wanted.

Ragna stood closer to the warriors, but was not to join. Sverin didn't force any of the warriors older than a certain age to fight. Shard shifted, hesitantly seeking the Widow Queen's gaze across the last of the gathering warriors. He expected to find anger there, disappointment to see him heading off to war under Sverin's command.

But her pale green eyes, eyes that matched his own, shone only with unwavering surety. *What does she look so sure of?* Shard tried to discern whether it was faith in him to do something, or pride—but it was neither. Something else filled her as she met his gaze, and Shard couldn't name it. Whatever it was, he didn't deserve it. Shame consumed him for all he'd done in those last days, back and forth between gryfon and wolf and Vanir and Aesir, and he had to look away.

All the warriors who planned to fight had arrived.

In silence, the king raised his head, flashed his wings for attention, and leaped from the cliff into the air. Clouds delayed the dawn, hanging tendrils to brush the sea with rain.

Even the sky is uneasy, Shard thought, thinking of the storms that wouldn't clear.

Kjorn jumped into the sky. Thyra, Halvden and Kenna leaped, along with copper Einarr and all the others, the entire throng of grown, tested warriors. And some young, untested but eager. Shard wanted to scream at them to stay. But they left behind only the fledges, old females, older males, and the fluffed kits from the spring whelping.

Shard crouched, hesitating, his gaze flicking through those remaining. Sigrun had already turned away. Ragna gazed on, as if she would watch him fly all the way to Star Isle. *Has she always watched me so, and I never saw?*

Grass whipped in the wind, stinging Shard's face, and he shoved into the sky.

They flew high over the Star Isle and the whole forest looked crouched, hunched under dark dawn clouds and tight, like a cornered creature waiting for attack.

The cornered creature is most dangerous, Shard thought wildly, staring down. The king put him on point, to lead the way to the ancient rowan tree. He thought of the birds, coming to his aid. He thought of wild boar. Shard feared what would happen if all of Star Isle tired of the presence of plodding, greedy Aesir. *Would other creatures fight?*

The raven, Hugin, had warned him to stay away from the Star Isle. *No. He told me not to leave Sun Isle.* Unease made his flight seem longer.

Seeing the clump of rowan leaf that dominated the pine wood, Shard banked and began to descend a good league out. They had to approach low, on foot.

Not one warrior spoke a word. As they landed in rough formation, they fanned out like the broad inner curve of a wing to surround the den, and stalked forward. Shard moved at Kjorn and Thyra's side. So different a feeling now than it had been on the boar hunt. Shard ruffled, shoving regret from his mind. The raven had flown in to give the wolf king news. Shard hoped it had been warning of the gryfons' change of plans. Maybe Catori had convinced some of her pack to flee. Maybe even proud Helaku would've seen sense and gotten to safety.

The birds sat silent in the trees, wary of the gryfon intruders. The scuttle of small animals fell quiet. The entire forest loomed dark and the smell of rain filtered in. No wolf smell came fresh with it. Shard laid his ears back, tight unease cramping his muscles. Ahead, he could see the cliff that broke up out of the ground, clenched together by rowan root and riddled with holes that were wolf dens.

The breeze brushed them and Shard lifted for scent. Stale. No fresh wolf scent. No movement. No sound.

The dens stood empty and black.

Relief stroked uneasily into Shard's breath. But something still felt wrong. Beside him, Thyra tensed. He felt tension and movement through the trees, then stillness and silence as the whole flight of warriors stopped where they stood. Kjorn swiveled to stare at Shard as if the empty dens were his fault, then strode forward into the clear, rocky space between trees and the den entrances.

"Cowards," he roared at the dens. "Show yourselves! I, Kjorn son-of-Sverin, prince of the Aesir, Summer King, future king of the Silver Isles, challenge you!"

Red Sverin stalked out of the trees. More colors drifted into Shard's view as gryfons milled forward, unsure. Above him, a raven screed and laughed, his mockery echoing long into the woods. It wasn't Hugin, that Shard knew. It was the other.

"No one is home to hear you, golden prince. Strut and fight the flying sparrows!" He laughed madly but Shard knew most of the gryfons only heard cackling shrieks.

Kjorn wasn't listening. A scent familiar to Shard drifted on the little breeze and all looked up for its source. Catori appeared at the top of the cliff that formed the wolf den, out of gryfon range but within their sight and hearing.

"They aren't here," she called.

"They ran?" Halvden's voice rang with contempt. Shard glanced over to see Sverin's face and found the gold eyes piercing him. Not Catori.

"They knew." The king took a step toward Shard. "Somehow."

"No!" Kjorn moved between them. "Shard remained on Sun Isle all through the night, Father. I saw sure of that. This is some other treachery. They couldn't have known. They—"

"They aren't here," Catori called, more firmly, the only wolf to face the entire front of gryfon warriors. In confusion, no one moved to attack her. "Because they traveled through the night. Through the caves. I thought I could convince my father against it, but I failed." Her mournful, bright gaze and voice focused on Shard. "They left, not to go into hiding, but—"

"To Sun Isle," Shard breathed, whirling to face Sverin. "Sire, the wolves will attack the nesting cliffs!"

"Impossible," snapped the king.

"They will, my Lord, an ambush! There are caves under the Isles! We must fly!"

Sverin stared at Shard, saw the truth in him, and crouched.

"I tried to warn you," Catori cried. "I sent a raven to Stigr, and Hugin to you to—"

"*Fly!*" roared the Red King, and shoved from the ground. "Fly! Back to the Sun Isle! We've been tricked! Ambush!"

Others milled, trapped tight in the trees and against the cliff face, only able to lift off two or three at a time. Shard crouched, waiting for a clear space. No one spared him a glance.

Soon he was the only gryfon remaining, and he saw that Catori wasn't the only wolf. One, tawny gold who seemed vaguely familiar, and one of her brothers, stepped up beside her. Shard stared hard at him, thinking how they were the same, and not. One twin was always the aggressor. One always followed. But not this time.

"Ahanu," he called, and the wolf dipped his head. Shard looked to the tawny wolf beside him. "I'm sorry. I don't know you."

"I am Tocho, windbrother. You saved me from Hallr, this spring past. I will not attack your family."

Shard's mind reeled. He mantled to the wolves. "Ahanu. Tocho. Catori. I will always remember that you didn't follow your father and king to attack my pride."

Ahanu raised his head again. "And we will remember always that you came to us, warned us, and tried to make peace."

"Tried," Shard whispered, then leaped back into the sky.

27
THE FALL OF THE KING

THERE WAS NO TIME TO assess injuries or deaths, or to truly hear the furious keening of new gryfon mothers, only pick a target and dive. Scanning from high, Shard saw a wolf chasing down a stumbling fledge and hurtled toward it. His eagle scream crashed in with the rest. Roars, snarls, shrieks. Feathers, fur and blood scattered the ground.

In trying to make everything right, Shard had created a horror beyond reckoning. *Betrayed by my own weak plans and indecision.*

At falcon speed he slammed into the big wolf, smashing against the ground. They flipped and rolled, tearing grass. Fury lanced up every muscle.

The wolf lunged up and Shard whirled away, his legs and sinew trained and moving on instinct from long days with Caj and Stigr. They circled each other and Shard saw an opening. Then he recognized his opponent.

"Ahote," he choked out the name. "I would have been your friend."

But it was not Ahote before him. Blood hunger, rage, and the mad light of the hunt gleamed in his eyes. Witless with hate.

226

Nameless. The wolf that Shard had known lurched forward and Shard ramped to his hind legs, clapping his wings together before spinning away. They tangled and at some point Shard felt warmth ooze down his ribs. Blood.

Somewhere, another fledge yelped in pain. Or death.

Red boiled up behind Shard's eyes and he shrieked, spinning to knock Ahote aside and in a rough, quick wrestle, slammed him to the hard earth. The wolf had too many wounds to survive the battle much longer. Hate drove him.

"Ahote of the Star Isle," Shard rasped. Ghosts whispered in his head. *The Nameless will know themselves.* "Stop this! You're dying."

Wild golden eyes flared at him, slather dripped from his fangs, and Shard clenched talons against his throat.

"Ahote. Son of Helaku. Hear me. You fought well, brother."

The wolf panted and squirmed and then, at the final word, the emptiness washed from his gaze. He stared at Shard, and knew him. "I…would have been king, after my father."

"We are all kings," Shard whispered, "in the Sunlit Land."

"You gave me back my name," Ahote whispered, and Shard heard blood in his throat. "Give me my honor."

The Nameless shall know themselves, the ghosts whispered. Ahote's head lolled. Shard finished him by the throat and looked up only in time to see an emerald fury swooping down on him.

"Traitor!"

Shard leaped forward under Halvden's dive and his claws raked empty air.

Halvden swooped by and wheeled around, talons sweeping wide as if to show Shard the battle. "This is your doing."

Shard remained on the ground to draw Halvden in. He didn't want to try his luck in an aerial battle against the bigger gryfon.

"No," he said firmly as Halvden circled low, seeking an opening. "I only ever tried to do what was right."

Halvden shrieked and dove again. This time he saw Shard's move
to dodge and met him sideways, catching Shard's wings to toss him
over on his side. Stunned, Shard rolled to gain his feet but Halvden
fell onto him, a mountain of weight and beak and claw.

Shard curled to protect his throat, panic bursting. Halvden's beak
slashed through the feathers of Shard's neck. Shard saw a blaze of
white. Halvden snarled in surprise as another gryfon plowed into him.
Freed, Shard leaped to his feet.

Ragna.

Amazement struck Shard to see the widow, a fury of white and
flashing talon, as quick as any young gryfess protecting her kit. Her
kit. *Me,* Shard thought. Another gryfon lunged up in a run, dusty
black and bloody.

"Stigr!" Shard shouted in relief. Catori's raven had reached him,
and of course he had come to Shard's aid.

Stigr and Ragna, brother and sister, fought Halvden off. They
were older, slower, but smarter. The green gryfon retreated, swearing,
and sought wolves to attack instead.

"Fly, my prince!" Stigr shouted. "Fly to safety!" Shard stood like a
stone. Thunder boomed across the sky as the wind brought in a third
storm.

I can't run. But who can I fight? He still tasted Ahote's blood. He
couldn't attack his own pride. He couldn't attack the wolves, despite
all. He crouched, backing away, staring around him. Neither gryfon
nor wolf showed strategy, plan, or thought to their attack and defense.
Animal fighting roiled across the field. Kjorn fought two older, scarred
wolf warriors. Thyra and coppery Einarr defended a wailing huddle
of fledges from two more.

Stop! Shard's mind screamed.

A cobalt blur. Caj thumped down between himself, Stigr and
Ragna.

"Didn't I drive you once from this isle?" he boomed at Stigr, who
crouched with a hiss. Ragna edged away toward Shard.

"You owe me an eye." Stigr leaped and Caj met him, cracking together like thunderclouds. *I can't let them fight.* Shard took two steps forward to break them up before Ragna shouldered him aside.

"Shard, fly to Black Rock," she pleaded. "I cannot risk you here!" But he barely heard. At the sound of shrieking fledges, Caj broke free of Stigr and flew off. Stigr didn't pursue.

Clouds boiled over them from the sea. A flash of skyfire drew Shard's gaze up. *Something has to stop this. Someone!*

Like a spell, a thunderclap broke the sky, shook the cliff and drew the attention of every warrior. As one, drawn by a sudden, twin knowing, wolves and gryfons lifted their heads to stare at the rise of the king's rocks, where they saw Sverin meet Helaku.

The Great Hunter and Red King battled each other to the top of the ancient stones, a tangle of black fur and red fury against the blackening dawn.

Gold flashed by Shard. "Father!"

Shard lunged after Kjorn, tripping him and catching his wing. "Stop, Kjorn, look at them!"

Pale Thyra lunged up beside them, panting, her feathers bloodied and flanks scarred. Wolves milled, howling and barking as a few gryfons took flight, finally dragging fledges away from the scene.

"Look," Shard urged Kjorn again, holding him back.

"They're mad," Thyra gasped. Both kings slashed and tore and snarled with the savagery of wild, witless beasts. Sverin's metal bands protected him from Helaku's worst bites at his throat and forelegs. The wolf king's heavy coat acted as armor against Sverin's talons.

"Let me go to him!" Kjorn spun tightly, snapping at Thyra and Shard. They fell back and the prince leaped, flapping hard against the wind to land at his father's side. He tried to shove the king back from Helaku. Sverin spun with an eagle scream knocked Kjorn away with a violent thrust of his wings. Kjorn lost footing and slid down the rocks, stunned. Thyra clambered to him, with Shard close behind.

Gryfons milled, seeking the young and the injured, or flew. Wolves circled, howling for their king, but he did not hear. Shard saw some injured wolves trail toward the woods and the Nightrun.

The cave entrance must be near the river.

The kings, oblivious, fought. They rolled, kicking and snapping, Sverin's red wings tearing the air, Helaku's growls like rolls of thunder. Sverin knocked the wolf king to his side with a twist of wing and talon. Helaku wrenched around, trying to gain his feet, and left his throat open.

Shard saw it. Sverin saw it, too.

Shard leaped forward, shouting. It was too late. Too far.

Thunder buried the last cry of the old wolf king.

Any wolves who hadn't fled gave wrenching cries as if it were their own death, turned, and sprinted to the woods. Gryfon warriors, renewed by the sight of the dying wolf king, leaped and chased them down.

Sverin roared, breaking to an eagle scream, and his wild golden eyes turned toward the fleeing wolves. Rain spat down.

This has to stop, Shard thought wildly. *They only want to escape now.* Even as he thought it, words bellowed from his own chest.

"Sverin!"

The Red King stilled, wings stretched up above his body, and stared down at Shard. Shard drew himself up, unfolding his own wings to mirror the king. "Son of Per! End this."

A raven swooped down around Sverin and the dead wolf king. "Behold, Sverin, behold the true king!" Circling, laughing, the raven fled when Sverin swiped at him. The battle seemed to hold its breath, bloody, panting wolves staring at their dead king, gryfons with wild eyes on Sverin, waiting for his command.

Sverin turned mad eyes on Shard, then his gaze darted to nearest wolf, a wounded, terrified yearling. Gryfons tensed. Wolves snarled, and the king crouched to pounce.

Shard leaped forward. "End this. Or fight me. I, Rashard son-of-Baldr, challenge you!"

"Shard!" Kjorn cried, and Sverin laughed in disbelief.

"Stay away from him, my son." The gryfon king's golden eyes pierced through the gloom to burn Shard like twin suns. "I told you what comes of trusting Vanir."

Rain pelted down. The king stretched his wings wide, red flames against the storm.

"I should have seen it. I should have known the Vanir had a secret. The Night King was too willing to fall." Sverin raised his head, his laugh breaking into a snarl. "Baldr the Nightwing threatened my father with tales of Vanir magic. *We never die,*" he rasped at the air, then snarled and crouched on top of the rocks. Shard tensed, lifting his wings for flight. The Red King lashed his tail. "I mean to prove him wrong."

And with a shrieking roar, he leaped down, talons wide. But Shard launched himself away from the king's furious charge, and swept fast into the sky. Sverin's scream echoed across the sky as he followed Shard up into the storm.

28
SON OF THE NIGHTWING

B LINDED BY WHIRLING DARK CLOUDS and rain, Shard pumped his wings hard, high into the storm. Skyfire lanced out over the sea and all his feathers prickled with the nearness of it. Peering back, he saw Sverin closing. Shard whirled, straining to hold his position for three breaths.

"I'm not your enemy! If you'd ever trusted me, my Lord, I told Kjorn—"

But the king's eagle scream cut him off and Shard snapped his wings shut to drop under the charge. Sverin's talons, streaked with Helaku's blood, scraped his shoulders.

"Vanir traitor," Sverin shouted, folding his wings to dive after Shard. Wind sucked the breath from Shard. He gasped, diving, then pulled up and banked, trying to lose Sverin in the winds. At least he was speaking. At least he was not fully mad.

"Give up! I see now. I see now I must rid the islands of wolves and Vanir if my pride is ever to have peace."

He snarled as Shard swooped over his head, doubling back, and banked to follow, slower, but full of power.

Shard turned to face Sverin, trying to meet his gaze. "I am your pride! All I ever did was to serve—"

"You are nothing!" Sverin's shriek broke into a roar and thunder smashed overhead. Shard stooped again as the king caught up to him, talons slicing the air, then Shard's hind leg. Warm blood ran down his leg, a crimson stream washed away in the downpour.

The silver and black waves below crested high in the wind, beaten by rain.

Shard's heart felt ready to burst, his breath scraping his throat. On each wing stroke his muscles quivered and twitched. He strained into the storm, but he could barely see. The Red King would never stop chasing him. But an Aesir couldn't fly in the rain forever. Sverin's furious shouts chased him through the rain.

"You are nothing! Nothing! Son of a dead king who would not fight! As he died, so will you!"

Helaku had said the same. Had called him nothing. New fire bloomed under Shard's feathers, flushing his skin, giving him strength against the rain. *I am the son of the Nightwing. I am the son of Ragna the White.* But Helaku had seen his father die. *Killed by the grandsire of the prince you call brother. He fell into the sea and all his visions died with him.*

All his visions died with him.

"No," Shard whispered to the storm. He thought of flying as high as he could, as high as he had ever practiced, as high as an Aesir could fly, to outpace the king. But Sverin would follow him to any height. Shard wondered if he would follow to any depth.

He whirled to face the Red King.

Dark red, feathers soaked, the wolves' blood washed from him by the storm, Sverin swooped around Shard once. But rather than attack head-on again, he flapped and strained to gain height. Shard circled tightly and didn't follow him up.

"My father lives, Severin!" Shard eyed the king's ascent, shouting to bait him down, stripping him of title and respect. "He lives in me!"

Severin laughed, narrowed his wings, and hurtled straight toward Shard. His talons stretched out for the kill. His razor beak opened wide.

Shard braced.

Severin slammed into him, talons smashed together, beak slashing, his weight like a boulder. "Then I will kill him at last," he growled.

Locked together, wings beating, they tumbled through the air. The Red King slashed and snarled, so close to victory. Shard strained and squirmed to avoid a killing bite. The wind battered around them. They wrenched and flipped so that for a heartbeat Shard rolled Severin beneath him. *Perfect.*

Shard drew a breath, then closed his wings. He might as well have turned to stone.

Not even the king could lift so heavy a weight.

They fell.

Severin shrieked when he realized what Shard was doing and they plummeted toward the wild sea. "Release me!" He tossed his head, his massive, drenched wings already struggling with his own weight and the metal bands he wore. "Traitor! You called my son wingbrother and then turned on us all! I will kill you!"

Shard freed one foreleg and grabbed the king's throat, forcing the wild gold eyes to his.

The scent of salt and brine tossed around them.

Now they could hear the waves.

So close, Shard could whisper, *"The Vanir never die."*

Then he unlocked his talons from the king's, wrenched loose, and dove. The wind yanked his breath. Waves lunged toward him. Severin's drenched wings stroked the air desperately and Shard saw distant colors, gryfons coming to aid their king.

Sverin shrieked curses and rage.

But he didn't follow as Shard broke through wind, terror and rain to plunge alone into the black and crashing sea.

A GRYFON, PALE GRAY, landed before him. They stood on a shore of the Star Island, a real place of rock and wave, as if Shard were awake. Waves washed nearby, birds sang and Shard's ears twitched. He felt light, tireless, and knew it was a dream, for his waking body would be full of aches and weariness. Or perhaps he was dead, and this was the Sunlit Land, free of pain and weariness forever. He felt a curious lack of sorrow.

"I'm proud of you, Shard."

"Are you Baldr? Are you my father?" It could be no other. Shard clung to his sense of the world, trying to steer the dream, refusing to be distracted. Hungrily, he studied the gryfon before him, the Nightwing. His father. His feathers weren't black, as Shard realized he'd pictured; black, like Stigr. He was raincloud gray. He was fit, compact, smaller than red Sverin and even old Stigr, and his lion haunches were pale, silvery gray.

"I am that part of him that passed into you. Your courage freed my spirit from the sea, and before I fly on, I can cling here a moment with you."

"Then you are dead. And so am I."

"The Vanir—"

"—never die," Shard finished with him, and their voices were so similar they could have been the same gryfon. "Tell me what to do."

Baldr stretched his wings, looking so alive that Shard twitched to step forward. But it wasn't life. Either it was a dream, or he was dead. Either way he was sure he wouldn't have the gift of touching his father.

"Only the Summer King can end this war the right way, for his is a name that stretches back into the memory of all creatures, and there may be more than gryfons battling by the time all is done."

"But what must I do? Am I truly the Summer King? Or is it some other? Someone stronger?"

The pale gryfon blinked slowly at him, as if he were looking through him. "Being dead gives me no more answers than being alive does. Death is beyond this realm, my son. Only life, only your tie to the earth and the sky and the beating life of the world will give you a vision of what may come, or what has been."

"I need help," Shard said, feeling desperate. "If not you, then who?"

"You will have help." Baldr watched him with an expression Shard hadn't known a spirit, or memory, or whatever this vision was, could possess. Pride. Love. It almost shattered him. "When the Aesir first came to us, I offered peace and shelter and help in their plight. They didn't come at first as conquerors."

"That's what Stigr thought," Shard murmured. He turned to pace and his limbs started to feel heavier. Little aches needled up his wings. Something tugged him, like waves, tried to drag him from his father.

He was waking. So he wasn't dead. And his father was a dream.

"If you can discover why they fled their homeland, you may find an answer."

"They think I'm dead. Kjorn would never speak to me again after my betrayal. What you ask is impossible."

"Then give up," murmured the gray gryfon. The dead king. His father. "Give up, sink into the sea and join me here in peace forever."

Shard stared at him. "I won't do that."

A sound, vaguely familiar, filled Shard's ears. Waves? Rain? A voice, screaming?

Shard!

The Nightwing didn't seem to hear. "Good. Then see the vision I saw, the very eve of the day the Aesir came to us, with gold and kits in their grasp."

"I think I dreamed it—"

Baldr opened his wings.

Red flashed in the sky and went dark, and they stood on a sunlit plain. Vast stretches of waving grass sprawled before him, broken by towering pillars and arches of marbled red rock. Above, a black gryfon soared across the cloudless blue, a bolt of skyfire in his talons. Again Shard saw the white mountains, heard the roar of the earth deep within.

"But I don't understand it," Shard whispered. Invisible waves dragged at him and he dug talons into the dream sand, clinging.

"Neither did I." They stood again on the beach of Star Island. "And maybe that was my undoing." More voices called for Shard, voices that Baldr didn't hear. Shard clenched his talons into the gravel and sand but it began to slip through them like wind. Like water.

"But the Aesir came the morning after. Per was too proud. I offered help and he played the invader and took our land and suppressed our ways." Stone-gray eagle eyes bored into Shard. "But I had another vision, one of peace, where gryfons ran with wolves in the woods, and had the strength of the Aesir and the peace of the Vanir within. I should have known I couldn't have that vision without understanding the meaning of the first. And so I died for something that couldn't yet be."

"But how can I—"

"Shard! He's there!"

"I can't reach—"

"Shard, wake!"

Shard whirled and saw no one. His paws slipped under him as if he stood on water, not sand. The Nightwing watched him quietly. "You must learn the truth. Talons and anger alone will not end this war. You must fly on the Silver Wind."

"How?" Shard leaped forward as the Nightwing stepped back into a crouch, poised to fly. "What truth?"

"He listens to all who speak," sang the dead king, "and speaks to all who hear—"

"Wait, please! I need you! I don't know what to do here, alone."

"And his voice is the song of summer." Baldr the Nightwing hesitated, eyes bright. He stretched his wings and they looked less gray, more silver in the growing light. The sand whirled to waves under Shard and the green forest of Star Island cracked with thunder, trees roiling into clouds.

"Tyr and Tor call me to the Sunlit Land. The best of me remains here." He gleamed with pride, watching Shard. *"I live on in you, Shard. And I'm with you. Every place my foot touched, in every wind that circled the world after lifting my wings, in your mother's love, in the sea. I'm with you, Shard."*

"You can't leave now!"

"Always. Fair winds, my son. You must wake now. I can bear you aloft no longer. Wake, and rise."

Shard surged forward as Baldr flapped his wings, but the gray gryfon flared into a bright light and vanished. Shard's talons splashed not on sand but in black water.

He screamed an eagle's rage into the bright light.

SALT WATER STREAMED DOWN his feathers and into his eyes.

"Shard!"

"Fly!"

Stigr's voice yanked Shard from the last of the dream, just as a black wave slapped the side of his face and dragged him under the water.

The storm. The king.

He had dived into the sea.

Hacking salt water, Shard stroked his wings under the water like massive fins, feeling the hard pull of the entire ocean on his muscles. Blind and thrashing, he felt terror and shock seize his muscles at passing from his vision to a battle against the sea.

Wake, and rise.

The terror slipped from him with the echo of his father's voice. He didn't have to relive his father's last fall again. Dragging his wings forward, Shard pierced a scream up to let Stigr know he could swim. Ragna flew with him. They swooped in circles above.

Shard slashed wings and paws through the water, freeing his feathers, his wings. He kicked, shoved, and with a lion's roar, surged from the water. The sea rolled from his wings like a leaden wind. Gasping, forcing wing beats through lancing aches and salt stings, Shard rejoined his mother and uncle in the sky, to the sound of thunder and Stigr's wild, victorious laughter.

29
SHARD'S VISION

"**N**OT SINCE THE DAYS OF Ivar the Bold has anyone, *anyone,* seen a flight like that!"

Stigr laughed as they landed on a beach of Star Isle, sheltered by a looming cliff. The rain slacked; the storm had drained itself of fury. Stigr slapped his wing against Shard's head in congratulations. "Nor are they likely to again. They will call him the Stormwing—"

"Be still, brother," white Ragna murmured. Shard followed her gaze to see others approaching from the beach and sky. Two wolves, loping up the beach, and three gryfons gliding in to land. Shard tensed, then saw Sigrun was among them, along with a copper brown male who looked familiar, and a female Shard didn't know. Overwhelmed, he backed up three steps. The wolves, Catori and Ahanu, paused and circled, sniffing the sand, ears perked.

"Shard," Sigrun breathed, trotting up to check him for injury. Shard stood obediently, trying to catch up with himself.

"Wingsister," murmured Ragna. Shard stared at her over Sigrun's head, and the Widow Queen looked away. Shard lashed his tail.

"What's happened? Severin—"

"Is in his nest," Sigrun said, "with injuries mending. As you should be."

Shard blinked at her. "I can't go back to the Sun Isle."

"Of course not." Stigr stepped between them. Sigrun lashed her tail, stepping away. "You'll stay with me now."

"Or with us," Catori murmured, stepping forward. "The prince of the Vanir is always welcome on the Star Isle."

"But, your father's death. It's my fault."

"He chose his death," Ahanu said, head raised, ears perked. "We mourn, but none blame you for that."

It took Shard a moment to realize he was looking now at the new, young king of Star Island, one who had just lost a father and brother. He mantled low. "Thank you."

Sigrun dipped her head to point at Shard's injuries. "You need to let me tend these." The slash on his leg oozed, and Ahote's claw marks across his ribs stung from the salt in the water. He drew a slow breath, turning an ear to the two strange gryfons who stood politely as if waiting their turn to see him. *Surely they haven't come to see me?* The storm rumbled distantly now and a cool wind rushed up the beach, tangy salt and rain-washed sand.

"I will, Mother." He paused after the word, and regret flashed over Sigrun's face. Shard leaned over to touch his beak to her shoulder. Late morning light crept out to them through the breaking clouds, and gulls began venturing out to find their meals. Their cries sounded too much like gryfon kits in the battle.

Shard looked to Ragna. "You saved my life."

She watched him with a loving hunger, an expression he hadn't recognized when he didn't know her. Pride. Love. As his father had watched in his dream. "You would have fought Halvden off," she said. "I only helped."

"I meant before," Shard whispered. "In the Conquering when you lied to Per the Red. You and, Sigrun." He looked between them both. "There is no repayment for that...Mother."

"My son," Ragna whispered. "My prince. There was nothing else for us to do. How could I let you die?"

Hesitating, Shard stepped forward, and bent his head to touch his brow lightly to the white widow's. "We'll come to know each other better," he promised softly. "For now, I—"

"I know," she murmured, though didn't move from his affection. "You were raised with one mother. I'm content with your safety, your happiness."

"I don't know what to do," he whispered, and felt her shift to lean back and look at him. "I saw him," he told her. "My father."

She perked her ears, eyes bright. "Then you're on the right path. You will be guided. When it's time."

"For now," Sigrun said firmly, "you must heal and rest."

Shard lowered his head in assent, then looked to Stigr. "And you, Uncle. You were my father's wingbrother, weren't you?" Stigr merely dipped his head. "You stayed in these islands, living among the dead, so that one day you could teach me…" He trailed off, thinking of all Stigr had given up. "I can never repay you."

"You already have."

Shard ruffled his wingfeathers as gratitude warmed his chest. Weakness and aches stalked up into his exhausted limbs.

"We should get under the trees," Stigr continued. "In case Sverin sends patrols."

Shard nodded, and Catori and Ahanu led the way up the cliffside on a crumbling deer trail. As they walked, Shard spoke to the two gryfons he didn't know. Each had a gnawing familiarity to them. "How do I know you?"

The copper brown spoke first. "We never properly met. I am Dagr, son-of-Vidar."

"Einarr's brother!" Shard blurted. The memory snapped back to the day of the boar hunt. The copper gryfon Sverin had banished. "I'm glad you're well."

"How could I not be?" He inclined his head. "The true Vanir prince has risen and Sverin lies humiliated in his nest."

Shard couldn't chuckle at the cheerful statement. There was too much left undone, and he thought of what Sverin's defeat would mean for Kjorn. "You should know that Einarr is well. He won a fair mate this summer, and has been a friend to me."

Dagr inclined his head deeply. "Thank you for watching over him, my prince."

Surprised by the gratitude, Shard had no answer but to nod.

They climbed through whispering sea wheat and a crumbly, muddy trail to the top, pausing there to swivel ears and check the wind. Vetch flowers stood bright purple and yellow against the wet grass and Shard breathed deeply. He glanced to the strange female.

"And you?"

She stepped up and mantled low. The sight of a gryfon bowing before him made Shard shift his feet uneasily. It made him unsure if he could be a prince, or a Summer King. Certainly none of the Vanir believed it was Kjorn, but Shard wasn't so sure he was it, either.

"I am Maja, my prince, daughter-of-Traj." As she introduced herself, they walked on toward the forest. "You're too young to have known my mate, for he died in the Conquering, along with my kits by him."

Stigr and Catori chose a patch of wood and they followed, weary, wary, moving as one like a little herd of deer. Shard studied Maja. Suddenly the cant of her head looked familiar, a rhythm in her voice and the way she walked. "You're Halvden's mother."

She angled her head proudly. "I'm honored you know me. After Hallr met his end, I knew I could no longer live pressed under the talon of a red king. I serve you, Shard son-of-Baldr, until my last breath."

"I'll try to be worthy of that," Shard murmured, trying to think of what Kjorn would've said to such a statement. The thought that she would leave her son and his new mate to serve Shard, that she would leave the pride and prefer exile, quickened his heart. If only the others like Halvden could see the possibility for peace. There stood a group of gryfons and wolves together, peaceful.

He had hope, he realized, staring at this circle of gryfons and wolves all looking to the future, for peace, as his father had seen it.

"What now?" Stigr looked around their quiet circle. Birds twittered around them, whispering excitedly, listening. The old exile looked to Ragna and Sigrun. "You can't go back to Sverin's pride."

Sigrun's eyes narrowed. "We must. He won't grudge himself a healer or a huntress, not with the...the losses."

"Mother," Shard began, and both Sigrun and Ragna looked to him. He flushed under his feathers. "I mean, Sigrun. The losses. Who?"

"Kjorn is fine," Sigrun murmured. "Thyra, Einarr and his mate fought well. Small injuries. Many kits and fledges were killed. And the old." Her voice fell measured and quiet, a healer's assessment. Shard knew how she would mourn, later, tucked away from the pain and death under Caj's wing. He had seen it as a kit, when a gryfon faced an injury or sickness she could not mend.

She cast a sidelong look at Catori and Ahanu, but neither wolf looked away. They hadn't joined the attack, and felt no shame, Shard saw. "Kenna and Halvden were injured, but survived as well."

"A relief," Stigr grumbled. Ragna nipped his feathers before speaking to Shard.

"The newly mated will need us over the winter, to carry their kits through to spring." Shard began to argue but she caught his gaze, her head high. He had no place to argue. Ragna had lived under Sverin's rule for ten years, and wasn't afraid.

Sigrun flexed her wings, nodding once in agreement. "There are injuries to guard from infection, broken bones. I cannot abandon the pride."

Stigr watched her blankly. "Are you mad? He'll kill you."

"My mate will protect me."

"Caj?"

"Caj." She stood firm, and the others shuffled and glanced away. "As he has, all these years."

For a moment it was silent again, and then understanding dawned in Shard's mind. "He knew all this time. He knows who I am and what you did."

Sigrun merely dipped her head. Stigr, his one eye wild, stared now at white Ragna who fluffed her wings in a shrug. "I don't fear Sverin. As my sister says, he'll need every hunter he can have over the winter. The pride is weak."

"The time to roust him," growled Stigr.

"No," Shard said quickly. After a gruesome battle and all that death, he couldn't call himself a prince of the Vanir if he swooped in and caused more fighting. It would mean attacking his own family. It would mean attacking Kjorn. "That isn't the answer. Not that way." *Only the truth will end this war…his voice is the song of summer.* His father's words and promises overlapped like waves and Shard clung to the sense of them.

"Then what?" Stigr turned on Shard, lifting his wings. The others backed off a step; Catori and Ahanu trotted back, ears perked and wary.

"I had a vision," Shard said slowly. "And I'm still sorting its meaning." For a moment it was quiet, but Shard decided not to share it with them just yet. "Uncle, you told me there are more Vanir. Those who left the Silver Isles to seek a life elsewhere."

Stigr inclined his head. Above them, birds gossiped and twittered. "Yes." He glanced to Dagr. "When your father was banished, he flew to seek the lands beyond the nightward sea, where some Vanir fled right after the Conquering."

Dagr perked his ears, lifting his wings. "He lives?"

"That, I can't be sure. But I haven't had wind of his death from the traveling birds."

Shard felt a heat in his chest, restless, ready but unsure of his own course. "Maybe there are more Vanir there, still."

Maja opened her wings. "I know Vanir who fled on the starward wind, seeking safety and wisdom at the top of the world."

Shard looked from her to Dagr. "We must gather our lost pride. This is their home." He hesitated. The next was a lot to ask of any gryfon and he didn't feel worthy. "Will you fly for me, the son of the Nightwing? Fly and gather the lost Vanir, in my father's name?"

Dagr and Maja glanced at each other, and Maja stepped toward Shard. "We will fly in *your* name. For you, our prince."

"For you," Dagr echoed.

Sunlight spread wings in Shard's heart. He inclined his head deeply to them.

"And we will watch over the pride on the Sun Isle," Ragna said. "As we have these years."

"And we will guard you on the Star Island," Catori said, raising her head, ears forward. "If you have need of us, we will fight for you, Shard."

"For peace," Ahanu echoed.

"For justice," Stigr growled. "What will you have me do, Shard? There are Vanir who took a chance, flying across the windward sea to make a home on the greatland, the home of Per the Red and the other clans of the Aesir."

And whatever he fled from, Shard thought. He watched Stigr and stepped forward. "It may be that we cross the windward sea. But not yet." His words tightened in his throat as he beheld his family, as he thought of losing Kjorn, and of all the answers he didn't know. He looked at Stigr, the first to show him his birthright.

"But whatever happens, you'll stay with me? You'll fly with me?"

"To end of the earth, my nephew. My prince." He bowed.

The others bowed, murmuring, 'To the end of the earth, to the end, my prince.'

Their strength lent strength to the ember glowing in Shard's heart. As they rose he said, "And I pledge the same to you, as your brother. As your prince. We will have peace in the Silver Isles."

Ragna returned to the Sun Isle, unafraid. Maja and Dagr flew that very afternoon, starward and nightward, to seek the lost Vanir. Catori and Ahanu disappeared into the forest to see to their pack, and Sigrun lingered to tend to Shard and Stigr's injuries. They rested under the cover of a rowan grove, and the sound of a stream trickled nearby. Stigr and Sigrun had left Shard napping in the shade. Now he roused and padded deeper into the forest to find them.

They sat by the stream.

He paused; they were speaking softly. He turned one ear their way, though he knew he shouldn't listen in. Sigrun sat staring resolutely dawnward as Stigr paced around her.

"I must know," the old warrior was saying. "If the Aesir hadn't come, that Daynight. Would you have flown with me?"

"But they did come," murmured the healer, and wouldn't look at him. "I waited as long as I could for you, Stigr, but you were busy being the king's best. Then the Aesir came. You lost, and fled, and Caj chose me. He chose me. And you chose exile."

"Did you choose him too?" The old exile's voice was raw.

"He is my true mate." She looked up at Stigr at last, so he would know it was true. "I came to love him and nothing will part us. I love the daughter he gave me. He protected Shard, too. You don't know him as I do."

"But if they hadn't come—"

"They did come," she said again, her ears settling back to a gentle expression. "Don't live in the past, Stigr."

"You sound like an Aesir."

She fluffed and resettled her wings. "Sometimes, they have the right of it. There is too much in the future to worry about. Thank you for being brave enough to lead Shard to his destiny. Without you—"

"Sigrun," he pleaded.

"Take care of him." She stood, and paused. "And yourself. Shard!"

Shard stared with fascination at the ferns, then turned as if he'd only just heard her.

Don't wait too long to choose a mate, Stigr had said to him. At last he understood. Regret and anger for his uncle flared and then died.

Don't live in the past.

Sigrun padded over to him, giving one last check over his injuries. Seeming satisfied, she bumped her head to his neck. "I will always think of you as my own," she whispered, and Shard's feathers fluffed with happiness. Then he ducked his head, struggling with sorrow. His family had unraveled before him, his life, and now, he barely knew which way to turn.

He stepped away from Sigrun and raised his head, forcing strength into his voice. "And I'll make you proud." He looked to Stigr.

Sigrun clicked her beak softly, and then, to Shard's surprise, stretched out her forelegs in a bow and mantled. "Until then, my prince."

With a final glance at Stigr, Sigrun turned and trotted briskly away, her wings half open at her sides until she found a clearing and leaped into the sky.

Shard and Stigr walked in silence out of the forest, to stand on the abandoned cliffs of Windwater. No gryfon would return there. They were in mourning, regathering, watching over each other and their king. Evening wind buffeted around them and even through his aches, Shard yearned to fly.

"My greatest fear used to be exile," Shard whispered, realizing it had, in some way, come to pass. "That I would lose my place in Sverin's pride."

Stigr was silent, and Shard regretted speaking. His uncle had his own troubles, Shard realized at last, his own sorrows and regrets. *He sought redemption for all things through me.*

"I had a vision, but I don't know what it means. I'm the son of the Nightwing, but I'm not him, and everyone expects me to be."

"No." Stigr shook himself and looked firmly at Shard. "That isn't what anyone expects. They honor his memory in you, but they flew for you. They know you, Shard, and they bowed before you. They honor you for finding yourself, for your brave and honest heart. As I love and honor you."

Shard looked down and away at the waves, then to the sky, hoping for another flash, a vision, an answer. Somewhere, across that broad, endless stretch of blue sea, lay Sverin's homeland and whatever had driven his pride to the Silver Isles. Somewhere, there was an answer.

Shard drew a slow breath. For now, Sverin's pride would heal. The wolves would heal and remain in safety, and the war would be stalled. As for the rest…

You will be guided, his father had promised.

"You may have lost your place in Sverin's pride," Stigr rumbled, and Shard perked his ears, "but now it's time to find your place in the the world."

Shard watched him a moment, then without speaking leaped from the cliff and flared his wings to catch the evening wind. Stigr laughed and jumped after him. They would have peace. Shard had sworn it, though he didn't know the way. He had lost the pride, but even at that moment those loyal to him flew to gather the lost Vanir. His mother lived. His father's spirit was at rest. Shard knew who he was, if not which way to go. As the songs promised, by seeing Sverin and Aesir clearly, he had come to know his own heart.

"*It was only in knowing the other,*" Shard whispered into the breeze, "*that they came to know themselves.*"

Shard spread his wings wide, basking in Tyr's last light, and savored the rush of wind that sent him soaring over the Silver Isles and into the open stretch of evening sky.

THE END

ACKNOWLEDGEMENTS

I T'S NEARLY IMPOSSIBLE TO THANK everyone involved in the making of a book, because who knows where stories really begin? All the authors I've read who inspire me, all the artists, the friends, the teachers who encouraged me and the friends who pushed me have all become *Song of the Summer King.*

So while it's impossible to thank everyone, I want to call out a few key people who helped get Shard off the ground.

To my wingsisters and fellow artists in their own right: Tracy Davis, Kate Washington, Lauren Head, and Monica Hart Warren for being my "readers" and asking questions and giving answers and insight. Thank you!

To my editor Joshue Essoe, who helped me past everything from simple grammatical stumbling blocks to the big questions; the gryfons wouldn't be flying quite as clean or high without your insight.

Author and mentor David Farland, who confirmed that yes, the story was worth telling, and encouraging me when I decided to self-publish.

To my cover artist Jennifer Miller, who went above and beyond with her magical work to make this look like a "real" book, and Terry

Roy of TERyvisions who saved my lettering inside and out and made me look professional.

Finally, to the generous backers of my Kickstarter project to fund the printing of the hardback version of this story. From the large to the small, thank you. To Bookworks of Whitefish, the Whitefish Library, and all the others who donated generously but asked for no reward, thank you!

This is to all of you, and I particularly want to call out those who were able to pledge over $100. In no order whatsoever, thank you so much the "Gryfon Hunters": Rhel ná DecVandé, Anthony Bova, Charlotte "pandemoniumfire" McCarthy, Joe 'Treyvan' Denton, Signe Stenmark, Kevin Wegener (Silberwolf), Kate M Washington, John Idlor, and Tom Greendyk. And to the "Wolf Pack Friends:" Tracy Davis, Troy Evans & Heather McLarty, Dan! Hartmann, Snowstorm, Jessica Thorsell, Lycanthrophile, J. Patrick Walker, Chrissandra Porter, Beat Hubmann Widmer, Cody Rademacher, Roberta Miller, and Sarah Huxley. And to the "King & Queen of the Pride," Jill Evans and John Owen. To my last backer who wished to remained anonymous, thank you.

Fair winds.

Other Books by
Jess E. Owen

The Summer King Chronicles

Song of the Summer King

Skyfire

A Shard of Sun

By the Silver Wind

Anthologies

The Starward Light

PHOTO BY JESSICA LOWRY WWW.JESSICALOWRY.COM

ABOUT THE AUTHOR

J ESS HAS BEEN CREATING WORKS of fantasy art and fiction for over a decade, and founded her own publishing company, Five Elements Press, to publish her own works and someday, that of others. She's a proud member of the Society of Children's Book Writers and Illustrators and the Authors of the Flathead. She lives with her husband in the mountains of northwest Montana, which offer daily inspiration for creating worlds of wise, wild creatures, magic, and adventure. Jess can be contacted directly through her website, www. jessowen.com, or her Facebook page, http://www.facebook.com/authorjessowen.

Would you like to be the first to know when
the new books come out?
Join the Gryfon Pride and sign up for the newsletter here:
http://eepurl.com/bHtzND

A Preview of

SKYFIRE

BOOK II
of the
SUMMER KING CHRONICLES

1
THE HIGHEST PEAK

ICY WIND LASHED ALONG VERTICAL slabs of black mountain rock near the highest peak of the Sun Isle. Few creatures ever ventured there.

Shard clung to the mountainside, talons caught in tiny crags, hind paws purchased on a feather-thin groove in the rock below. The wind soared past and Shard tightened his wings to his sides, swinging his long feathered tail out for balance. Snow swirled, stinging his eyes, and the wind howled like a wolf close to the kill.

The mountain was angry.

One wing stroke, then another. Unbidden, his uncle Stigr's voice came to him. *One foot in front of the other.* Even though he wasn't on the mountainside with Shard, his mentor's advice stuck, and the words made him groan. He perked his ears and peered down to check his height.

Surely the peak is close. This is mad, mad, mad. He sought a vision on the mountain, at what felt like the top of the world. The past summer had changed everything he knew. Now it was his responsibility to solve the injustices he'd discovered—but he had no path.

His idea to seek his vision on the mountain top seemed less and less like a good idea, for at that moment, he saw nothing.

A whorl of white and gray met his eagle stare. Not even his gaze could pierce the wall of wind and snow. No longer able to see the floor of the canyon between the jagged peaks, Shard turned his face upward and shoved his muscles back into a sluggish, lurching climb.

The wind shifted again, dry as wood and cold from the top of the world. Shard ground his beak and shoved his talons up higher. *One. Foot.*

"In front of the other," he gasped. Snow soaked even his wings, oiled and resistant to water from his diet of fish. The climb, hours in the wind and snow, had broken down all of his defenses. If Shard tried to open his wings he would meet his end smashed into the cliff face. The wind changed direction and angle every three breaths, made it impossible to fly. The snow made it impossible to see more than two leaps ahead. Everything felt impossible. He dragged himself another notch higher, muscles beginning to lock and quiver.

He hadn't eaten in five days.

The memory of another's voice drifted into his head, a she-wolf from another, much warmer place, *"Only when we are empty as pelt do we know what truly lies under fur or feather and bone."*

Her words, the wolf song sending him on his way, and his uncle's advice flickered in and out of his mind like falling feathers. He knew he was still climbing, but it seemed to happen without him. A ledge loomed above. If he could drag over the top of that ledge, he was sure he would be close to the pinnacle, or at least high enough for his challenge.

One will rise higher.

Another voice. His father. His dead father. That spirit had spoken to him so clearly once, appeared before him as if in flesh, advised him, and then gone. Shard hadn't heard another word since then. He'd had no visions, no guidance, no ideas, and there were things he needed to know before winter came. The last time he'd made wrong decisions, too many lives were lost. He couldn't take that chance again.

We wolves go on a quest for our life vision, his friend had told him, a wolf seer named Catori. Her fur had burned bright and ruddy in the red autumn woods. In the lowland, it was the quarter of the year the wolves called the time of red rowan, not for the leaves, but for the berries that grew in red bursts. Cold stole the nights and the leaves of red and gold only served as a bright warning of winter.

The brisk chill of the lowlands was nothing compared to the White Mountain.

We wear down all that is flesh so the spirit may rise and show us the path.

Catori had told him her own vision that she'd dreamed as a pup before her eyes even opened. A gryfon nest and a whelping mother, but out of the mother's belly came wolf pups, and Catori knew by that vision that the future of wolves and gryfons was linked. They must befriend each other again, and she was to be a link between them.

It was autumn when it became clear to Shard that he didn't know what to do, and didn't like the choices he had, so Catori had encouraged him to go on a vision quest as the wolves did, and seek his answers that way.

> *He is borne aloft on the Silver Wind*
> *He alone flies the highest peak…*

Words from a song overlapped the memory of Catori and Shard shook his head, squinting up and around. Fast-flying snow stung his eyes and he ruffled his feathers, shaking it off again. The ledge loomed dark overhead.

There. That is as high as I can go. The place had to challenge him, to strip him to his essence. Then, as Catori said, a vision should come to him. The wolves didn't seek their visions on the White Mountain, but Shard had chosen the highest point on the largest island in all the Silver Isles. It felt right that a gryfon seek his vision there. He remembered choosing the point on a warm autumn evening, gazing at the distant peak, surrounded by friends and a warm sunset.

Shard would have laughed at his stupid choice if he'd had extra breath. A nice glide along the seashore, seeking his vision by sunset light, sounded better every moment.

One foot in front of the other.

He slapped talons against a solid-looking outcropping. The ice that had looked like rock cracked and crumbled under his weight. Shard swung down, clawing for purchase, shrieking. His voice fell dead in the wind, dry from thirst. His claws scraped as he slid down on rolling rocks and ice. Wild for balance, he flared one wing.

The wind swooped in, knocked his wing wide and threw him spiraling off the rock face into the air.

Shard kicked his hind paws out straight and lashed his tail into a fan to rudder himself, stretching the other wing to try soaring. Sick of climbing, blinded from snow, Shard ducked and curved with the wind. The long canyon between the two white peaks sent winds circling and lunging like caribou, knocking him toward one face, then the other.

Panicked, aching and blind, Shard forced his thoughts to leave him. He was nothing but wings and air. He knew only that he wanted the pinnacle of the mountain.

I won't be defeated by wind!

He twisted and flapped, testing the air, straining all his skill. At last he found what he needed–a sliver of wind slipped under his wing like a guiding friend. Latching onto it, he curved his wings to follow only that current. It was warmer than the others. The single, tiny, warmer current lifted him higher.

After wild moments that felt like hours, Shard saw where the mountain slopes met. The canyon between them ended in a solid wall of white snow and black rock. Ice crumbled down its face, chunks falling into the hazy gloom below. Shard, heart slamming, had barely enough strength to react.

Pull up pull up PULL UP! Even his wings screamed until Shard realized he was shrieking also, wordless, mindless as he flapped his wings against cold air, unable to fight the wind that he rode straight toward a solid face of rock.

Shard screamed an eagle cry into the wind and shut his eyes—

—and a warm draft shoved him straight up and over the canyon rim, and higher. Free of the circling winds, Shard angled his wings to catch the draft, soaring, soaring high until he saw a flat, round expanse jutting out from the highest peak. No wider than a gryfon at full stretch, it was large enough to land on.

The thin air made him gasp. Snow dragged his wings like stones. Happy to be freed from climbing like a wingless beast, Shard shoved through the gray air until he reached the ledge below the peak and landed, tumbling in the snow. Awkward and exhausted as a fledge after its first, miserable flight, Shard lay panting, barely comprehending the blanket of snow under him, and that now the wind was whispering and soft.

Snow fell gently around him.

He had landed in the shadow of the great, pointed peak of the mountain, sheltered from the wind. It felt like a calm winter day.

In the corner of his vision, something moved, like a little hump of snow.

Shard tried to stand, but his legs quivered and collapsed under him. He lay on his belly, beak resting on the snow, and perked his ears as the hump of snow became an owl.

"Son-of-Baldr," sang the owl, and her deep voice perked his ears again. "Son of the Nightwing. Rashard, son-of-Ragna the White."

The sounds and words became his name and Shard blinked slowly and raised his head. He had, for a moment, forgotten his name. Forgotten that he had one. With his name, everything else snapped back. Why he had come, his need for guidance, the wolves singing him away with blessings on his vision quest.

"I know you," he whispered. "You guided me once before, in the forest. What are you doing here? You can't live up here."

He failed to keep the disappointment from his voice. In that moment he realized keenly that he'd craved to see his father again, and nothing else. Instead, his deadly, awkward flight had attracted the attention of this creature, an old friend. Or at least an acquaintance. He wondered if this flesh and blood owl could answer his questions any better than a sparrow could. She had helped Shard before, when he was lost. Perhaps she meant to again, but he would've preferred a vision of his father.

Still, it was good not to be alone.

"My prince. I came here for you. " The white owl stretched her rounded wings in a bow, and blinked large fierce eyes, yellow as the summer moon. "What brings you to the brow of the Sun Isle?"

"I need help," Shard whispered. His tongue stuck to his beak. Warmth rushed his head. Then the owl lost focus in front of him, the mountain slanted, ready to tip him back down to the bottom of the world, and he fell from blinding white into blackness.

Look for

SKYFIRE

THE SUMMER KING CHRONICLES BOOK II

at your favorite bookseller

.

Made in the USA
Columbia, SC
05 April 2019